"I am no seducer of innocents." Indignation had him vaulting out of the bed.

A crowd of interested bystanders were peering into his room with a mixture of shock and disapproval.

With a low snarl, he stalked stark naked across the room and slammed the door shut on the whole crowd of them.

Then shot the bolt home for good measure.

He turned, slowly, wondering just exactly what sort of female he had found in such a ramshackle inn, in such a dreary little town. He took a good look at the girl who was sitting up in the bed, with the covers clutched up to her chin.

Contrary to what he'd half expected, she was a pretty little thing, with a cloud of chestnut curls and a pair of huge brown eyes.

Which was an immense relief. He may have lost his memory, but at least he hadn't lost his good taste.

Annie Burrows

In Bed with the Duke

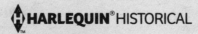

Recycling programs
for this product may
not exist in your area.

ISBN-13: 978-0-373-29880-8

In Bed with the Duke

Copyright © 2016 by Annie Burrows

All rights reserved. Except for use in any review, the reproduction or
utilization of this work in whole or in part in any form by any electronic,
mechanical or other means, now known or hereinafter invented, including
xerography, photocopying and recording, or in any information storage
or retrieval system, is forbidden without the written permission of the
publisher, Harlequin Enterprises Limited, 225 Duncan Mill Road,
Don Mills, Ontario M3B 3K9, Canada.

This is a work of fiction. Names, characters, places and incidents are
either the product of the author's imagination or are used fictitiously,
and any resemblance to actual persons, living or dead, business
establishments, events or locales is entirely coincidental.

This edition published by arrangement with Harlequin Books S.A.

For questions and comments about the quality of this book,
please contact us at CustomerService@Harlequin.com.

® and TM are trademarks of Harlequin Enterprises Limited or its
corporate affiliates. Trademarks indicated with ® are registered in the
United States Patent and Trademark Office, the Canadian Intellectual
Property Office and in other countries.

Printed in U.S.A.

Annie Burrows has been writing Regency romances for Harlequin since 2007. Her books have charmed readers worldwide, having been translated into nineteen different languages, and some have gone on to win the coveted Reviewers' Choice Award from CataRomance.com. For more information, or to contact the author, please visit annie-burrows.co.uk, or you can find her on Facebook at Facebook.com/annieburrowsuk.

Books by Annie Burrows

Harlequin Historical

Brides of Waterloo

A Mistress for Major Bartlett

Stand-Alone Novels

One Candlelit Christmas
"The Rake's Secret Son"
The Earl's Untouched Bride
A Countess by Christmas
Gift-Wrapped Governess
"Governess to Christmas Bride"
Captain Corcoran's Hoyden Bride
An Escapade and an Engagement
Never Trust a Rake
Reforming the Viscount
Portrait of a Scandal
Lord Havelock's List
The Captain's Christmas Bride
In Bed with the Duke

Harlequin Historical Undone! ebooks

Notorious Lord, Compromised Miss
His Wicked Christmas Wager

Visit the Author Profile page
at Harlequin.com for more titles.

Once again, my thanks to the Novelistas for constant support, brainstorming when necessary, and cake.

Chapter One

'Vile seducer of women!'

Gregory winced and pulled the quilt up over his ears. What kind of inn was this? Surely even travellers to such a Godforsaken backwater shouldn't have to put up with deranged females bursting into their rooms and screeching at them before breakfast?

'Oh! What wickedness!'

Pulling the quilt up round his ears clearly wasn't a strong enough hint that deranged females weren't welcome in his room. For the voice was definitely getting louder. Coming closer.

'What is the world coming to?'

Just what he'd like to know, he thought resentfully, dragging his eyelids open and seeing the owner of the strident voice standing right over him, jabbing a bony finger at his face.

'How could you?' the bony-fingered, screeching woman shouted into his face. *Right* into his face.

Enough was enough. He knew that public inns were of necessity frequented by...well, by the public. But surely even here a man was entitled to some privacy? At least in his own bedchamber?

'Who,' he said, in the arctic tone that normally caused minions to shake in their shoes, 'let you into my room?'

'Who let me into your room? Why, I let *myself* in, of course.' She smote her breast theatrically. '*Never* have I been so shocked!'

'Well, if you will invade a man's chamber what can you expect?'

'Oh!' the woman cried again, this time laying the back of one hand across her brow. 'Was *ever* there such a villain? Truly, your soul must be stained black with depravity if you can treat the seduction of innocence with such levity!'

Seduction of innocence? The woman must be fifty if she was a day. And *she'd* invaded *his* room. Nothing innocent about that.

'And as for you!' The screeching woman's finger moved to a point somewhere to his left side. 'You… you *trollop*!'

Trollop? There was a trollop in his bed as well as a hysterical woman standing next to it?

A brief foray with his left foot confirmed that, yes, indeed there was another pair of legs in his bed. A slender pair of legs. Belonging, he had to suppose, to the trollop in question.

He frowned. He wasn't in the habit of taking trollops to his bed. Nor any other kind of woman. He always, but *always*, visited theirs. So that he could retire once he'd reduced them to a state of boneless satiation and get a peaceful night's sleep at home. In his own bed. Where he heartily wished he was now. For there wouldn't be a strange woman in his bed if he'd stayed at home. Nor, which was more to the point, would *anybody* be daring to stand over him screeching.

'How could you repay me by behaving like this?' The hysterical woman was still ranting. 'After all I have done for you? All the sacrifices I have made?'

Her voice was rising higher and higher. And getting louder and louder. But even so there seemed to be a sort of fog shrouding his brain. He couldn't for the life of him pierce through that fog to work out why there was a woman in his bed. He couldn't believe he'd hired her. Because he had never needed to hire a woman. So how did she come to be here?

How, for that matter, did *he* come to be here?

And how was he to work it out with that harpy shrieking at him?

He put his hands over his ears.

'You ingrate!'

No use. He could still hear her.

'Madam,' he said coldly, removing his hands from his ears, since ignoring her in the faint hope that she might go away wasn't working. 'Lower your voice.'

'Lower my voice? *Lower my voice?* Oh, yes, that would suit you just fine, would it not? So that your vile misdeed might be covered up!'

'I have never,' he said in outrage, 'committed *any* vile misdeed.' Nor used the kind of language that more properly belonged on the stage.

He pressed the heels of his hands to his temples. His throbbing temples. How much must he have had to drink last night to wind up in bed with a trollop he couldn't remember hiring and be parroting the vulgar phrases of a woman who seemed intent on dragging him into some kind of…*scene*?

'Get out of my room,' he growled.

'How dare you order me about?'

'How dare *I*?' He opened his eyes. Glared at the screeching woman. Sat up. 'No. How dare *you*? How dare you walk into my room and address me in that impudent manner? Fling accusations at me?'

'Because you have seduced my own lamb! My—'

Indignation had him vaulting out of the bed.

'I am no seducer of innocents!'

The woman shrieked even more loudly than before. Covered her eyes and stumbled towards the door. The *open* door. Where she had to push her way through a crowd of interested bystanders. Who were all peering into his room with a mixture of shock and disapproval.

Except in the case of a plump girl he recognised as the chambermaid. She was gazing at him round-eyed and slack-jawed.

At which point he realised he was stark naked.

With a low snarl he stalked across the room and slammed the door shut on the whole crowd of them.

Then shot the bolt home for good measure.

He had a brief flash of his nurse, clucking her tongue and quoting that proverb about shutting the stable door after the horse had bolted.

No horse. He shook his head. A horse was about the only thing that *didn't* appear to have wandered into his room while he lay sleeping.

Sleeping like the dead. Which made no sense. How had he managed to get to sleep at all? When he'd decided to rack up here for the night he'd suspected he wouldn't be getting a wink of sleep. Other, similar inns in which he'd stayed had made a restful night wellnigh impossible. If it wasn't travellers in hobnailed boots tramping up and down the corridor at all hours, or coaches rattling into the inn yard with their guards blowing their horns as though it was the last trump, it was yokels with lusty voices bellowing at each other in the tap. Over which his room was always inevitably situated.

Although this chambermaid had brought him to a room right up in the eaves. So the noise wouldn't have been an issue. Had he been so exhausted after the events of the past few days that he'd slipped into a state resembling a coma?

It wasn't likely. And it didn't explain the muzzy feeling in his head. That felt more as though he'd taken some kind of sleeping draught.

Except that he'd never taken a sleeping draught in his life. And he couldn't believe he'd suddenly decided to do so now.

He rubbed his brow in a vain effort to clear his mind. If he could only recall the events of the previous night.

He concentrated. Ferociously.

He could remember having a brief wash and going down for dinner. And being served with a surprisingly good stew. The beef had melted in his mouth. And there had been cabbage and onions and a thick hunk of really good bread to mop up the rich gravy. He remembered congratulating himself as he'd come up the stairs on stumbling across an inn that served such good food.

After that—nothing.

Could the overseer and his accomplice have attacked him on the way upstairs? Had they followed him and sneaked up on him, intent on getting revenge? He felt the back of his head but didn't find any lumps or cuts. No sign that anyone had struck him with a blunt instrument. It was about the only thing they *hadn't* used.

They certainly hadn't hesitated to use their boots when they'd managed to knock him to the ground.

Not that he'd stayed down for long. A feeling of satisfaction warmed him. He flexed the fingers of his right hand, savouring the sting of grazed knuckles. It was one thing practising the science in a boxing saloon, where due deference was always given to regular customers, quite another to rise triumphant from an impromptu mill with a brace of bullies who had neither known who he was nor fought fair.

But, still, that didn't answer the question of why this harridan had burst, shrieking, into his bedroom, nor the female he'd apparently taken to his bed without having any recollection of so much as meeting her.

He turned slowly, wondering just exactly what sort of female he had found in such a ramshackle inn, in such a dreary little town.

He took a good look at the girl, who was sitting up in the bed with the covers clutched up to her chin.

Contrary to what he'd half expected she was a pretty little thing, with a cloud of chestnut curls and a pair of huge brown eyes.

Which was an immense relief. He might have lost his memory, but at least he hadn't lost his good taste.

Prudence rubbed her eyes. Shook her head. She'd never had a dream like this before. Not as bad as this, at any rate. She had sometimes had nightmares featuring her aunt Charity, for despite her name her mother's sister was the kind of cold, harsh woman who was bound to give a girl the occasional nightmare, but never—not in even the most bizarre ones that had invaded her sleep when she'd been feverish—had her aunt spoken such gibberish. Nor had she ever had the kind of dream in which a naked man invaded her room. Her bed.

He'd stalked to the door and shut it, thankfully, though not before she'd realised that the landlord was staring at her chest. Her *bare* chest.

Why hadn't she checked to see if she was naked before sitting up? And why *was* she naked? Where was her nightgown? Her nightcap? And why wasn't her hair neatly braided? What was going on?

The naked man by the door was ruffling his closely cropped light brown hair repeatedly, as though his head hurt. And he was muttering something about horses and gravy.

Naked.

Man.

Her stomach lurched. She had a clear recollection of snuggling up against that man a few minutes ago. He'd had his arms round her. It had felt...lovely. But then she'd thought it was all part of a pleasant dream, in which someone was holding her, making her feel safe for once. Loved.

Instead he'd probably...

She swallowed. Heaven alone knew what he'd done to her.

And now he was standing between her and the door. The door he'd just bolted.

Don't come near me. Don't turn round. Don't turn round.

He turned round.

Looked at her searchingly.

Appeared to like what he saw.

Started walking back to the bed.

She opened her mouth to scream for help. But the

only sound that issued from her parched throat was a sort of indignant squeak.

She worked her tongue against the roof of her mouth, desperately trying to find some moisture so that she could call for help.

Though from whom? That landlord? The man who'd just taken a good look at her breasts?

Aunt Charity? Who'd come in here and called her a trollop?

Although…it didn't look as though she needed to call for help just yet. The man was standing still. Fists on his hips. Glaring down at her.

Glaring down from a face she suddenly recognised. Now that she was actually looking at it. And not at those broad, bare shoulders. Or the bruised ribcage. Or the… Well, she'd never seen a naked man before. She couldn't help looking at *that*. Even though she knew she shouldn't.

But anyway, now that she was looking at his face she knew she'd seen it before. Last night. In the dining room.

He'd been sitting in the corner, at a table all on his own. Looking dangerous. And it hadn't been just the bruise to his jaw, or the fact that one eye had been swelling and darkening, or that he'd had the grazed knuckles of a man who'd clearly just been in a fist fight. It had been the cold atmosphere that had surrounded him. The chill emanating from steel-grey eyes that had dared anyone to try and strike up a conversation, or walk too closely past his table, or serve him with anything that didn't meet his expectations.

She hadn't noticed him observing her. But he must have been doing so. He must have somehow known she was in a room on her own and followed her up here, and then…

But at that point her mind drew a blank.

He hadn't handled her roughly—that much she knew. Because she didn't feel the slightest bit sore anywhere. Though perhaps she hadn't put up much of a struggle. Perhaps she'd known it would have been useless, given the size of the muscles bulging out all over that huge, great body…

'It won't work!'

'Pardon?' The word just managed to crawl over her teeth.

'This—' The big, dangerous, naked man waved his arm round the room. Ended up pointing at her. 'This attempt to compromise me.'

Compromise? What an odd choice of word. Besides, if anyone was compromised it was her.

She tried clearing her throat, in order to point this out, but he'd whirled away from her. Was striding round the room, pouncing on various items of clothing that lay on the floor. He bundled them up and threw them at her.

'Get dressed and get out,' he snarled. And then, for good measure, he drew the hangings around the bed, as though to blot out the very sight of her.

Which at least gave her the privacy to scramble into what turned out to be the clothes she'd been wearing last night. Clothes which had been scattered all over the room as though they'd been torn off in a frenzy and dropped just anywhere.

Which wasn't like her at all. She was always meticulous about folding her clothes and placing everything she might need rising close at hand. It was a habit ingrained during the first dozen years of her life, when the ability to move out of a billet at a moment's notice might have meant the difference between life and death.

Still, she wasn't going to dwell on that. If ever there was a time to make a swift exit then that time was now. She needed to get decently dressed, as fast as was humanly possible, and out of this room before the gigantic, angry, naked man changed his mind about letting her go.

She untangled her chemise and pulled it on over her head. Reached for her stays. And considered. It would take some time to wriggle it into a comfortable position and do up all the laces. Better just to get her gown on and get out of here.

When she peeped out through the bed hangings she saw that he was sitting on a chair, stamping his feet into a pair of scuffed, rather baggy boots.

Which reminded her. Shoes. Where were her shoes?

There. Right by the door. Next to each other, although one was lying on its side.

She grabbed her stays and waited until the man—the no longer naked man, since he'd pulled on some breeches and a shirt—reached for his second boot. He didn't look like the kind of man who'd sacrifice his dignity by hopping after her. So as he started easing his foot down the leg of that boot she made a dash for the door.

As quickly as she could, she thrust her feet into her shoes, and went to open the door.

It wouldn't budge.

She tugged and tugged at it, but no matter how hard she pulled, or how frantically she turned the handle, she simply couldn't get it open.

And the man must have got his second boot on. Because she could hear him walking across the room. He was coming in her direction.

In panic, she dropped her stays so she could tug at the handle with both hands. But she wasn't quick enough. He'd come right behind her. Was reaching up. Over her head.

And drawing the bolt free.

The bolt. In her panic to escape she'd forgotten all about the bolt.

'Allow me,' said the man, opening the door and making a mockingly courteous gesture with one hand.

Before putting the other on her back.

And shoving her out onto the landing.

The beast. The rude, nasty, horrible man! He hadn't even let her pick up her stays! Not that she really wanted to be seen running round an inn with her stays in full view in her hands.

But still— Her lower lip trembled. If she'd had a drop of moisture in her parched body she was sure tears would have sprung to her eyes.

She rubbed at them, but got no relief. The gesture only made the landing spin, and then sort of ripple— the way the surface of a pond rippled when you threw in a pebble.

And there was something else odd about the landing. It all seemed to be the wrong way round. True, she hadn't spent much time exploring the place when they'd arrived, but it had been such an odd little space, up under the eaves, that it was bound to have stuck in her mind. The owner of the inn had made clever use of his attics, fashioning three rooms around three sides at the top of his property, with the head of the stairwell and a broad landing taking up the fourth side. Last night, when she'd come up the stairs, she'd had to go right round the narrow gallery which bordered the stairwell to reach her room. But now she was standing right next to the staircase, which meant she hadn't been in *her* room just now.

But his.

Why had she been in his room? Could she have stumbled, sleepily, into the wrong room last night?

No…no, that wasn't it. She distinctly recalled starting to get ready for bed and her aunt coming in with a drink of hot milk.

A sound from inside the room she'd just shared with a total stranger made her jump out of her skin.

She shouldn't be loitering here. Who was to say he wouldn't change his mind and drag her back inside?

With legs that felt like cotton wool, she made her way round the gallery. She passed the door to the room where her aunt and her… She shook her head. She still couldn't think of her aunt's new husband as her uncle. He was no relation of hers. It was bad enough having to share her home with him, let alone address the old skinflint as though he was family.

She stumbled to a halt in the doorway that stood open. *This* was her room. She was *sure* this had been her room. The bed was just where it should be. And the washstand. And the little dormer window with the seat underneath on which she'd knelt to peer down at the view. She'd been able to see along the road that led to the market square. Even from this doorway she could just spy the top of the market cross.

But—where were her things? Her trunk should be just there, at the foot of the bed. Her hatbox beside it. Her toiletries, brush and comb should be on the washstand.

Confused, she tottered round the landing to the back of the house, to the room her aunt and the vile Mr Murgatroyd were sharing. There was nothing for it. She'd have to intrude, even though they might be— she shuddered—*embracing*, which they tended to do with revolting frequency.

She braced herself and knocked on the door. When there was no reply she knocked again, and then gingerly tried the handle. The door opened onto an empty room. No luggage. No personal clutter on the washstand or dresser.

As if they'd gone.

She blinked a couple of times and shook her head. This must all be part of the same nightmare. That was it. In a minute she'd wake up, back in… Back in…

She pinched her arm—hard.

But nothing changed. She was still standing on the landing at the top of an inn, in a little town whose name she couldn't remember. After waking up in bed with a naked man.

It couldn't be happening.

Her aunt and her new husband must be downstairs. Paying the bill. That was it. They couldn't have abandoned her. They just *couldn't* have.

Her heart fluttering like a butterfly trapped in a jam jar, she turned away from the empty room and ran down the stairs.

Chapter Two

'We run a respectable establishment,' said the land-lady, glaring at Gregory as she folded her arms over her ample bosom.

'Really?' If this was what passed for a 'respectable' establishment, he hated to think what she considered *un*respectable. *Dis*respectable. He gave himself a mental shake. Why couldn't he think of the word for the opposite of respectable?

'So we'd be obliged if you'd pay your shot and leave.'

'I haven't had my breakfast.'

'Nor will we be serving you any. We don't hold with putting our guests through the kind of scene you caused this morning.'

'I didn't cause any kind of scene.'

Why was he bandying words with this woman? He never bandied words with *anyone*. People did as they were told or felt the force of his displeasure.

'Well, that's not what my Albert told me,' said the landlady. 'Came to me with tales of guests complaining they'd been woken up by screaming women in the halls, naked girls in rooms where they didn't ought to be, and—'

He held up one imperious hand for silence. Very well, he conceded there *had* been a scene. In which he'd become embroiled. Now that he came to think of it, did he really want to break his fast here? The last meal he'd eaten under this roof, although palatable, had ended with him sinking into a state of oblivion so profound it appeared a band of criminals had attempted to perpetrate some kind of…of crime against him.

Dammit, he'd thought his mind was getting clearer. He'd managed to summon up words like palatable and perpetrate. Why, for heaven's sake, had he been unable to come up with another word for crime?

It felt as though someone had broken into his head and stolen three-quarters of his brain. When he'd first awoken he'd likened it to the kind of haze that followed a night of heavy drinking. A state he disliked so much he'd only very rarely sought the form of release that alcohol promised. And then only when he'd been young enough to know no better.

And the landlady was still standing there, hands on her hips now, glaring past him at the state of his room as though expecting to see the naked girl he'd ejected the moment she'd put on her clothes. That sounded wrong. As though he'd only tolerated her in his room while she was naked. What he'd meant was that of course he wouldn't have thrown her out until she was dressed. That would not have been a decent thing to do.

While he was standing there, wondering why his thoughts were in such a muddle when he was used to making incisive decisions about complex issues in the blink of an eye, the landlady's eyes narrowed and her nostrils flared. He followed the direction of her fixed stare to see what had put that disgusted expression on her face. And spied a stocking. A lady's stocking. Dangling from the mirror over the washstand. Looking for all the world as though it had been thrown there during an explosion of frenzied undressing.

He stalked across the room, wrenched it from the mirror and shoved it into his pocket, feeling...cheated. If he really had torn that girl's clothing from her in a burst of passion so overwhelming he'd thrown her stockings clear across the room, then he ought to be able to remember it. Remember being so out of control that he'd not only scattered her clothing all over the room but his own, too.

He shivered in distaste at the recollection that his shirt had spent its night on the floor. A floor that was none too clean.

'I will be down directly,' he said, coming to a sudden decision to shake the dust of this place from his shoes. As he'd had to shake the dust from his shirt a short while ago.

The landlady gave him one last basilisk stare before very pointedly stepping over the stays that lay on the floor by the door through which she exited.

He strode to the door and slammed it shut after her. Picked up the stays. Glared at them. Wondered for a moment why he felt such reluctance to leave them lying exactly where they were.

Because he didn't want any trace of himself, or whatever had happened here, lingering after he'd gone, he decided. Which was why he thrust them into the one meagre little valise he'd brought with him. Then he went to the washstand and rolled up his shaving kit, tossed it into the valise with the stays and the rest of his things.

Not that the stays were his.

And who was likely to look in his valise and imply that they were?

Nobody—that was who. Not once he'd returned to where he belonged. Which he planned to do as soon as possible.

He paid his bill downstairs at the bar, rather than calling for the landlord to come and attend to him. The sooner he'd done with this place, the better. He needed to get outside and breathe fresh air. Perhaps even find a pump under which to douse his head with cold water. He certainly needed something to clear his head.

Instead of calling for someone to bring his gig round to the front of the inn, he decided to go and fetch it himself. Because there was bound to be a pump in the yard at the back. Or at least a trough for the horses.

He had to pause on the threshold when the spring sunshine assaulted his eyes. It seemed incredibly bright after the darkness of the inn.

When his eyes adjusted to the daylight he saw that there was indeed a pump in the stable yard. And that next to it were two people. One was an ostler. The other was the girl. The girl from the night before—or rather this morning. Heaven alone knew what had happened the night before.

She was inching backwards, round the pump. While the greasy-haired ostler was stalking her. Leering at her.

He frowned. Surely if she was plying her trade at this inn she ought not to be taking evasive action. Or looking so scared. She should be smiling coyly, attempting to wheedle as high a price from the ostler as he could afford to pay.

Come to think of it, she shouldn't have clutched the sheets to her chest, or dressed so hurriedly, or scrabbled at the door in what had looked like desperation to get away from him earlier, either.

'Hi, there. You! Ostler!'

The ostler suspended his pursuit of the girl. Recognising him as a customer, he pushed his hat to the back of his head with a grubby forefinger and shambled over.

'Leave that girl alone,' Gregory found himself saying. When what he'd meant to say was, *Harness up my gig*.

The ostler gave him a look that was very much like a sneer. 'Want to keep 'er to yerself, do yer?'

The girl was looking round the yard wildly, as though for a means of escape. The only way out of the yard was through an archway. To reach it she'd have to get past both him and the lecherous ostler.

'That is none of your business,' he replied. 'I want my gig. And I want it now.'

'Oh-ár,' said the ostler, apparently remembering what his job here actually was. He shot the girl a look that made her shudder as he went past her and into the stable.

Once the ostler had gone into the stable Gregory turned to look at the girl. She was pressed up against the far wall of the stable yard, as though trying to disappear into the plaster.

It didn't make sense. Well, nothing about this morning made sense. But the girl's behaviour, above all, was perplexing.

He didn't like it. He didn't like not being in complete control of any situation. He didn't like the feeling of stumbling about in the dark.

He'd thought all he wanted to do was get away from this inn and back to normality. But the mystery of this girl, and how she'd come to be in his bed when she clearly wasn't a professional, was plaguing him.

He'd never be at rest until he knew what had really happened here last night. He wanted answers. And the girl would have those answers.

He stalked towards her. And as he did so she pressed even deeper into the plasterwork, her eyes widening with alarm. He supposed she must fear the consequences of having perpetrated—ah, there was that word again—whatever deception it was she'd attempted last night. As well she might. When she'd attempted to perpetrate whatever it was she'd been attempting to perpetrate she'd picked the wrong man.

He came to a halt a scant foot from her, wondering how best to make her abandon any loyalty she might feel towards her accomplices and put her faith in him, instead. Only then would she tell him what he wanted to know. Which was how the deuce had they managed to penetrate his disguise and what would be their next move?

The answer came to him when the ostler led his gig out of the stable, giving the girl a knowing, triumphant grin as he hitched the reins to a ring in the wall. If she wasn't a whore yet she would be one by tonight, that look said. Willing or unwilling.

His whole being rejected the notion of abandoning any woman to such a fate. No matter what she'd tried to do to him.

Besides, he had his reputation to think of. Somehow

the screeching woman with the bony fingers must have worked out who he was.

Or been informed.

Ah, yes, that would explain everything. Even the confusion and panic on the girl's face. It would be just like Hugo to drag some unsuspecting third party into one of his pranks and leave them to pay the price.

And the devil of it was that Hugo knew *he* would do his utmost to hush it all up. That he would never let the family name be dragged through the mud.

'Once I have left this inn yard in that gig...' he pointed it out to the quaking girl '...you will be completely at that man's mercy.'

Her eyes flicked wildly from the gig to the ostler, who was ambling in their direction, and to him. Only once she was looking at him did he continue.

'You would do better to come with me. I will keep you safe.'

She didn't look as though she believed him. Her inference that he might not be telling the truth was an insult so grave she might as well have spat at him.

Drawing himself to his full height, he bit out, 'I give you my word.'

Something about his demeanour, or maybe the approach of the ostler, must finally have managed to convince her, because she nodded her head before shooting past him and clambering up into the gig.

The ostler's face fell. And *he* actually did spit. At the pair of them as they swept past him and out into what passed for the high street in this scruffy little town.

The girl had wrapped her arms around herself in a protective gesture the moment he'd climbed into the driver's seat. And he was so angry with her that for a while he didn't bother to reassure her that she really was safe with him. How dared she insinuate that he was the kind of man who told lies?

Though, to be fair, these last few days he *had* been somewhat economical with the truth.

But never—not under any circumstances—would he harm a helpless woman. Not even an *un*helpless woman. Oh, blast it all. There went his vocabulary again. There was no such word as unhelpless, was there?

The approach of a farm cart from the opposite direction caused him to abandon his vain attempt to find a suitable word to describe the girl sitting next to him. He needed all his concentration to get his vehicle past the cart in the narrow confines of the lane. Particularly since the farmer's horse appeared to annoy the one harnessed to his own gig. What with preventing his bad-tempered nag from biting the gentle, rather stupid mare belonging to the farmer, and convincing it that it really *did* need to progress further down the lane, even though it looked as if it would be better sport to make the farmer's horse back his cart into the wall, he had his hands—and his mind—completely full.

They were right out in the countryside, with the little town of Much Wapping far behind them, before he decided to speak to the girl again.

He found he was looking forward to coaxing her into speaking. The only word that had so far passed her lips had been huskily spoken. Like a velvet caress.

Velvet caress? Good grief, what was the matter with him that he was coming up with such bizarre ideas?

Anyway, he shouldn't have to coax her into speaking again. Females, in his experience, were never silent. Not for as long as this anyway. Not unless they were planning something. He gave her a sharp look. She still had her arms wrapped around her middle. Her fingers tucked under her armpits. It struck him that she didn't look merely defensive any longer. She looked cold.

Cold. Of *course* she was cold. She wasn't wearing a coat. Or a bonnet. Her rust-coloured gown was made of good quality kerseymere, but a brief glance at her feet revealed an expanse of bare skin between the tops of her sturdy shoes and the hem of that gown. And it might be sunny, but this early in the year it wouldn't be really warm until perhaps the middle of the afternoon. If then. She needed to put something else on. But she hadn't any luggage, had she?

Frowning, he cast his mind over what to do for her. It would be pointless to offer her the one stocking he had in his jacket pocket. She needed more than one stocking. She needed a coat.

He could lend her his own coat… But, no. It would swamp her. Even his jacket would probably come down to her knees. Though that, actually, might not be such a bad thing. She could tuck her hands inside the sleeves.

He couldn't just stop where they were and offer her his jacket, though. The lane was so narrow that if any other vehicle came from either direction they wouldn't be able to pass. But from now on he'd look for a place where he could safely pull over.

Before very much longer he spied a gate leading into a field, which gave him the chance to pull the gig off the road a little. He put on the brake, removed his gloves and swiftly unbuttoned his coat.

Just as he was leaning forward, with his left arm out of one sleeve, about to remove his right arm from the other, the girl gave him a hefty shove in the side. She caught him so off balance that he tumbled right out of the seat, landing between the gig's nearside wheel and the gatepost.

Dammit, why hadn't he seen that coming? Women were never as defenceless as they looked. *Obviously* she was going to try and steal his horse and gig the moment he let down his guard.

And *why* had he let down his guard? All she'd had to do was shiver and look a bit pathetic and he'd promptly forgotten the way they'd met. All he'd been able to think of was shielding her. Just the way he'd wanted to shield her from that repulsive ostler.

Well, no longer. He surged to his feet on a wave of absolute fury. He might despise the bad-tempered nag harnessed to the ramshackle gig he normally wouldn't have permitted in any of his stables, let alone take out onto a public road, but it was currently his only means of transport. And he was *not* going to relinquish it to a slip of a girl! He'd climb back into the driver's seat and wrest the reins from her hands. And then—

And then nothing. Because she wasn't in the driver's seat, whipping the horse into a gallop and leaving him standing in the lane. On the contrary—she'd scrambled out of the gig while he'd been picking himself up and was currently running away as fast as she could.

Back towards Much Wapping.

Her accomplices must still be there. Hang it all, why hadn't he thought of that? She must have been loitering in the stable yard awaiting them.

Well, he wasn't going to let her get back to them and…and do whatever it was she was planning to do. He'd had enough of stumbling about in ignorance. Of being chivalrous, and merciful, and all the rest of it. He was going to drag her back and shake the truth out of her, if that was what it took. For only by discovering the truth would he stand any chance of regaining the upper hand.

Prudence ran as fast as her legs could carry her. Though her shoes chafed against her bare feet and her legs still didn't feel as though they quite belonged to her.

But she wasn't going to be fast enough. She could hear the man's feet pounding down the road behind her. Getting closer and closer.

She wasn't going to be able to outrun him. She had to find another way to stop him. But what?

Just then she stumbled and half fell to the ground, which was littered with large chunks of jagged rock. Chunks of rock which looked as though they had come away from the dry stone wall that flanked this side of the lane.

She grabbed one. Turned. Faced the big, angry man who was planning to... Well, she didn't know what he planned to do with her once he caught her, but from the look on his face it wasn't anything she'd like.

In a sort of wild desperation she flung the rock at him as hard as she could.

To her surprise—and his—it caught him on the forehead.

He went down like a... Well, like a stone. Prudence stood rooted to the spot. Stared in horror at the blood which was trickling down his face.

The ungainly sprawl of his limbs.

His total stillness.

What had she done? She'd only meant to show him she meant business. To stop him pursuing her.

Instead she'd...she'd *killed* him!

Chapter Three

She ran to where he lay, sprawled on his back in the dirt, blood streaming across his forehead and into his hair. She dropped to her knees beside him. She couldn't believe she'd felled him like that. With one little stone. Oh, very well then, with a large chunk of rock. She pressed her hands to her mouth. He was such a big man. So full of life and strength. It was unnatural to see him lying so still.

And then he groaned. She'd never heard such a welcome sound in her life.

'Oh, thank God! You aren't dead.' She was almost sobbing.

He opened his eyes and shot her a cold, disbelieving look.

'No thanks to you,' he growled, then raised one hand to the cut and winced. He drew his hand away and held his fingers before his eyes, as though he couldn't believe he really was bleeding without seeing the evidence as well as feeling it.

She reached into the pocket of her skirt for something to dab at the wound. But there was nothing. She had no handkerchief. Her chemise was of fine lawn, though.

Its material would be as good. She hitched up her skirt and started tugging at her chemise.

'What,' asked the man warily—which wasn't surprising since she'd well-nigh killed him, 'are you doing?'

'I'm trying to tear a piece from my chemise,' she said, still desperately trying to rip the fabric that was proving more resilient than she'd expected.

'Why?' He looked baffled now, as well as wary.

'To do something about that cut on your head,' she said.

'The cut *you* caused by throwing a rock at me?'

'That's the one.'

'Wouldn't you rather get another rock and finish what you started?' he enquired mildly.

'No! Oh, no—I never meant to hurt you. I didn't think my aim was that good. Actually...' She sat back on her heels. 'My aim *wasn't* that good. Because I wasn't aiming at your head. I was just throwing the rock in your general direction, so you'd understand I wished you to leave me alone.'

'Why?'

While she'd been attempting to explain he'd been fishing in his own pockets and found a large, pristine white silk square which he handed to her with a sort of flourish.

'Thank you,' she said, taking it from him and applying it to the cut. 'Why what?'

'Why were you running away? Why didn't you just steal the gig? Or can you not drive?'

'Yes, I can drive. Of course I can drive. It just never occurred to me to steal your gig. I'm not a thief!'

He quirked one eyebrow—the one that wasn't bleeding—as though in disbelief. 'Not a thief?' he repeated dryly. 'How fortunate I feel on receipt of that information.'

She put her hand around the back of his head to hold it still, so that she could press down hard on the cut. 'Yes, you are fortunate,' she said tartly. 'I could have left you lying in the road for the…the next gang of thieves to come along and finish you off!'

'Well, that would have made more sense than this,' he said, making a vague gesture to his forehead.

She couldn't be sure if he meant her trying to stanch the flow of blood, or the fact she'd caused his injury in the first place.

'You had no reason to run off,' he said, a touch petulantly for a man who looked so tough. 'I told you I wouldn't harm you. But,' he said, drawing his brows down and narrowing his eyes with what looked like suspicion. 'I suppose you were desperate to get back to Much Wapping to collect your fee.'

'Fee?' She withdrew the handkerchief, noting with some relief that the bleeding was slowing already. 'I don't know what you mean.'

'It's no use playing the innocent with me. Hugo put you up to this, didn't he?'

'Hugo? I don't know anyone by that name.'

'A likely story. If you were not attempting to get back to Much Wapping and claiming your reward, why were you running away?'

'You scared me,' she admitted. 'When you started undressing.'

'Undressing? I was not undressing.' He frowned. 'Not precisely. That is, I *was* removing my coat, but only so that I could lend you my jacket. You looked cold.'

'Your…your jacket?' She sat back on her heels. The handkerchief slid from the man's brow to the ground on which he was still lying, glaring up at her. 'Because I looked cold? But… But…'

She pressed her hands to her mouth again for a moment. Looking back on his actions in the light of that explanation, it all looked very, very different.

'I'm so sorry. I thought… I thought…'

'Yes,' he said grimly. 'I can see what you thought.'

'Well,' she retorted, suddenly angered by the way he was managing to look down his nose at her even though he was flat on his back and she was kneeling over him. 'What would *you* have thought? I woke up in bed naked, in a strange room, with no idea how I came to be there. Aunt Charity was screaming at me, you were wandering about the place naked, shouting at me, too, and then I went to my room and it was empty, and Aunt Charity had gone with all my things, and the landlady called me names and pushed me out into the yard, and that man…that man…' She shuddered.

'I told you,' he said, reaching for the abandoned handkerchief and pressing it to his brow himself, 'that I would keep you safe. Didn't you believe me?'

'Of course I didn't believe you. I'm not an idiot. I only went with you because I was so desperate to get away from that dirty, greasy stable hand. And because at least *you* didn't seem…amorous. Even this morning, when we woke up together, you didn't seem amorous. Only angry. So I thought at least you'd spare me *that*. Except then you took me out into the middle of nowhere and started undressing. And I… I didn't know what to think. It's all like some kind of nightmare.' She felt her lower lip tremble. 'None of this seems real.' Her eyes burned with tears that still wouldn't quite form.

'No,' he said slowly. 'None of this seems real.'

And then he sat up.

Her instinct was to flinch away. Only that would look terribly cowardly, wouldn't it? So she made herself sit completely still and look him right in the eyes as he gazed into hers, searchingly.

'Your eyes look strange,' he said, reaching out to take hold of her chin. 'I have never seen anyone with such tiny pupils.'

For such a large man his touch was remarkably gentle. Particularly since he had every right to be angry with her for throwing that rock. And actually hitting him with it.

'My eyes *feel* strange,' she admitted in a shaky voice. The touch of his fingers on her chin felt strange, too. Strange in the sense that she would have thought, given all that had passed between them so far, she would want to recoil. But she didn't. Not in the slightest. Because for some strange reason his fingers felt pleasant. Comforting.

Which was absurd.

'My head is full of fog. Nothing makes sense,' she said, giving her head a little shake in a vain attempt to clear it of all the nonsense and start thinking sensibly again. It shook his fingers clear of her chin. Which was a pity.

No, it wasn't! She *didn't* want to take his hand and put it back on her face, against her cheek, so that she could lean into it. Not one bit.

'It is the same for me,' he said huskily.

'Is it?' That seemed very unlikely. But then so did everything else that had happened today.

'Yes. From the moment I awoke I could not summon the words I needed.'

Words. He was talking about words. Not wanting to put his hand back on her face.

'They seem to flit away out of reach, leaving me floundering.'

'It is my aunt and uncle who've flitted out of *my* reach,' she said bitterly. 'Leaving me floundering. Literally. And my legs don't seem as if they've properly woken up yet today.'

'And you really haven't heard of anyone called Hugo?'

Just as she shook her head in denial her stomach growled. Rather loudly.

He looked down at it with a quirk to his lips that looked suspiciously like the start of a smile.

'Oh, how unladylike!' She wrapped her arms around her middle.

'You sound as hungry as I feel,' he said, placing his hands on his own stomach. 'I didn't have any breakfast.'

'Nor me. But until my stomach made that noise I hadn't thought about being hungry,' she found herself admitting. 'I'm too thirsty.'

'I'm thirsty, too. And foggy-headed. And I don't feel as though my limbs want to do my bidding, either. I'm generally held to be a good whip, but I'm having real trouble controlling that broken-down hack that's harnessed to the gig. And what's more...' He took a breath, as though coming to a decision. 'I don't recall a thing about last night. Not after dinner anyway. Do you?'

She thought for a bit. Today had been so bizarre that

she hadn't done anything more than try to work her way through it. And that had been hard enough, without trying to cast her mind back to the day before.

'I went up to my room directly after dinner,' she said. 'I remember starting to get ready for bed, and Aunt Charity bringing me some hot milk which she said would help me sleep...'

A coldness took root in her stomach.

'After that,' she continued as a horrible suspicion began to form in her mind, 'I don't remember anything until I woke up next to you.'

'Then it seems clear what happened,' he said, getting to his feet and holding out his hand to her. 'She drugged you and carried you to my room.'

'No. *No.*' She shook her head as he pulled her to her feet. 'Why would she do such a horrid thing?'

'I wonder if *she* knows Hugo,' he mused. Then he fixed her with a stern look. 'Because if Hugo *isn't* behind this...' he waved his free hand between the pair of them '...then we're going to have to find another explanation. You will have to have a serious think about it on the way.'

'On the way where?'

He hadn't let go of her hand after helping her up, and she hadn't made any attempt to tug it free. So when he turned and began to stride back to the gig she simply trotted along beside him.

'On the way to Tadburne,' he said, handing her up into the seat. 'Where we are going to get something to eat in a respectable inn, in a private parlour, so that we can discuss what has happened and what we plan to do about it.'

She liked the sound of getting something to eat. And

the discussing of plans. But not of the private parlour. Now that he'd let go of her hand she could remember that he was really a total stranger. A very disreputable-looking stranger, in whose bed she'd woken up naked that morning.

But what choice did she have? She was hungry, and cold, and she had not the means to do anything about either condition since Aunt Charity had vanished with all her possessions. She didn't even have the small amount of pin money she was allowed. It had been in her purse. Which was in her reticule. The reticule she'd last seen the night before, when she'd tucked it under her pillow for safekeeping.

Oh, why hadn't she thought to go to the bed in that empty room and see if her reticule was there? At least she'd have a few shillings with which to… But there her mind ran blank. What good would a few shillings be at a time like this?

But at least she would have had a clean handkerchief.

Though it wouldn't have been clean now anyway. She'd have had to use it to mop up the blood. And then, if she'd needed one for herself later, she'd have had to borrow one from him anyway.

Just as she was now having to borrow his jacket, which he'd stripped off and sort of thrust at her, grim-faced.

'Thank you,' she said, with as much penitence as she could muster, and then pushed her arms gratefully into sleeves that were still warm from his body. Which reflection made her feel a bit peculiar. It was like having his arms around her again. The way they'd been before she'd woken up.

Fortunately he shot her a rather withering look,

which brought her back to her senses, then bent to retrieve the coat that had fallen into the road when she'd pushed him off the seat just a short while since.

'To think I was concerned about my *name* being dragged through the mud,' he muttered, giving it a shake. 'You managed to pitch me into the only puddle for miles around.'

She felt a pang of guilt. Just a small one. Because now not only was his eye turning black around the swelling he'd already had the night before, but he also had a nasty gash from the stone she'd thrown, spatters of blood on his neckcloth, and a damp, muddy smear down one side of his coat.

She braced herself for a stream of recrimination as he clambered back into the driving seat. But he merely released the brake, took up the reins, and set the gig in motion.

His face was set in a fierce scowl, but he didn't take his foul mood out on her. At least she presumed he was in a foul mood. Any man who'd just been accused of indecency when he'd only been trying to see to a lady's comfort, and then been cut over what must already be a sore eye, was bound to be in a foul mood.

'I'm sorry,' she said, after they'd been going for a bit. Because she felt that one of them ought to say something.

'For what, exactly?'

Oh. So he was the sort of man who sulked when he was angry, then, rather than one who ranted.

'For throwing the rock. For hitting you when normally I couldn't hit a barn door.'

'You are in the habit of throwing rocks at barn doors?'

'Of course not! I just meant… I was trying to apologise. Do you have to be so…so…?'

'You cannot think of the word you want?'

'No need to mock me.'

'I didn't mean to. It was an observation. I have already told you that I am struggling to find the words I want myself this morning. And, like you, none of this seems real. I suspect that when whatever drug we have both been given wears off I shall be rather more angry about the rock and your assumptions about me. But right now all I can think about is getting something to drink.'

'A cup of tea…' She sighed. 'That would be heavenly.'

'A pint of ale.'

'Some bread and butter.'

'A steak. With onions.'

'At breakfast?'

'Steak with onions is always good.'

She shuddered. 'I don't know about that. My stomach doesn't usually wake up first thing. I don't normally eat much before noon.'

'I don't bother with a break at noon. I'm usually out and about. Busy with estate business when I'm in the country. Or in my office with my secretary when I'm in town.'

'You have a secretary? What kind of business are you in?'

Did she imagine it, or did he look a little hunted?

'Never mind what business I'm in,' he said, rather defensively.

Oh, dear. Last night Aunt Charity had remarked that he was just the kind of disreputable person she'd been afraid they might encounter in such an out-of-the-way tavern. That he was probably a highwayman. Or a housebreaker. Though surely housebreakers didn't have secretaries? Still, the fact that he didn't want to answer any questions about his background made it more than likely that he was some sort of scoundrel.

But not a complete scoundrel. A complete scoundrel wouldn't have given her his jacket. Wouldn't have rescued her from the ostler or offered to buy her breakfast, either. No—a complete scoundrel would have left her to fend for herself. Climbed into the gig and driven away. If not the first time then definitely the second time, after she'd thrown a rock at him.

She rubbed at her forehead. He looked so villainous, and yet he wasn't acting like a villain. Whereas her aunt, who made a great display of piety at every opportunity… Oh, nothing made sense today! Nothing at all.

'I have just realised,' he said, 'that I don't even know your name. What is it?'

'Prudence Carstairs,' she said. 'Miss.'

'Prudence?' He gave her one sidelong glance before bursting out laughing.

'I don't see what's so funny about my being called Prudence,' she objected.

'P…Prudence?' he repeated. 'I cannot imagine a name *less* suited to a girl whom I met naked in bed, who gets chased around horse troughs by lecherous ostlers and throws rocks at her rescuer. Why on earth,' he said, wiping what looked like a tear from one eye, 'did they call you *Prudence*? Good God,' he said, looking at her in sudden horror as a thought apparently struck him. 'Are you a Quaker?'

'No, a Methodist,' she said, a touch belligerently. 'Grandpapa went to a revival meeting and saw the light. After that he became a very strict parent, so naturally my mother named me for one of the virtues.'

'Naturally,' he said. 'But why Prudence in particular?'

'Because it was the one virtue it was impossible for her to attain in any other way,' she retorted, without thinking.

'And did she feel she *had* attained it, once you grew old enough for her to discern your personality? I suspect not,' he observed. 'I think you are just like her.'

'No, I'm not! *She* ran off with a man she'd only known a week, because his unit was being shipped out and she was afraid she'd never see him again. Whereas *I* have never been dazzled by a scarlet jacket or a lot of gold braid. In fact I've never lost my head over *any* man.'

'Good for you.'

'There is no need to be sarcastic.'

'No, no—I was congratulating you on your level head,' he said solemnly, but his lips twitched as though he was trying to suppress a smile.

'I don't think so.'

'So,' he said, ignoring her retort. 'Your mother ran off with a soldier, I take it, and regretted it so much that she gave you a name that would always remind her of her youthful folly?'

'She did no such thing! I mean, yes, Papa was a soldier, but she never regretted eloping with him. Not even when her family cut her out of their lives. They were very happy together.'

'Then why—?'

'Well, doesn't every parent want a better life for their child?'

'I have no idea,' he said.

He said it so bleakly that she stopped being angry with him at once.

'And I have no patience with this sort of idle chatter.'

What? She'd hardly been chattering. All she'd done was answer the questions he'd put to her.

She'd taken a breath in order to point this out when he held up his hand to silence her.

'I really do need to concentrate for a moment,' he said brusquely. 'Although I am familiar with the area, in a general sort of way, I have never travelled down this road.'

They had reached a junction to what looked like a high road.

'I think we need to turn left,' he muttered. 'Yes, I'm almost sure of it.'

He looked to the right, to make sure nothing was coming, before urging the horse off the rutted, narrow lane and out onto a broad road that looked as though it saw a lot of traffic.

'So how come,' he said, once they were trotting along at a smart pace, 'you ended up falling into such bad company? If your mother was so determined you would have a better life than she did how did you end up in the power of the termagant who invaded my room this morning?'

'That termagant,' she replied acidly, 'happens to be my mother's sister.'

'You have my sincere condolences.'

'She isn't usually so—' She flared up, only to subside almost at once. 'Actually, that's not true. Aunt Charity has never been exactly easy to get along with. I did my best. Well, at least at first I did my best,' she confessed. 'But eventually I realised that she was never going to be able to warm to me so it didn't seem worth the effort.'

'Why should she not warm to you?'

He looked surprised. As though there was no earthly reason why someone shouldn't warm to her. Did that mean *he* had?

'It was all to do with the way Mama ran off with Papa. The disgrace of it. I was the result of that disgrace. A constant reminder of it. Particularly while my father was still alive.'

'He sent you back to your mother's family while he was still alive?'

'Well, not deliberately. I mean…' Oh, why was it so hard to explain things clearly? She screwed up her face in concentration, determined to deliver the facts in a logical manner, without getting sidetracked. 'First of all Mama died. And Papa said that the army was no place for a girl my age without a mother to protect her. I was getting on for twelve, you see.'

'I *do* see,' he grunted.

'Yes… Well, he thought *his* family would take me in. Only they wouldn't. They were as angry over him marrying a girl who "smelled of the shop" as Grandpapa Biddlestone was that his daughter had run off with a sinner. So they sent me north. At least Mama's family took responsibility for me. Even though they did it grudgingly. Besides, by then Aunt Charity had also angered Grandpapa Biddlestone over her own choice of husband. Or at least the way he'd turned out. Even though he was of the Methodist persuasion he was, apparently, "a perpetual backslider". Though that is neither here nor there. Not any more.'

'By which you mean what?'

'He'd been dead for years before I even reached England. I cannot think why I mentioned him at all.'

'Nor can I believe I just said, *By which you mean what.*'

'It doesn't matter that your speech isn't very elegant,' she said consolingly. 'I knew what you meant.'

The sort of snorting noise he made in response was very expressive, if not very polite.

'Well anyway, Grandpapa decided I should live with Aunt Charity until my father could make alternative arrangements for me, since she was a woman and I was of an age to need female guidance. Or that was what he said. *She* told me that Grandpapa didn't want the bother of raising a girl child who couldn't be of any use to him in his business.'

'And why didn't your father make those alternative arrangements?'

'Because he died as well. Only a couple of years later.'

'That makes no more sense than what I originally thought,' he said in disgust.

'*What* did you originally think?'

'Never mind that,' he said tersely. 'I need to concentrate on the traffic now that we're approaching Tadburne. This wretched animal—' he indicated the horse '—seems to wish to challenge anything coming in the other direction, and I need to keep my wits about me—what little I appear to have remaining this morning—if you don't want to get pitched into the road.'

She could understand that. She'd already noted that

he was having increasing difficulty managing his horse the nearer they drew to the town she could see nestling in the next valley.

'However,' he said, 'I should like you to consider a few things.'

'What things?'

'Well, firstly, why would your own aunt—your own flesh and blood—drug you, undress you, and deposit you in my bed? And, worse, abandon you in that inn after removing all your possessions, leaving you completely at the mercy of strangers? Because, Miss Prudence Carstairs, since you deny having any knowledge of Hugo and you seem to me to be a truthful person, then I feel almost sure that is what happened.'

Chapter Four

'You are wrong,' Prudence said. 'Aunt Charity is a pillar of the community. Positively steeped in good works. She couldn't have done anything like that.'

Though why could she recall nothing after drinking that warm milk?

He made no answer.

It must have been because he was negotiating a tricky turn before going under the archway of an inn. The inn was, moreover, right on a busy crossroads, so that traffic seemed to be coming at them from all directions. It was concentration that had put the frown between his brows and made his mouth pull into an uncompromising line.

It wasn't because he disagreed with her.

Of course he was wrong. Aunt Charity couldn't possibly have done what he said.

Yet how else could she have ended up in bed with a stranger? Naked? She would never, ever have gone to his room of her own accord, removed every stitch of clothing, flung it all over the place, and then got into bed with him.

And the man denied having lured her there.

He brought the gig to a halt and called over an ostler.

Well, no, he hadn't exactly denied it, she reflected as he got down, came round to her side and helped her from the seat. Because she hadn't accused him of doing any luring. But from the things he'd said he seemed to think *she'd* been in some kind of conspiracy against *him*. And he was also unclear about what had happened last night after dinner. Claimed to have no recollection of how they'd wound up in bed together, either.

So what he was saying was that someone else must be responsible. Since she wasn't. And he wasn't.

Which left only her aunt.

And uncle.

Or this Hugo person he kept mentioning.

'Come on,' he said a touch impatiently.

She blinked, and realised she'd been standing still in the bustling inn yard, in a kind of daze, while she struggled with the horrid notion he'd put in her head.

'Well, I want some breakfast even if you don't,' he said, turning on his heel and stalking towards the inn door.

Beast!

She had no choice but to trot along in his wake. Well, no acceptable choice anyway. She certainly wasn't going to loiter in another inn yard, populated by yet more greasy-haired ostlers with lecherous eyes. And she *did* want breakfast. And she had no money.

When she caught up with him he was standing in the doorway to what looked like the main bar. Which was full of men, talking and swigging tankards of ale. It must be a market day for the place to be so busy and for so many men to look so inebriated this early.

'Stay here,' he growled, before striding across to the

bar. 'I want a private parlour,' he said to the burly man in a stained apron who was presiding over the bar. 'For myself and…' he waved a hand in her direction '…my niece.'

His *niece*? Why on earth was he telling the landlord she was his niece?

The answer came to her as soon as she looked at the burly tapster and saw the expression on his face as he eyed their appearance. Bad enough to have been called a trollop by the landlady of the last inn she'd been inside. At least if people thought she was this man's niece it gave an acceptable explanation for them travelling together, if not for the way they were dressed.

'And breakfast,' her 'uncle' was saying, as though completely impervious to what the burly man might be thinking about his appearance—or hers. 'Steak, onions, ale, bread and butter, and a pot of tea.'

The burly man behind the bar looked at her, looked over the rowdy market-day crowd, then gave a sort of shrug.

'Well, there ain't nobody in the coffee room at present, since the Birmingham stage has just gone out. You're welcome to sit in there, if you like.'

'The coffee room?'

Her muddy-coated, bloodstained companion looked affronted. He opened his mouth to make an objection, but as he did so the landlord's attention was snagged by a group of men at a far table, all surging to their feet as though intending to leave. They were rather boisterous, so Prudence wasn't all that surprised when the burly man came out from behind the bar to make sure they all paid before leaving. Her newly acquired 'uncle', however, looked far from pleased at being brushed aside as though his order for breakfast was of no account. He must be really hungry. Or spoiling for a fight. Things *really* hadn't been going his way this morning, had they?

Some of the boisterous men looked as though they were spoiling for a fight, too. But the burly landlord dealt with them deftly, thrusting them through the doorway next to which she was standing one by one the moment he'd extracted some money from them. She wouldn't be a bit surprised to learn that he'd been in the army. He had that look about him—that confidence and air of authority she'd seen fall like a mantle over men who had risen through the ranks to become sergeants. She'd heard such men talk about opening taverns when they got out, too...

Her suppositions were rudely interrupted by a couple of the boisterous men half falling against her on their way out, knocking her against the doorjamb. She decided enough was enough. It was all very well for her *uncle* to stand there looking indignant, but it wasn't getting them anywhere. Ignoring his command to stay where she was, she threaded her way through the tables to his side and plucked at his sleeve to gain his attention over the uproar.

'Can we go into the coffee room, please...er... Uncle?' she said.

He frowned down at her with displeasure.

She lifted her chin. 'I'm really not feeling all that well.' In fact the hot, crowded room appeared to be contracting and then expanding around her, and her head swam unpleasantly.

The frown on his face turned to a look of concern. 'You will feel better for something to eat and that cup of tea,' he declared, slipping his arm round her waist. 'I am only sorry we cannot have complete privacy, because what we have to discuss will of necessity be rather...'

'It certainly will,' she muttered, rather shocked at how good it felt to have him supporting her into the coffee room, when not half an hour since she'd been trying to escape him. 'Perhaps,' she suggested as he lowered her gently into a chair, 'we should discuss things right now, before anyone comes in.'

'We will be able to think more clearly once we've had something to eat and drink,' he said.

'How do you know? Have you ever been drugged before?'

He quirked one eyebrow at her as he drew up a chair next to her. Then leaned in so that he could speak quietly. 'So you *do* accept that is the case?'

She clasped her hands in her lap. 'Couldn't there have been some sort of mistake? Perhaps I stumbled into your room by accident?'

'And tore off all your clothes and flung them about in some sort of mad fit before leaping into my bed? It isn't likely. Unless you are in the habit of sleepwalking?'

She flushed as he described the very scenario she'd already dismissed as being completely impossible. Shook her head at his question about sleepwalking.

'Then what other explanation can there be?'

'What about this Hugo person you keep asking if I know?'

'Yes,' he said grimly. 'I still wonder if he could somehow be at the back of it. He has good reason to meddle in the business that brought me up here, you see. Only...'

He rubbed his hand over the back of his neck, looking troubled. Then shook his head.

'Only he isn't a bad lad—not really. Only selfish and thoughtless. Or so I've always thought.'

'Always? You have known him a long time?'

'Since his birth,' said Gregory. 'He is my cousin. My nearest male relative, in point of fact. Ever since he left school I have been attempting to teach him all he needs to know should he ever have to step into my shoes. He couldn't have thought it through. If it *was* him.'

'But how on earth could he have persuaded my aunt to do such a thing? Let alone my uncle?'

'He might have put the case in such a way that your aunt would have thought she was acting for your benefit.'

'My *benefit*? How could it be of any benefit to…to humiliate me and abandon me? Anything could have happened. If you were not the kind of man who…that is if you were not a… I mean…although you don't look it… I think you are a gentleman. You could easily have taken advantage of me. And you haven't. Unless… Oh! Are you married?'

'No. Not any more.'

'I am so sorry. I did not mean to make you uncomfortable by mentioning a topic that must surely cause you sorrow.'

'It doesn't.' He gave a sort of grimace. Then explained, 'My wife has been dead these eight years.'

'Oh, that's good. I mean…not that she's dead, but that it is long enough ago that you are past the worst of your grief. But anyway, what I was going to say was that perhaps you are simply not the sort. To break your marriage vows. I know that even the most unlikely-looking men can be doggedly faithful…'

His gaze turned so icy she shivered.

'Not that you look like the *un*faithful sort,' she hastily amended. 'Or the sort that… And anyway you have been married, so… That is… Oh, dear, I do not know what I mean, precisely.'

She could feel her cheeks growing hotter and hotter the longer she continued to babble at him. But to her relief his gaze suddenly thawed.

'I think I detected a sort of compliment amongst all those observations,' he said with a wry smile.

'Thank goodness.' She heaved a sigh of relief. 'I mean, it is not that I *intended* to compliment you, but…'

He held up his hand. 'Just stop right there, before you say anything else to embarrass yourself. And let me bring you back to the point in question. Which is this: perhaps your aunt thought to put you in a compromising position so that she could arrange an advantageous match for you.'

'An *advantageous match*? Are you mad?' She looked at his muddy coat, his blackened eye, the grazes on his knuckles.

And he pokered up.

'Although,' she said hastily, in an attempt to smooth down the feathers she'd ruffled by implying that someone would have to be mad to consider marrying the likes of *him*, 'of late she *has* been growing increasingly annoyed by my refusal to get married. On account of her wanting a particular member of her husband's family to benefit from my inheritance.'

'Your inheritance?'

Oh, dear. She shouldn't have blurted that out. So far he had been behaving rather well, all things considered. But once he knew she would come into a great deal of money upon making a good marriage it was bound to

bring out the worst in him. He had told her he was no
longer married. And, whatever line of business he was
in, acquiring a rich wife would be a definite asset.

Why hadn't she kept quiet about it? Why was she
blurting out the answers to all his questions at all?

She rubbed at the spot between her brows where once
she'd thought her brain resided.

'You don't think,' he persisted, 'that your aunt chose
to put you into *my* bed, out of the beds of all the single
men who were at that inn last night, for a particular
reason? Or that she chose to stay at that particular inn
knowing that I would be there?'

She kept on rubbing at her forehead, willing her brain
to wake up and come to her rescue. But it was no use.

'I don't know what you mean!' she eventually cried
out in frustration. 'We only stopped there because one
of the horses went lame. We were supposed to be pushing on to Mexworth. Uncle Murgatroyd was livid when
the postilions said we'd have to put up at the next place
we came to. And Aunt Charity said it was a miserable
little hovel and she'd never set foot in it. And then the
postilion said she could sleep in the stable if she liked,
but didn't she think she'd prefer a bed with sheets? And
then they had a rare old set-to, right in the middle of
the road…'

'I can just picture it,' he put in dryly.

'The upshot was that we didn't have any choice. It
was sheer coincidence that we were staying at the same
inn as you last night. And I'm sure my aunt wouldn't
have wanted to compromise you into marriage with
me anyway. She made some very derogatory remarks
about you last night at supper. Said you looked exactly

the sort of ruffian she would expect to find in a dingy little tavern in a town she'd never heard of.'

He sat back then, a thoughtful expression on his face.

'How much money, exactly, will you receive when you marry?'

Or was it a calculating expression, that look she'd seen?

She lowered her eyes, feeling absurdly disappointed. If he suddenly started paying her compliments and… and making up to her, the way so many men did when they found out about her dowry, then she would…she would…

The way she felt today, she'd probably burst into tears.

Fortunately he didn't notice, since at that moment a serving girl came in with a tray bearing a teapot, a tankard and a jug. He was so keen on getting on the outside of his ale that she might have thrown a tantrum and she didn't think he'd notice.

She snapped her cup onto its saucer and threw two sugar lumps into it before splashing a generous dollop of milk on top. She removed the lid from the teapot and stirred the brew vigorously.

'What will happen,' he asked, setting down his tankard once he'd drained it, 'to the money if you don't marry?'

'I will gain control of it for myself when I am twenty-five,' she replied dreamily as she poured out a stream of fragrant brown liquid. Oh, but she was counting the days until she need rely on nobody but herself.

She came back to the present with an unpleasant jerk the moment she noticed the pale, unappealing colour of the brew in her cup. She'd put far too much milk in first. Even once she stirred it it was going to be far too weak.

'And in the meantime who manages it for you?'

'My trustees. At least…' She paused, the teaspoon poised in mid-air as yet another horrible thought popped into her head. 'Oh. Oh, *no*.'

'What? What is it you've thought of?'

'Well, it is probably nothing. Only Aunt Charity re-married last year. *Mr Murgatroyd*.'

She couldn't help saying the name with distaste. Nothing had been the same since he'd come into their lives. Well, he'd always been there—right from the first moment she'd gone to live with her aunt. But back then he'd just been one of the congregation into which her aunt had introduced her. She hadn't disliked him any more than any other of the mealy-mouthed men who'd taken such delight in making her life as dreary as possible. It hadn't been until he'd married her aunt that she'd discovered how nasty he really was.

'He persuaded my trustees,' she continued, 'that he was a more proper person to take over the management of my money once he became the husband of my guardian.'

'And they agreed?'

'To be honest there was only one of them left. They were all older than my grandfather when he set up the trust in the first place. And the one who outlived him wasn't all that…um…'

'Capable?'

'That's a very good word for it.'

He looked into his tankard with a stunned expression. 'I always thought drink addled a man's brains. But this ale appears to have restored my intellect. That's the first time since I awoke this morning that I have been able to come up with an appropriate word.'

'Good for you,' she said gloomily, then took a sip of the milky tea. Which wasn't strong enough to produce any kind of restorative effect.

'And your uncle—this man your aunt has married—is now in charge of handling your inheritance? Until such time as you marry? Do I have it correct?'

'Yes.'

He set his tankard down on the table with a snap. 'So when shall I expect him to come calling? Demanding I make an honest woman of you?'

She shrugged. 'I would have thought he would have done so this morning, if he was going to do it at all. Instead of which he left the inn, taking all my luggage with him. You'd better pour yourself another tankard of ale and see if it will give you another brilliant idea, Mr—' She stopped. 'You never did tell me your name.'

'You never asked me for it.'

'I told you mine. It is only polite to reciprocate when a lady has introduced herself.'

He reared back, as though offended that she'd criticised his manners.

'A lady,' he replied cuttingly, 'would never introduce *herself*.'

'A gentleman,' she snapped back, 'would not make any kind of comment about any female's station in life. And you still haven't told me your name. I can only assume you must be ashamed of it.'

'Ashamed of it? Never.'

'Then why won't you tell me what it is? Why are you being so evasive?'

He narrowed his eyes.

'I am not being evasive. Last time we came to an introduction we veered off into a more pressing conversation about bread and butter I seem to recall. And this time I…' He shifted uncomfortably in his chair. 'I became distracted again.' He set down his tankard and pressed the heels of his hands against his temples, closing his eyes as though in pain.

'Oh, does your head hurt? I do beg your pardon. I am not usually so snappish. Or so insensitive.'

'And I am not usually so clumsy,' he said, lowering his hands and opening his eyes to regard her ruefully. 'I fear we are not seeing each other at our best.'

He'd opened his mouth to say something else when the door swung open again, this time to permit two serving girls to come in, each bearing a tray of food.

Prudence looked at his steak, which was smothered in a mountain of onions, and then down at her plate of bread and butter with a touch of disappointment.

'Wishing you'd ordered more? I can order you some eggs to go with that, if you like?'

She shook her head. 'I don't suppose I could eat them if you *did* order them, though it is very kind of you. It is just the smell of those onions…' She half closed her eyes and breathed in deeply. 'Ohhh…' she couldn't help moaning. 'They are making my mouth water.'

He gave her a very strange look. Dropped his gaze as though he felt uncomfortable. Fumbled with his knife and fork.

'Here,' he said brusquely, cutting off a small piece of meat and depositing it on her plate. 'Just a mouthful will do you no harm.'

And then he smiled at her. For the very first time. And something inside her sort of melted.

She'd never known a man with a black eye could smile with such charm.

Though was he deploying his charm on purpose? He certainly hadn't bothered smiling at her before he'd heard she was an heiress.

'Are you ever,' she asked, reaching for a knife and fork, 'going to tell me your name?'

His smile disappeared.

'It is Willingale,' he said quickly. *Too quickly?* 'Gregory Willingale.'

Then he set about his steak with the air of a man who hadn't eaten for a se'ennight.

Thank goodness she hadn't been fooled by that charming smile into thinking he was a man she could trust. Which, she admitted, she had started to do. Why, she hadn't talked to anyone so frankly and freely since her parents had died.

Which wouldn't do. Because he had secrets, did her *uncle Gregory.* She'd seen a distinct flash of guilt when he'd spoken the name Willingale.

Which meant he was definitely hiding something.

Chapter Five

Perhaps his real name wasn't Gregory Willingale at all. Perhaps he was using an alias, for some reason. But what could she do about it anyway? Run to the burly bartender with a tale of being abandoned by her aunt and left to the mercy of a man she'd never clapped eyes on until the night before? What would that achieve? Nothing—that was what. She already knew precisely what people who worked in inns thought of girls who went to them with tales of that sort. They thought they were making them up. At least that was what the landlady of the last inn had said. Before lecturing her about her lack of morals and throwing her out.

Earlier this morning she'd thought the woman must be incredibly cruel to do such a thing. But if Prudence had been the landlady of an inn, with a business to run, would *she* have believed such a fantastic tale? Why, she was living through it and she hardly believed it herself.

She cleared her throat.

'So, Mr Willingale,' she said, but only after swallowing the last of the sirloin he'd shared with her. 'Or should I call you *Uncle* Willingale? What do you propose we do next?'

Her own next step would depend very much on whatever *his* plans were. She'd only make up her mind what to do when she'd heard what they were.

'I am not sure,' he said through a mouthful of beef. 'I do not think we are in possession of enough facts.'

Goodness. That was pretty much the same conclusion she'd just drawn.

'Though I do think,' he said, scooping up a forkful of onions and depositing it on her plate, 'that in some way your guardians are attempting to defraud you of your inheritance.'

'Thank you,' she said meekly. 'For the onions, I mean,' she hastily explained, before spreading them on one of the remaining slices of bread and butter, then folding it into a sort of sandwich.

'You're welcome. Though how abandoning you in a small hostelry in the middle of nowhere will serve their purpose I cannot imagine. Surely the disappearance of a wealthy young woman will not go unnoticed wherever it is you come from?'

Since her mouth was full, she shook her head.

'It might not be noticed,' she admitted, as soon as her mouth was free to use it for anything other than eating. 'Not for a very long time anyway. Because we were on our way to Bath.'

'Bath?'

Why did he look as though he didn't believe her?

'Yes, Bath. Why not? I know it isn't exactly fashionable any more, but we are far from fashionable people. And I did tell you, didn't I, that Aunt Charity had been trying to get me to marry…? Well, someone I don't much care for.'

'A relative of her new husband?' he said grimly.

'Yes.'

'And then she suddenly changed her tack, did she? Offered to take you somewhere you could meet a young man you might actually like?'

'There's no need to say it like that!' Though she *had* been rather surprised by her aunt's sudden volte-face. 'She said she would rather see me married to anyone than have me create talk by moving out of her house to set up home on my own.'

'My mental powers are growing stronger by the minute,' Gregory said sarcastically, sawing off another piece of steak. 'Do go on,' he said, when she glowered at him over the rim of her teacup. 'You were about to tell me why nobody will be raising a hue and cry.'

'I have already told you. Aunt Charity finally saw that nothing on earth would induce me to marry…that toad. So she told everyone she was going to take me to Bath and keep me there until she'd found me a match, since I had turned up my nose at the best Stoketown had to offer.'

'Stoketown? You hail from Stoketown?'

'Yes.'

'And your aunt claimed she was taking you to Bath?'

'Yes.'

He laid down his knife and fork. 'You are not very bright, are you?'

'What? How *dare* you?'

'I dare because you were headed in entirely the wrong direction ever to end up in Bath. You should have gone in a south-westerly direction from Stoketown.

Instead you had been travelling in completely the opposite direction. Wherever it was your guardians were planning to take you, it most definitely wasn't Bath.'

'I don't believe you. That cannot be true.' Though why would he say such a thing if he didn't think it?

'Would you like me to ask the landlord to bring us a road map?' he asked her calmly. 'He probably has one, since this inn is on a staging route.'

'I've had enough of landlords for one day,' she said bitterly. 'The less I have to do with the one of this tavern, the better.'

'So you believe you were not headed in the direction of Bath?'

She turned her cup round and round on its saucer for a few moments, thinking as hard as she could. 'I cannot think of any reason why you should say that if it weren't true,' she said pensively. 'But then, I cannot think of any reason why Aunt Charity should claim to be taking me there and actually be taking me in the opposite direction, either.'

'Nor why she should give you something that would make you sleep so soundly you wouldn't even wake when she carried you to the room of the most disreputable person she could find, undressed you, and put you into bed with him? Aha!' he cried, slapping the tabletop. 'Disreputable. *That* was the word I was searching for.'

'Do you have to sound so pleased about it?'

'I can't help it. You have no idea how irritating it has been, not being able to come up with the words I want,' he said, wiping the gravy from his plate with the last slice of her bread.

Her bread. The bread *she'd* ordered.

Though, to be fair, he had shared some of his own

meal with her. If he had taken the last slice of her bread, at least he'd made up for it by sharing his steak and onions.

'I wasn't talking about that,' she protested.

'What, then?'

'I meant about the conclusions you have drawn.'

'Well, I'm pleased about them, too. That is that things are becoming clear.'

'Are they?'

'Yes.' He finished the bread, picked up his tankard, emptied that, and sat back with a satisfied sigh. 'I have ruled Hugo out of the equation. You,' he said, setting the tankard down on the tabletop with a sort of a flourish, 'are an heiress. And villains are trying to swindle you out of your inheritance. First of all they told everyone they were going to take you to Bath, and then set off in the opposite direction. Where exactly they planned to take you, and what they planned to do when they got there, we may never know. Because one of the horses went lame and they were obliged to rack up at The Bull. Where they were shown to rooms on the very top floor.'

He leaned forward slightly.

'There were only three rooms on that floor, if you recall. Yours, mine, and I presume theirs?'

She nodded.

'Your aunt saw me, reached an unflattering conclusion about my integrity on account of my black eye and travel-stained clothing, and decided to make the most of what must have looked like a golden opportunity to dispose of you. You have already admitted that you believe your aunt gave you some sort of sleeping draught.'

'Well, I suppose she might have done. I didn't think it was anything more than hot milk at the time, but—'

'How they managed to administer something similar to me is a bit of a puzzle,' he said, cutting her off mid-sentence. 'But let us assume they did. Once I lay sleeping heavily they carried you to my room, safe in the knowledge that there would be no witnesses to the deed since we were isolated up there.'

She shuddered. She couldn't bear to think of Mr Murgatroyd touching her, doing who knew what to her while she was insensible. Oh, she hoped he'd left the room before her aunt had undressed her. At least she could be certain he hadn't done *that* himself. Aunt Charity would never have permitted it.

'Then, in the morning,' Gregory continued, 'they set up a bustle, pretending to search for you. They must have summoned the landlord and dragged him up all those stairs, attracting a crowd on the way so that they could all witness you waking up naked in my bed.'

'There is no need to look so pleased about it. It was horrid!'

His expression sobered.

'I beg your pardon,' he said. 'But you see I have led a very dull, regulated sort of existence until very recently. Suffocatingly boring, to be perfectly frank. And I had come to the conclusion that what I needed was a bit of a challenge. What could be more challenging than taking on a pair of villains trying to swindle an heiress out of her inheritance? Or solving the mystery of how we ended up naked in the same bed together?'

She wished he wouldn't keep harping on about the *naked* part of it. How did he expect her to look him in the eye or hold a sensible conversation when he kept reminding her that she'd been *naked*?

She had to change the subject.

'Pardon me for pointing it out,' she said, indicating his black eye and then the grazes on his knuckles, 'but you don't look to me as though you have been leading what you call a dull sort of existence.'

'Oh, this?' He chuckled as he flexed his bruised hands. 'This was the start of my adventure, actually. I'd gone up to Manchester to deal with a…ah…a situation that had come to my attention. I was on my way… er…to meet someone and report back when I…' He looked a bit sheepish. 'Well, to be perfectly honest I took a wrong turning. That's why I ended up at that benighted inn last night. So Hugo *couldn't* have done it!' He slapped the table. 'Of *course* he couldn't.' He smiled at her. 'Well, that's a relief. I shan't have to hold him to account for what has happened to you. I don't think I could have forgiven him this.'

His smile faded. He gave her a look she couldn't interpret, then glared balefully at his empty tankard.

He took a deep breath. 'I'm going to take you to the place where I've arranged to meet him. Straight away.'

She wasn't at all sure she liked the sound of that.

'Excuse me, but I'm not convinced that is the right thing to do.'

'I beg your pardon?' He looked completely stunned. 'Why should you not wish to go there?'

'I know nothing about it, that's why.' And precious little about *him*, except that he had recently been in a fight and was being downright shifty about what it had been about.

Oh, yes—and she knew what he looked like naked.

'It is a very comfortable property in which a relative of mine lives,' he snapped. 'A sort of aunt.'

She gave an involuntary shiver.

'You need not be afraid of her. Well...' He rubbed his nose with his thumb. 'I suppose some people *do* find her impossible, but she won't behave the way your aunt did—I can promise you that.'

'I would rather,' she said tartly, 'not have anything to do with *any* sort of aunt—particularly one you freely admit is impossible.'

'Nevertheless,' he said firmly, 'she can provide you with clean clothes, and we will both enjoy good food and comfortable beds. In rooms that nobody will invade,' he said with a sort of muted anger, 'the way they did at The Bull. And then, once we are rested and recovered, I can contact people who will be able to get to the bottom of the crime being perpetrated against you.'

'Will you? I mean...thank you very much,' she added doubtfully.

If he really did mean to take her to the home of a female relative who lived in some comfort, even if she *was* a touch difficult to get on with, and contact people on her behalf to right the wrongs done her, then it was the best thing she could think of.

It was just that coming from a man with a black eye and bruised knuckles it sounded a bit too good to be true.

He shot her a piercing glance. 'Don't you believe me?'

'I am sorry,' she said, a touch defiantly. 'But I am having trouble believing *anything* that has happened today. But if you say you mean to help me, then I shall...' She paused, because she'd been brought up to be very truthful. 'I shall *try* to believe you mean it.'

'Of course I mean it. Your guardians picked the wrong man to use as their dupe when they deposited you in my bed. I will make them rue the day they attempted to cross swords with *me*.' He flexed his bruised, grazed hands.

'Did you make *them* rue the day as well?'

She'd blurted out the question before she'd even known she was wondering about it. She looked up at him in trepidation. Only to discover he was smiling. True, it wasn't what she'd call a very *nice* sort of smile. In fact it looked more like the kind of expression she imagined a fox would have after devastating a hen-house.

'Yes, I made a whole lot of people sorry yesterday,' he said.

She swallowed. Reached for the teapot.

Something about the way she poured her second cup of tea must have betrayed her misgivings, because his satisfied smile froze.

'I don't generally go about getting into brawls, if that's what you're afraid of,' he said.

'I'm not afraid.'

He sighed. 'I wouldn't blame you if you were. Look…' He folded his arms across his chest. 'I'll tell you what happened, and why it happened, and then you can judge for yourself.'

She shrugged one shoulder, as if she didn't care, and took a sip of her tea. This time, thankfully, it had much more flavour.

'It started with a letter from a man who worked in a…a manufactory. In it he described a lot of double-dealing, as well as some very unsavoury behaviour towards the female mill workers by the foreman, and he asked the owner of the mill whether he could bear having such things going on in his name. He couldn't,' he said, with a decisive lift to his chin. 'And so I went to see if I could get evidence of the wrongdoing, and find a way to put a stop to it.'

So he was employed as a sort of investigator? Which explained why he had a secretary. Someone who would help him keep track of the paperwork while he went off doing the actual thief-taking. It also explained why he was reluctant to speak of his trade. He would have to keep a lot of what he did to himself. Or criminals would see him coming.

She took a sip of tea and suddenly saw that that couldn't be the right conclusion. Because it sounded like rather an exciting sort of way to make a living. And he'd said he had lived a dull, ordered existence. She sighed. Why did nothing make any sense today?

'I soon found out that it wouldn't be possible to bring the foreman to trial for what he was doing to the women under his power, because not a one of them would stand up in court and testify. Well, you couldn't expect it of them.'

'No,' she murmured, horrified. 'So what did you do?'

'Well, Bodkin—that's the man who wrote the letter—said that maybe we'd be able to get the overseer dismissed for fraud if we could only find the false ledgers he kept. He sent one set of accounts to…to the mill owner, you see, and kept another to tally up what he was actually making for himself. We couldn't simply walk in and demand to see the books, because he'd have just shown us the counterfeit ones. So we had to break in at night, and search for them.'

'Aunt Charity said you looked like a housebreaker,' she couldn't help saying. Though she clapped her hand over her mouth as soon as she'd said it.

He frowned. 'It's funny, but I would never have thought I'd be keen to tell anyone about Wragley's. But you blurting out things the way you just did… Perhaps it's something to do with the drug we were given. We can't help saying whatever is on our minds.'

'I…suppose that might be it,' she said, relieved that he wasn't disposed to take her to task for being so rude. 'Although…' She paused.

'What?'

'Never mind,' she said with a shake of her head. She didn't want to admit that for some reason she felt as though she could say anything to him. 'You were telling me about how you tried to find the second set of books?'

'Oh, yes. Well, long story short, we found them. Only the night watchman saw the light from our lantern, called for help and came after us. It was touch and go for a while, but eventually we got clean away,' he ended with a grin.

So even if he wasn't a professional thief-taker, he certainly enjoyed investigating crime and seeing villains brought to book. A man who could speak of such an adventure with that look of relish on his face would be perfect for helping her untangle whatever it was that Aunt Charity and Uncle Murgatroyd thought they'd achieved last night.

Someone who could fight for her. Defend her. And he was certainly capable of that. She only had to think of all those bulging muscles. The ones she'd seen that morning as he'd gone stalking about the bedroom, stark naked and furious.

Oh, dear, there was that word again. The one that made her blush, since this time it wasn't just her own nudity she was picturing but his.

She pushed it out of her mind. Instantly it was replaced by the memory of him handing her his jacket. And that after she'd almost brained him with a rock.

Which helped her come to a decision.

'I should like you to make Aunt Charity and Uncle Murgatroyd sorry, too. Because I think you are right. I think they *are* trying to take my money. Trying to make me disappear altogether, actually. If it was them who put me in your room—'

'Who else could it have been?'

'I know, I know. You're clearly very good at working out how criminals think. It still isn't very pleasant to accept it. But...' She drew a deep breath. 'Very well, *when* they put me in your room,' she said, although her stomach gave a little lurch, 'they probably did take advantage of the way the rooms were isolated up there— particularly after they saw the way you looked and behaved at dinner. I do think they believed that of all the men in that place you looked the most likely to treat me the worst.'

'For that alone I should break them. How dare they assume any such thing?'

And that was another thing. He had a vested interest in clearing his own name, too. Now that she'd heard the lengths to which he'd gone to right the wrongs being done to the women at that mill, she felt much better about going to the house of which he'd spoken. They would need somewhere to go and hatch their plans for... not revenge. Justice. Yes, it was only justice she wanted.

'So you will help me track them down and make them pay?'

Make them pay? 'I most certainly will,' he said.

He would set his people on their trail. He would

tell them it was their top priority. From what Prudence had told him so far, he wouldn't be surprised to learn they'd actually been heading for Liverpool. Possibly with a view to leaving the country altogether, if her uncle had actually swindled her out of all her money. On the off-chance that the case was not as bad as all that, he'd make sure his staff found out everything about their business dealings, too, and gained control of any leases or mortgages they had. He would throw a cordon around them so tight that they wouldn't be able to sneeze without his permission.

And if it turned out that they *had* stolen Prudence's inheritance, and hadn't had the sense to get out of the country while they could, then he would crush them. Utterly.

Just then the door opened and the landlord came in.

'Next coach's due in any time now,' he said without preamble. 'Time for you to make off.'

Gregory deliberately relaxed his hands, which he'd clenched into fists as he'd been considering all the ways he could make Prudence's relatives pay for what they'd done. 'Bring me the reckoning, then,' he said. 'I am ready to depart.'

He turned to see Prudence eyeing him warily.

'Hand me my purse, would you, niece? It's in my pocket.'

She continued to stare at him in that considering way until he was forced to speak to her more sternly.

'Prudence, my purse.'

She jumped, but then dug her hand into one of the pockets of the jacket he'd lent her. And then the other one. And then, instead of handing over his purse, she pulled out the stocking he'd thrust in there and forgotten all about. She gazed at it in bewilderment.

Before she could start asking awkward questions he darted round the table, whipped it out of her hand and thrust it into his waistcoat. And then, because she appeared so stunned by the discovery of one of her undergarments that she'd forgotten to hand him his purse, he decided he might as well get it himself.

It wasn't there. Not in the pocket where he could have sworn he'd put it. A cold, sick swirl of panic had him delving into all the jacket pockets, several times over. Even though it was obvious what had happened.

'It's gone,' he said, tamping down the panic as he faced the truth. 'We've been robbed.'

Chapter Six

'Ho, robbed, is it?' The landlord planted his fists on his ample hips. 'Sure, and you had such a fat purse between you when you come in.'

'Not a fat purse, no,' said Gregory, whirling round from his crouched position to glare at the landlord. 'But sufficient. Do you think I would have asked for a private parlour if I hadn't the means to pay for it?'

'What I think is that there's a lot of rogues wandering the highways of England these days. And one of them, or rather two,' he said, eyeing Prudence, 'have fetched up here.'

'Now, look here…'

'No, *you* look here. I don't care what story you come up with, I won't be fooled, see? So you just find the means to pay what you owe or I'm sending for the constable and you'll be spending the night in the roundhouse.'

There was no point in arguing. The man's mind was closed as tight as a drum. Besides, Gregory had seen the way he'd dealt with that bunch of customers in the tap. Ruthlessly and efficiently.

There was nothing for it. He stood up and reached

for the watch he had in his waistcoat pocket. A gold hunter that was probably worth the same as the entire inn, never mind the rather basic meal they'd just consumed. The very gold hunter that Hugo had predicted he'd be obliged to pawn. His stomach contracted. He'd already decided to go straight to Bramley Park rather than wait until the end of the week. But that was *his* decision. Pawning the watch was not, and it felt like the bitterest kind of failure.

'If you would care to point me in the direction of the nearest pawn shop,' he said, giving the landlord a glimpse of his watch, 'I shall soon have the means to pay what we owe.'

'And what's to stop you legging it the minute I let you out of my sight? You leave the watch with me and I'll pawn it if you don't return.'

Leave his watch in the possession of this barrel of lard? Let those greasy fingers leave smears all over the beautifully engraved casing? He'd rather spend the night in the roundhouse.

Only there was Prudence to consider. Spending a night in a roundhouse after the day she'd had… No, he couldn't possibly condemn her to that.

'I could go and pawn it,' put in Prudence, startling them both.

'That ain't no better an idea than to let *him* go off and not come back,' said the landlord scathingly.

He had to agree. She was sure to come to some harm if he let her out of his sight. He'd never met such a magnet for trouble in all his life.

'You do realise,' he said, folding his arms across his chest, and his gold watch to boot, 'that I have a horse and gig in your stables which would act as surety no matter which of us goes to raise what we owe?'

The landlord gave an ironic laugh. 'You expect me to believe you'd come back if I let either one of you out of my sight?'

'Even if I didn't return you'd still have the horse.' Which would serve him right. 'And the vehicle, too. I know the paint is flaking a bit, but the actual body isn't in bad repair. You could sell them both for ten times what we owe for breakfast.'

'And who's to say you wouldn't turn up the minute I'd sold 'em, with some tale of me swindling and cheating you, eh? Trouble—that's what you are. Knew it the minute I clapped eyes on yer.'

'Then you were mistaken. I am not trouble. I am just temporarily in a rather embarrassing state. Financially.'

Good grief, had he really uttered the very words he'd heard drop so many times from Hugo's lips? The words he'd refused to believe any man with an ounce of intelligence or willpower could ever have any excuse for uttering?

'What you got in that case of yours?' asked the landlord abruptly, pointing to his valise.

Stays—that was the first thing that came to mind. And the landlord had already spied the stocking Prudence had extracted from his jacket pocket.

'Nothing of any great value,' he said hastily. 'You really would be better accepting the horse and gig as surety for payment.'

The landlord scratched the lowest of his ample chins thoughtfully. 'If you really do have a horse stabled here, I s'pose that'd do.'

Gregory sucked in a sharp stab of indignation as the

landlord turned away from him with a measuring look and went to open one of the back windows.

'Jem!' the landlord yelled through the window. 'Haul your hide over here and take a gander at this sharp.'

Gregory's indignation swelled to new proportions at hearing himself being described as a 'sharp'. He'd never cheated or swindled anyone in his life.

'It's horrid, isn't it?' said Prudence softly, coming to stand next to him. 'Having persons like that—' she jerked her head in the landlord's direction '—doubt your word.'

'It is indeed,' he replied. It was especially so since, viewed dispassionately, everything he'd done since entering this inn had given the man just cause for doing so.

'Though to be fair,' she added philosophically, 'we don't look the sort of people *I* would trust if I was running this kind of business.' She frowned. 'I put that very clumsily, but you know what I mean.' She waved a hand between them.

'Yes,' he said. 'I do know exactly what you mean.'

He'd just thought it himself. Her aunt had marked him as a villain the night before just because of his black eye. Since then he'd acquired a gash, a day's growth of beard, and a liberal smear of mud all down one side of his coat. He'd been unable to pay for his meal, and had then started waving ladies' undergarments under the landlord's nose.

As for Prudence—with her hair all over the place, and wearing the jacket she'd borrowed from him rather than a lady's spencer over her rumpled gown—she, too, now looked thoroughly disreputable.

Admirably calm though, considering the things she'd

been through. Calm enough to look at things from the landlord's point of view.

'You take it all on the chin, don't you? Whatever life throws at you?'

'Well, there's never any point in weeping and wailing, is there? All that does is make everyone around you irritable.'

Was that what had happened to her? When first her mother and then her father had died, and one grandfather had refused to accept responsibility for her and the other had palmed her off on a cold, resentful aunt? He wouldn't have blamed her for weeping in such circumstances. And he could easily see that bony woman becoming irritated.

He wished there had been someone there for her in those days. He wished there was something he could do for her now. Although it struck him now that she'd come to stand by his side, as though she was trying to help *him*.

To be honest, and much to his surprise, she had succeeded. He *did* feel better. Less insulted by the landlord's mistrustfulness, at any rate.

'We do look rather like a pair of desperate criminals,' he admitted, leaning down so he could murmur into her ear. 'In fact it is a wonder the landlord permitted us to enter his establishment at all.'

Just then a tow-headed individual poked his head through the open window.

'What's up, Sarge?'

'This 'ere *gent*,' said the landlord ironically, 'claims he has a horse and gig in your stable. Know anything about it?'

As the stable lad squinted at him Gregory's heart

sped up. Incredible to feel nervous. Yet the prospect that Jem might fail to recognise him was very real. He'd only caught a glimpse of him as he'd handed over the reins, after all.

Prudence patted his hand, as though she knew exactly what he was thinking. Confirming his suspicions that she was trying to reassure him all would be well.

'Bad-tempered nag,' Jem pronounced after a second or two, much to Gregory's relief. 'And a Yarmouth coach.'

Yes, that was a close enough description of the rig he'd been driving.

'Right,' said the landlord decisively. 'Back to work, then.'

Jem withdrew his head and the landlord slammed the window shut behind him.

Gregory resisted the peculiar fleeting urge to take hold of Prudence's hand. Focussed on the landlord.

'So, we have a deal?' he said firmly.

'I suppose,' said the landlord grudgingly. 'Except now I'm going to have your animal eating its head off at my expense for the Lord knows how long.'

'Fair point. How about this? If I'm not back within the space of one week from today, with what we owe for the meal we've eaten, plus the cost of stabling the horse, you can sell the beast and the…er…Yarmouth coach.'

'One week from today?' He narrowed his eyes. 'I s'pose that'd do. But only if you put something in writing first.'

'Naturally. Bring me pen and paper and you may have my vowels.'

The landlord screwed up his face and shook his head, indicating his reluctance to let them out of his sight even for the length of time it would take to fetch writing implements. Instead, he rummaged in his apron pocket and produced what looked like a bill and a stub of pencil, then slapped both on the table.

As Gregory bent to write the necessary phrases on the back of the bill he heard the sound of a coaching horn. Closely followed by the noise of wheels rattling into the yard. Then two surprisingly smart waiters strode into the coffee room, bearing trays of cups and tankards.

The landlord swept Gregory's note and the pencil back into his pocket without even glancing at them, his mind clearly on the next influx of customers.

'Get out,' he said brusquely. 'Before I change my mind and send for the constable anyway.'

Gregory didn't need telling twice. He snatched up the valise with the incriminating stays with one hand, and grabbed Prudence's arm with the other. Then he dragged her from the room against the tide of people surging in, all demanding coffee or ale.

'Come on,' he growled at her. 'Stop dragging your heels. We need to get out of here before that fat fool changes his mind.'

'But…' she panted. 'How on earth are we going to get wherever it is you planned to take me without your gig?'

'Never mind that now. The first thing to do is find a pawn shop.'

'It will be in a back street somewhere,' she said. 'So that people can hope nobody will see them going in.'

'It isn't a very big town,' he said, on a last flickering ray of hope. 'There might not even be one.'

'If there wasn't the landlord would have said so,' she pointed out with annoyingly faultless logic.

Condemning him to the humiliating prospect of sneaking into some back street pawn shop. After all the times he'd lectured Hugo about the evils of dealing with pawnbrokers and moneylenders.

'And I don't see why you have to walk so fast,' she complained. 'Not when we have a whole week to raise the money.'

'We?' He couldn't believe she could speak of his possessions as though they were her own. As though she had some rights as to how he should dispose of them. '*I* am the one who is going to have to pawn *my* watch.'

'I'm sorry. I can see how reluctant you are to part with it. But you know I don't have anything of value.'

'Not any more,' he fumed. 'Thanks to you.'

'What do you mean, thanks to *me*?'

'I mean that *you* had my purse. Which contained easily enough money to last until the end of the week. I can't believe how careless you are.'

'Careless? What do you mean? Are you implying it's *my* fault you lost your purse?'

'Well, you were wearing my jacket when those oafs jostled it out of the pocket.'

'What oafs?' She frowned. 'Oh. You mean when we came in here?'

He could see her mind going over the scene, just as his own had done the moment he'd realised the purse wasn't where he'd put it.

'So,' she added slowly. 'You think that is when the purse went missing, do you?'

'When else could it have gone?'

'How about when you fell out of the gig?'

'You mean when you pushed me out of the gig?'

They were no longer walking along the street but standing toe to toe, glaring at each other. Though what right *she* had to be angry, he couldn't imagine. He was the one who was having to abandon every principle he held dear. She was the one whose fault it was.

Yet she was breathing heavy, indignant breaths. Which made her gown strain over her bosom.

Her unfettered bosom.

Since her stays were in his hand. At least they were in his valise, which was in his hand.

'Right,' she said, and drew herself up to her full height and lifted her chin.

He probably ought to warn her to pull his jacket closed. She could have no idea how touchable and tempting she looked right now.

Tempting? No. She wasn't tempting. She was *not*.

No more than she'd been when she'd moaned in ecstasy at the flavour of his steak and onions. There was still something the matter with his brain—that was what it was. Some lingering after-effect from the drug. It explained why he'd spilled out almost the entire story of his adventure at Wragley's. And why he kept on being afflicted by these inconvenient, inappropriate surges of lust.

Though part of it *was* down to her. The way she looked all wild and wanton in the grip of anger, so much more alive and vital than any other woman he'd ever known. The way she openly stood up to him in a way nobody had ever dared before.

Though he'd even found her appealing when she'd looked drugged and dazed and helpless. Helpless, she aroused his protective instincts. Angry she just aroused…more basic instincts.

'Right,' she said again. And with a toss of her head turned round and strode away from him.

'Where do you think you are going?' The insufferable wench was obliging him to follow her if he didn't wish to lose sight of her.

'I'm going,' she tossed over her shoulder, 'to sort out the mess you have plunged us into.'

'Mess *I* have plunged us into? You were the one who got robbed—'

'You were the one who left the purse in my pocket, though, once it became an outside pocket after you removed your coat.'

'I—' Dammit, she was correct. *Again.* He should have kept hold of the purse himself.

'In my defence,' he pointed out resentfully, 'I had just suffered a stunning blow to the head.'

'Trust you to bring that up,' she said, rounding on him. And then, taking him completely by surprise, she reached up and snatched off his hat.

'You don't mind me borrowing this, do you?'

'For what, pray?'

'To collect the money.'

'Collect the...what?'

She didn't seriously mean to go begging through the streets, did she? That would be worse by far than anything that had happened to him yet.

'Yes, I do mind,' he said, reaching round her to retrieve his property.

But she twitched it out of his reach. And slapped his hand for good measure. And carried on walking down the street towards the market square.

'Prudence,' he warned her. 'I cannot permit you to do this.' It was unthinkable. If anyone ever found out that he'd been seen begging… The very thought sent cold chills down his spine.

'*Permit* me?'

If he thought she'd looked angry before it was as nothing compared to the way she looked now. She came to an abrupt halt.

'You have no say over anything I do,' she said, poking him in the chest with her forefinger. A habit she'd no doubt picked up from that bony aunt of hers. 'I shall do as I please.'

'Not with my hat, you won't.'

He made a move to get it back. But she was still too quick for him, nimbly leaping out of his reach with the agility of a professional fencing master.

'Prudence,' he snapped. 'Don't you realise you can be arrested for begging?'

'Begging?' She gave him a disbelieving look over her shoulder. 'I have no intention of begging.'

Well, that was a relief. But still… 'Then what *do* you plan to do? With my hat?'

'It's market day,' she said, as though the statement should be self-explanatory. And then added for his benefit, as though he were a total simpleton, 'People expect entertainers to come to town on market day.'

'Yes. But you are not an entertainer. Are you?'

'No,' she said indignantly. 'But I do have a very fine singing voice.'

'Oh, no…' he muttered as she made for the market cross with his hat clutched in her determined little fingers. 'You cannot mean to perform in the street for pennies, surely?'

'Well, do you have a better idea?'

'Yes.'

'Which is…?' She planted her hands on her hips and pursed her lips again.

Dammit, nobody *ever* questioned his decisions. If he said he had an idea people always waited to hear what it was, with a view to carrying out his orders at once. They didn't plant their hands on their hips and look up at him as though they didn't believe he had ever had a plan in his life.

'I see no reason,' he said, affronted, 'why I should tell you.'

'Just as I thought,' she scoffed. 'You haven't a plan. Except to pawn your watch and then go crawling back to that nasty landlord, with your tail between your legs, in order to retrieve a horse you despise and a gig that you have trouble steering.'

'I do not!'

He was a notable whip.

Normally.

'And I have no intention of crawling. I *never* crawl.'

'Really?'

She raised one eyebrow in such a disdainful way it put him in mind of one of the patronesses of Almack's, depressing the pretensions of a mushroom trying to gain entrance to their hallowed club.

'Really,' he insisted.

'So, how do you propose to treat with the landlord?'

'Once I've pawned my watch—'

'Look,' she said, in the kind of voice he imagined someone using on a rather dim-witted child. 'There will be no need for you to pawn that watch. Because I intend to rectify the situation *I* have caused by being so *careless* as to lose the purse you entrusted to my keeping without informing me you had done so. If it *was* actually there when you draped your jacket around my shoulders,' she said with an acid smile. 'For all I know you dropped it at The Bull. A lot of things went missing there. Why not your purse?'

'Because I distinctly recall paying my shot there— that's why.'

'Well, then. It's clearly up to me to make amends,' she flung at him, before mounting the steps of the market cross and setting his hat at her feet.

'Not so fast,' he said, striding after her and mounting the steps himself.

'You cannot stop me,' she said, raising one hand as though to ward him off. 'I will scream,' she added as he reached for the open edges of his jacket.

But she didn't. Not even before she realised that all he was doing was buttoning it up.

'There,' he growled. 'At least you no longer run the risk of being arrested for indecency.'

She clapped her hands to her front, glancing down in alarm. While he stalked away to seek a position near enough to keep watch over her, yet far enough away that nobody would immediately suspect him of being her accomplice.

Once he'd found a suitable vantage point he folded his arms across his chest with a glower. Short of wrestling her down from the steps, there was no way to prevent the stubborn minx from carrying out her ridiculous threat. Let her sing, then! Just for as long as it took her to realise she was wasting her time. They'd never get as much money from what amounted to begging as they would by pawning his watch.

And then she'd have to fall in with his plans, meek as a lamb. A chastened lamb. Yes, he'd wait until the citizens of Tadburne had brought her down a peg, and then he'd be…magnanimous.

He permitted himself a smile in anticipation of some of the ways in which he could be magnanimous to Miss High-and-Mighty Prudence Carstairs while she cleared her throat, lifted her chin, shifted from one foot to the other, and generally worked up the nerve to start her performance.

The first note that came from her throat wavered. He grimaced. If that was the best she could do they weren't going to be here very long. He'd pull her down off the steps before the locals started pelting her with cabbages, naturally. He didn't want a travelling companion who smelled of rotting vegetables.

Prudence cleared her throat and started again. This time running through a set of scales, the way he'd heard professional singers do to warm up.

By the time she'd finished her scales the notes coming from her throat no longer squeaked and wavered. They flowed like liquid honey.

Prudence hadn't exaggerated. She did indeed have a fine singing voice. In keeping with the husky, rather sensuous way she spoke, she sang in a deep, rich, contralto voice that might have earned her a fortune in London.

Blast her.

Every time he looked forward to gaining the advantage she somehow managed to wrest it back.

So why did he still find her so damned attractive?

Oh, Lord, if Aunt Charity could see her now! She'd be shocked. Horrified. That a Biddlestone should resort to singing in a public street… Although, had Aunt

Charity not abandoned her in The Bull, there would have been no need to do any such thing. Or if Mr Willingale hadn't lost his purse and chosen to blame *her* instead of shouldering it like a gentleman.

No, she mustn't get angry. Anger would come out in her voice and ruin her performance. One of the singing teachers she'd had intermittently over the years had told her always to think pleasant thoughts when singing, even if the ballad was a tragic one, or it would make her vocal cords tense and ruin her tone.

So she lost herself in the words, telling the story of a girl in love with a swain in the greenwood. She pictured the apple blossom, the rippling brook and the moss-covered pebbles about which she was singing.

She would *not* look at Mr Willingale, whose expression was enough to turn milk sour. Or at least not very often. Because, although it was extremely satisfying to see the astonishment on his face when she proved that not only could she sing, she could do so to a very high standard, it made her want to giggle. And nobody could sing in tune when they were giggling. It was worse than being angry, because it ruined the breath control.

Far better to look the other way, to where people were starting to take note of her. To draw near and listen. To pull out their hankies as she reached the tragic climax of the ballad and dab at their eyes.

And toss coppers into the hat she'd laid at her feet.

She did permit herself to dart just one triumphant glance in Mr Willingale's direction before launching into her next song, but only one. There would be time enough to crow when she could tip the shower of pennies she was going to earn into his hands.

She'd show him—oh, yes, she would. It had been so

insulting of him not to trust her to pawn his watch. He'd looked at her the way that landlord had just looked at him. How could he think she'd run off with his watch and leave him there?

He'd assumed she would steal his gig, too, earlier, and leave him stunned and bleeding in the lane.

He was the most distrustful, suspicious, insulting man she'd ever met, and why she was still trying to prove she wasn't any of the things he thought, she couldn't imagine.

Why, she had as much cause to distrust *him*—waking up naked in his bed like that.

Only honesty compelled her to admit that it hadn't been his doing. That was entirely down to Aunt Charity and her vile new husband. There really could be no other explanation.

She came to the end of her second ballad and smiled at the people dropping coins into Mr Willingale's hat. How she wished she had a glass of water. Singing in the open air made the voice so dry, so quickly. Perhaps she could prevail upon Mr Willingale to fetch her some? She darted a hopeful glance in his direction. But he just grimaced, as though in disgust, then turned and strode off down a side street.

He had no intention of helping her—not when he was opposed to her plan. The beast was just going to leave her there. Probably hoping she'd become nervous once he was out of sight and run after him, begging him not to leave her alone.

Well, if he thought she would feel afraid of being alone in the middle of a strange town then he didn't know her at all. Why, she'd been in far more dangerous places than an English town on market day.

Though then she'd been a child. With her parents to protect her. Not to mention the might of the English army at her back. Which was why she'd never felt this vulnerable before.

Not even when she'd realised her aunt had abandoned her at The Bull. Though that had probably been largely due to the fact that she'd been numb with shock and still dazed from the sleeping draught at that point this morning. But now she was starting to think clearly.

What was to become of her?

She had no money. Only the few clothes she stood up in. And no real idea where she was or where she was going. In just a few short hours she'd become almost totally reliant on Mr Willingale. Who'd just disappeared down that alley. For a second, panic gripped her by the throat.

But she was not some spineless milk-and-water miss who would go running after a man and beg him not to abandon her to the mercy of strangers. She was a Carstairs. And no Carstairs *ever* quailed in the face of adversity.

Defiantly, she lifted her chin and launched into her third ballad.

Chapter Seven

Prudence had hardly got going when a trio of young men emerged from a side street and sauntered in her direction. She could tell they were trouble even before they pushed to the front of the crowd who'd gathered to hear her sing.

She did her best not to display any sign of nervousness. But it was difficult not to feel anxious when one of them pulled out a quizzing glass, raked her insolently from top to toe, and said, 'Stap me, but I never thought to find *such* a prime article in *such* an out-of-the-way place.'

She carried on singing as though she hadn't heard him.

One of his companions, meanwhile, turned to look at the farmer standing next to him. With a supercilious sneer he pulled out a handkerchief and held it to his nose. The yokel turned a dull, angry shade of red and shuffled away.

The three young bucks had soon had the same effect on all her audience. By the time she'd reached the end of her song they'd all dispersed. Leaving her alone on the steps of the cross.

Time to leave. Her voice was past its best anyhow. What with having nobody to bring her a glass of water…

She darted the bucks a smile she hoped was nonchalant as she bent to pick up the hat.

'Allow me,' said the one with the quizzing glass, snatching it from the ground before she could get to it. He smirked at his companions, who chuckled and drew closer.

'Thank you,' she said, holding out her hand in the faint hope that he'd simply give her the hat. Though she could tell he had no intention of doing any such thing.

'Not much to show for your performance,' he said, glancing into the hat, then at her. 'Hardly worth your trouble, really.'

The others sniggered.

'It is to me,' she said. 'Please hand it over.'

He took a step closer, leering at her. 'Only if you pay a forfeit. I think a hatful of coins is worth a kiss, don't you?'

His friends found him terribly amusing, to judge from the way they all hooted with laughter.

He pressed forward, lips puckered as though to make her pay the forfeit.

She backed up a step. 'Absolutely not,' she protested.

'A kiss for each of us,' cried the one who'd driven the farmer away with his scented handkerchief.

All three were advancing on her now, forcing her to retreat up the steps until her back was pressed to the market cross.

'Let me pass,' she said, as firmly as she could considering her heart was banging against her ribs so hard.

'If you are going to give my friends a kiss just for letting you pass,' said the ringleader, 'I should demand something more for the return of your takings, don't you think?'

The look in his eyes put her forcibly in mind of the greasy ostler from The Bull. And when he leaned forward, as though to follow through on his thinly veiled threat, her whole being clenched so hard she was convinced she was about to be sick.

'You will demand *nothing*, you damned insolent pup,' said someone, in such a menacing growl that all three bucks spun round to see who was trying to spoil their fun.

It was Mr Willingale. Oh, thank heavens.

'I will take that,' he said, indicating the hat.

Miraculously, they didn't argue, but meekly handed it over and melted away, muttering apologies.

Or perhaps it wasn't such a miracle. He'd looked disreputable enough last night for her aunt to select him to act as the villain in her scheme. With the addition of a day's growth of beard and a furious glare in those steely grey eyes he looked as though he might easily rip three slender young fops to ribbons and step over their lifeless corpses without experiencing a shred of remorse.

She forgot all about her determination to prove she didn't need him to look after her as she stumbled down the steps and flung her arms round his neck.

'I've never been so glad to see anyone in my life,' she sobbed. 'I thought you'd gone! Left me!'

'Of course not,' he snapped, standing completely rigid in the circle of her arms. As though he was highly embarrassed.

'Oh, I do beg your pardon,' she said, unwinding her arms from his neck and stepping hastily back.

'That's quite all right,' he said gruffly, patting her

shoulder in an avuncular manner. 'You had a fright. Here,' he said then, tipping the small change from the hat into her hands. 'Your takings.'

Then he clapped the hat back onto his head and tipped it at an angle that somehow magnified the aura of leashed power already hanging round him.

A tide of completely feminine feelings surged through her. Feelings he'd made it very clear he found embarrassingly unwelcome. She bent her head to hide the blush heating her cheeks, pretending she was engrossed in counting her takings.

Fourpence three farthings. Better than she'd have thought, considering her audience hadn't looked all that affluent.

'Well?'

His dry, sarcastic tone robbed her of what little pleasure she might have felt at her success if he hadn't already made her feel so very awkward, and foolish, and helpless, and...*female*.

'Well, what?'

'Do you have enough to pay the landlord for our breakfast?'

'You know very well I haven't.'

'So we shall have to pop my watch after all.' He grimaced. 'I can't believe I'm using such a vulgar term. I suppose I must have caught it from Hugo. He is always being obliged to "pop" something or other to "keep the dibs in tune", or so he informs me.'

'Not necessarily.'

'What do you mean?'

'Well, we have this,' she said, jingling her coins.

'Oh, please,' he huffed. 'We've already established you've hardly made anything there.'

'It's enough to buy some bread and cheese,' she pointed out. 'Which will keep us going for the rest of the day. We have a week before we have to pay the land-lord what we owe him. A week in which to raise the money some other way.'

'That's true,' he said, with what looked suspiciously like relief.

'And if all else fails, or if we run into any other dif-ficulties, we will have your watch in reserve.'

'And knowing you,' he muttered, 'we are bound to run into more difficulties.'

'And what is that supposed to mean?'

'Just that you seem to have a propensity for stum-bling from one disaster to another.'

'I never had any disasters until I met you.'

'That is not true. We would not have met at all had you not already been neck-deep in trouble. And since then I have had to rescue you from that ostler, *and* your penury, *and* your foolish attempt to evade me, and now a pack of lecherous young fops.'

For a moment his pointing all this out robbed her of speech. But she soon made a recovery.

'Oh? Well, I do not recall asking you to do *any* of those things!'

'Nevertheless I have done them. And what's more I fully intend to keep on doing them.' He halted, frown-ing in a vexed way at the clumsiness of the words that had just tumbled from his lips. 'That is,' he continued, 'I am going to stick to your side until I know you are safe.'

'Well, until we reach wherever it is that your dragon of an aunt lives and you hand me over to her, I reserve the right to…to…'

'Be mean and ungrateful?'

'I'm not ungrateful.' On the contrary, she'd been so grateful when he'd shown up just now and sent those horrible men packing that she'd fallen on his neck and embarrassed him. Embarrassed herself. In fact she suspected that half the reason she was suddenly so cross with him again was because she was ashamed of appearing clingy and weepy. Right after vowing she wasn't going to rely so totally on him.

'Of course I'm grateful for everything you've done,' she said. 'But that doesn't give you the right to…to… dictate to me.'

'Is that what I was doing? I rather thought,' he said loftily, 'I was making helpful decisions which would keep you from plunging into further disaster.'

'Oh, did you indeed?'

All of a sudden his manner altered.

'No, actually, I didn't,' he said, rubbing the back of his neck with one hand. 'You are quite correct. I *was* being dictatorial.'

'What?'

'Ah. That took the wind out of your sails,' he said with a—yes—with a positive *smile* on his face. 'But, you see, I am rather used to everyone doing as I say without question. You are the first person in a very long while to argue with me.'

'Then I expect I will do you a great deal of good,' she retorted.

'I shouldn't be a bit surprised,' he replied amiably. 'Just as being in my company will be an improving experience for *you*. Because you,' he said, taking her chin between his long, supple fingers, 'are clearly used to having your every whim indulged.'

'I am *not*,' she objected, flinching away from a touch that she found far too familiar. And far too pleasant.

'You behave as though you have been indulged all your life,' he countered. 'Pampered. Spoiled.'

'That is so very far from true that…' She floundered to a halt. 'Actually, when my parents were alive they did cosset me. And Papa's men treated me like a little princess. Which was what made it such a dreadful shock when Aunt Charity started treating me as though I was an unwelcome and rather embarrassing affliction.'

Just as Gregory had done when she had rushed up to him and hugged him. That was one of the reasons it had hurt so much. He'd made her feel just as she had when she'd first gone to live with Aunt Charity, when everything she'd done had been wrong. She'd already been devastated by having lost her mother, being parted from her father, and then being spurned by both grandfathers. But instead of receiving any comfort from Aunt Charity she'd been informed that she had the manners of a hoyden, which she'd no doubt inherited from her morally bankrupt father.

'I suppose it must have been.'

They stood in silence for a short while, as though equally surprised by her confession. And equally bewildered as to how to proceed now they'd stopped quarrelling.

'Look,' said Prudence, eventually, 'I can see how difficult you are finding the prospect of parting with your watch.'

'You have no idea,' he said grimly.

'Well, then, let us consider other options.'

'You really believe we have any?'

'There are always other options. For example, do we

really need to redeem your horse? I mean, how far is it, exactly, to your aunt's house?'

'Exactly?' He frowned. 'I couldn't say.'

'Guess, then,' she snapped, barely managing to stop herself from stamping her foot. 'One day's march? Two?'

'What are you suggesting? *Marching?*'

'I don't see why not. We are both young—relatively young,' she added, glancing at him in what she hoped was a scathing way. 'And healthy.' *He* most certainly was. She'd never seen so many muscles on a man. Well, she'd never seen so *much* of a man's muscles, to be honest, but that wasn't the point. 'And the weather is fine.'

He placed his hands on his hips and gave her back a look which told her he could rise to any challenge she set. And trump it.

'We *could* cut across country,' he admitted. 'I don't believe it is all that far as the crow flies.'

'Well, then.'

'There is no need to look so smug,' he growled.

'I beg your pardon,' she said, although she couldn't help smiling as she said it. 'It is just that, having grown up in an army that always seemed to be on the move, I am perhaps more used than you to the thought of walking anywhere I wish to go, as well as having more experience of adapting to adversity than you seem to.'

There—that had been said in a conciliating manner, hadn't it?

'What do you mean by that?'

'Well, you said yourself that your life has been rather dull and unpredictable up to now. Obviously I assume I am more used to thinking on my feet than you.'

'Ah.' He gave her a measured look. 'Strange though

it may seem, I do not regard my time with you as being one of unalloyed adversity, exactly. And thinking on my feet is…' He paused. 'Exactly the kind of challenge I was looking for when I set out. So, instead of regarding the loss of my horse as a problem, I agree— we *could* look upon it as the perfect excuse for taking a stroll through what looks to be a rather lovely part of the countryside.'

Now he was catching on.

'And having a picnic?' she suggested. 'Instead of having to eat in yet another stuffy inn.'

'A picnic…' he said, his eyes sliding to her takings. 'We would only need to purchase a bit of bread, some cheese, and an apple or two.'

'And what with it being market day,' she added, 'there will be plenty of choice. Which generally means bargains.'

'I shall take your word for it,' he muttered.

'You won't have to. Until you have seen an army brat haggle over half a loaf and a rind of cheese you haven't seen anything,' she informed him cheerfully.

And then wished she hadn't. For he was looked at her in a considering manner that had her bracing herself for some kind of criticism. Hadn't Aunt Charity always said that her life in the army was not a suitable topic of conversation—indeed, forbidden her ever to mention it?

'Then lead on,' he said, picking up his valise in one hand and crooking his other arm for her to take. 'And haggle to your heart's content.'

She let out her breath in a whoosh of relief. And took his arm with pleasure. She couldn't remember the last time anyone had allowed her to be herself, let alone appeared to approve of it.

It felt as if she were stepping out of an invisible prison.

Morals, Gregory decided some time later that day, could be damned inconvenient things to possess. For if he didn't have so many of them he could be making love to Miss Prudence Carstairs instead of engaging only in stilted conversation.

He'd been thinking about making love to her ever since she'd flung back her head and started singing. That rich, melodious voice had stroked down his spine like rough velvet. And had made him see exactly why sailors leaped into the sea and swam to the rock on which the Sirens lived. Not that she'd been intentionally casting out lures, he was sure. For one thing she'd been covered from neck to knee by his jacket, whereas the Sirens were always depicted bare-breasted.

Ah, but he *knew* that her breasts were unfettered beneath his jacket and her gown. He had her stays in his valise to prove it. Which knowledge had given him no option but to take himself off for a brisk walk while reciting the thirteen times table. Fortunately he'd just about retained enough mental capacity to keep half an eye on her, and had made it to her side before those three drunken young fops had done more than give her a bit of a fright.

He'd have liked to have given *them* a fright. How dared they harass an innocent young woman? A woman under *his* protection? He could cheerfully have torn them limb from limb.

Though who, his darker self had kept asking, had

appointed *him* her guardian? To which he had replied that he'd appointed himself. And he knew of no higher authority.

Besides, what else was he to do after the way she'd rushed to him and hugged him and said she'd never been so pleased to see anyone in her life? Nobody had ever been that pleased to see him. He hadn't known how to react. And so he'd stood there, stunned, for so long that eventually she had flinched away, thinking he hadn't liked the feel of her arms round him.

Whereas the truth was that he'd liked her innocent enthusiasm for him far too much. Only his response had been far from innocent. Which put him in something of a dilemma. She wasn't the kind of girl a man could treat as a lightskirt. For one thing she came from the middling classes. Every man knew you didn't bed girls from the middling classes. One could bed a lower class girl, for the right price. Or conduct a discreet affair with a woman from the upper classes, who'd think of it as sport.

But girls from the middling class were riddled with morals. Not that there was anything wrong with morals, as a rule. It was just that right now he wished one of them didn't have so many. If only Prudence didn't hail from a family with Methodist leanings, who called their daughters things like Prudence and Charity. Or if only he wasn't fettered by his vow to protect her. Or hadn't *told* her of his vow to protect her.

Or if only she hadn't gone so damned quiet, leaving him to stew over his own principles to the extent that he was now practically boiling over.

What was the matter with her? Earlier on she'd been a most entertaining companion. He'd enjoyed watching her haggle her way through the market. She'd even induced many of the stallholders to let her sample their wares, so that they'd already eaten plenty, in tiny increments, by the time they'd left the town with what they'd actually purchased.

But for a while now she'd been trudging along beside him, her head down, her replies to his few attempts to make conversation monosyllabic.

Had he done something to offend her?

Well, if she thought he was going to coax her out of the sullens, she could think again. He didn't pander to women's moods. One never knew what caused them, and when they were in them nothing a man did was going to be right. So why bother?

'How far?' she suddenly said, jolting him from his preoccupation with morals and the vexing question of whether they were inconvenient encumbrances to a man getting what he wanted or necessary bars to descending into depravity. 'How far is it to wherever you're planning to take me?'

'Somewhat further than I'd thought,' he replied testily. When people talked about distances as the crow flies, the pertinent fact was that crows *could* fly. They didn't have to tramp round the edges of muddy fields looking for gates or stiles to get through impenetrable hedges, or wander upstream and down until they could find a place to ford a swiftly running brook.

'So when do you think we might arrive?'

He glanced at the sky. 'It looks as though the weather is going to stay fair. It should be a clear night. If we keep going we might make it some time before dawn tomorrow.'

She made a noise that sounded suspiciously like a sob.

'Prudence?' He looked at her. Really looked at her for the first time since they'd left the outskirts of town. 'Prudence, you aren't crying, are you?'

She wiped her hand across her face and sniffed. 'No, of course not,' she said.

'Of course not,' he agreed, though she clearly was. Which gave him a strange, panicky sort of feeling.

There must be something seriously wrong for a woman like Prudence to start weeping. A woman who'd been abandoned by her guardians, left to the care of a total stranger, had thought up the notion of singing for pennies with which to buy provisions so he could keep back his gold watch for emergencies, and then gone toe to toe with him about how to spend money she was proud of having earned herself—no, that wasn't the kind of person who burst into tears for no good reason.

Was it?

'Look, there's a barn over there,' he said, pointing across the rise to the next field. 'We can stop there for the night if you like,' he offered, even though he'd vowed only two minutes earlier not to pander to her mood. After all, it wasn't as if she was crying simply to get attention. On the contrary, she looked more as though she was ashamed of weeping, and was trying to conceal her tears behind sniffles and surreptitious face-wiping.

'You will feel much more the thing in the morning.'

'Oh.'

She lifted her head and pushed a handful of wayward curls from her forehead in a gesture that filled him with relief. Because when they'd first set out she'd done so at regular intervals. Without a bonnet, or a hairbrush to tame her curls, they rioted all over her face at the slightest provocation. But as the day had worn on she'd done so less and less. She'd been walking for the last hour with her head hanging down, watching her feet rather than looking around at the countryside through which they were trudging.

'Well, I don't mind stopping there if *you* wish to rest,' she said.

She was drooping with exhaustion, but would rather suffer in silence than admit to weakness.

All of a sudden a wave of something very far from lust swept through him. It felt like…affection. No, no— not that! It was admiration—that was all. Coupled with a completely natural wish to put a smile back on that weary, woebegone face.

As they got nearer the barn he started casting about in a very exaggerated manner. Tired as she was, she couldn't help noticing the way he veered from side to side, stooping to inspect the ground.

'What are you looking for?' She turned impatiently, as though getting inside that barn was crucial.

'A rock,' he said.

'A rock?' She frowned at him. 'What on earth do you want a rock for? Aren't there enough in your head already?'

'Oh, very funny,' he replied. 'No, I was just thinking,' he carried on, with what he hoped was an expression of complete innocence, 'of giving you some practice.'

'Practice?'

'Yes. You claimed you weren't able to hit a barn door when you threw that rock at me. I just thought that now we have a barn here for you to use as target practice you might like to…'

'In the morning,' she said, her lips pulling into a tight line, 'I may just take you up on your generous offer of using this poor innocent building as target practice. For now, though, all I want to do is get inside, get my shoes off and lie down.'

So saying, she plunged through the door, which was hanging off its hinges, and disappeared into the gloomy interior. Leaving him to mull over the fact that, in spite of deciding that coaxing a female out of the sullens was beneath him, he'd just done precisely that.

With about as much success as he'd ever had.

Chapter Eight

The barn was almost empty. It looked as though the farmer had used up most of last year's crop of hay over the winter. Though there was enough, still, piled up against the far wall, to provide them with a reasonably soft bed for the night.

Clearly Prudence thought so, because she made straight for it, sat down, and eased off her shoes with a little moan of relief.

His own progress across the barn was much slower. She was too tempting—in so many ways.

'Miss Carstairs…' he said.

Yes, that was a good beginning. He must not call her Prudence. That had probably been where he'd gone wrong just now. He'd called her Prudence when he'd thought she was crying, and then he'd started trying to think of ways to make her smile, rather than ignoring her poor mood. He had to preserve a proper distance between them, now more than ever, or who knew how it would end? With him flinging himself down on top of her and ravishing her on that pile of hay, like as not. Because he was too aware that she had noth-

ing on beneath her gown. That her breasts were easily accessible.

He'd tell her that he had her stays in his valise and
beg her to put them back on in the morning—that was
what he would do.

Though that would still leave her legs bare. From her
ankles all the way up to her... Up to her... He swallowed. All the way up. Whenever he'd caught a brief
glimpse of her ankles today that was all he'd been able
to think of. Those bare legs. And what awaited at the
top of them.

Now that she'd removed her shoes, her feet were
bare, too. Whatever he did, he must not look at her
toes. If thoughts of her breasts and glimpses of her ankles had managed to work him up into such a lather,
then seeing her toes might well tip him over the edge.
There was something incredibly improper about toes. A
woman's toes, at any rate. Probably because a man only
ever saw them if he'd taken her to bed. And not always
then. Some women preferred to keep their stockings on.

Just as he was thinking about the feel of a woman's
stockinged leg, rubbing up and down his bare calves,
Prudence flung herself back in the hay with a little
whimper. And shut her eyes.

All his good resolutions flew out of the door. He
strode to her bed of hay. Ran his eyes along the whole
length of her. Not stopping when he reached the hem
of her gown. His heart pounding, and sweat breaking
out on his forehead, he breached all the barriers he'd
sworn he would stay rigidly behind. And looked at her
naked toes.

'Good God!'

Her feet—the very ones he'd been getting into such a

lather about—were rubbed raw in several places. Bleeding. Oozing. He dropped to his knees. Stretched out a penitent hand.

'Don't touch them!'

He whipped his hand back.

'No, no, of course I won't. They must be agonisingly painful.' Yet she hadn't uttered one word of complaint. 'Why didn't you tell me you were getting blisters, you foolish woman?'

'Because…because…' She covered her face with her hands and moaned. 'I was too proud,' she muttered from behind her fingers. 'It was my idea to walk wherever it is we are going. When I haven't walked further than a mile or so since I was sent to England. And I *boasted* about being young and healthy. And I *taunted* you for not thinking of it. So how could I admit I wasn't coping?'

'Prudence,' he said gently, immediately forgetting his earlier vow to address her only as Miss Carstairs, and removing her hands so that he could look into her woebegone little face. 'You would have struggled to get this far even if you'd had stockings to cushion your skin. Those shoes weren't designed for walking across rough ground. It would have been different if you had been wearing stout boots and thick stockings, but you weren't. You should have said something sooner. We could have…'

'What? What could we possibly have done?'

He lowered his gaze to her poor abused feet again. And sucked in a sharp breath. 'I don't know, precisely. I…' It seemed as good a time as any to explain about the stocking she'd found in his pocket. 'If I'd had both your stockings I could have given them to you. But I didn't. There was only the one this morning…'

She looked up at him as though she had no idea what he was talking about. He'd been trying to explain that he wasn't the kind of man who kept women's underthings about his person as some kind of trophy. It made him even more aware of the immense gulf separating them. Of his vast experience compared to her complete innocence.

Though not the kind of experience that would be of any use to her now. He had no experience of nursing anyone's blisters. Of nursing anyone for any ailment. 'They probably need ointment, or something,' he mused.

'Do you *have* any ointment?' she asked dryly. 'No, of course you don't.'

'We could at least bathe them,' he said, suddenly struck by inspiration. 'There was a stream in the dip between this field and the next. I noticed it before, and thought it would come in handy for drinking water. But if it is cool that might be soothing, might it not?'

'I am not going to walk another step,' she said in a voice that was half-sob. 'Not even if the stream is running with ice-cold lemonade and the banks are decked with bowls of ointment and dishes of strawberries.'

He took her meaning. She was not only exhausted and in pain, but hungry, too.

'I will go,' he said.

'And fetch water how?'

He put his hand to his neck. 'My neckcloth. I can soak it in the water. Tear it in half,' he said, ripping it from his throat. 'Half for each foot.'

She shook her head. 'No. If you're going to rip your neckcloth in two, I'd much rather we used the halves to wrap round my feet tomorrow. To stop my shoes rubbing these sores even worse.'

She was so practical. So damned practical. *He* should have thought of that.

'I have another neckcloth in my valise,' he retorted. See? He could be practical, too. 'And a shirt.' Though it was blood-spattered and sweat-soaked from his exploits at Wragley's. He shook his head. How he detested not having clean linen every day. 'Plenty of things we can tear up to bind your feet.'

As well as her stays.

He swallowed.

'Why on earth didn't you say so earlier?'

'I would have done if only you'd admitted you were having problems with your shoes. I could have bound your feet miles ago, and then they wouldn't have ended up in that state,' he snapped, furious that she'd been hurt so badly and he hadn't even noticed when he was supposed to be protecting her.

Though how was he to have guessed, when she hadn't said a word? She had to be the most provoking female it had ever been his misfortune to encounter.

'You weren't even limping,' he said accusingly.

'Well, both feet hurt equally badly. So it was hard to choose which one to favour.'

'Prudence!' He gazed for a moment into her brave, tortured little face. And then found himself pulling her into his arms and hugging her.

Hugging her? When had he ever wanted to hug anyone? Male or female?

Never. He wasn't the kind of man who went in for hugging.

But people gained comfort from hugging, so he'd heard. And since he couldn't strangle her, nor ease his frustration the only other way that occurred to him, he supposed hugging was the sensible, middling course to take. At least he could get his hands on her without either killing or debauching her.

Perhaps there was something to be said for hugging after all.

Prudence let her head fall wearily against his chest. Just for a moment she could let him take her weight, and with it all her woes—couldn't she? Where was the harm in that?

'You've been so brave,' he murmured into her hair.

'No, not brave,' she protested into his shirtfront. 'Stubborn and proud is what I've been. And stupid. And impractical—'

'No! I won't have you berate yourself this way. You may be a touch proud, but you are most definitely the bravest person I've ever met. I don't know anyone who would have gone through what you have today without uttering a word of complaint.'

'But—'

'No. Listen to me. If anyone is guilty of being stupidly proud it is I. I should have swallowed my pride at the outset and pawned the watch. I should have done everything in my power to liberate that horse and gig from the stable so you wouldn't have to walk. I will never forgive myself for putting you through this.'

'It isn't your fault.'

'Yes, it is. Oh, good grief—this isn't a contest, Prudence! Stop trying to outdo me.'

'I'm not.'

'Yes, you are. Even when I admit to a fault,' he said, as though it was an immense concession to admit any such thing, '*you* have to insist your fault is greater.'

'But I *feel* at fault,' she confessed.

It was easy to maintain her pride when he was being grumpy and aloof, but so much harder when he was trying to be kind.

'It was my fault you lost all your money.' She'd known it from the start, but had been so angry when he hadn't scrupled to accuse her of carelessness that she'd refused to admit it. 'It was my fault you got into this…this escapade at all. If my aunt and her new husband, whom I refuse to call my uncle, hadn't decided to steal my inheritance…or if you hadn't had a room up on our landing…'

'Then we would never have met,' he said firmly. 'And I'm *glad* we have met, Miss Prudence Carstairs.'

Her heart performed a somersault inside her ribcage. She became very aware of his arms enfolding her with such strength, and yet such gentleness. Remembered that he'd put them round her of his own volition.

And then he looked at her lips. In a way that put thoughts of kissing in her head.

'Because before I met you,' he said, with a sort of intensity that convinced her he meant every word, 'I have never admired or respected any female—not really.'

What would she do if he tried to kiss her? She had to think of something to say—quickly! Before one of them gave in to the temptation to close the gap that separated their faces and taste the other.

What had he just said? Something about never admiring a female before? Well, that was just plain absurd.

'But…you were married.'

He let go of her. Pulled away. All expression wiped from his face. Heavens, but the mention of his late wife had acted upon him like a dousing from a bucket of ice water. Which was a *good* thing. If she'd let him kiss her or, even worse, started kissing him, who knew how it would have ended? A girl couldn't go kissing a man in a secluded barn, on a bed of sweet-smelling hay, without it ending badly.

'Instead of sitting here debating irrelevancies, I would be better employed going to that stream and soaking my neckcloth in it,' he said in a clipped voice. Then got to his feet and strode from the barn without looking back.

A little shiver ran down her spine as she watched him go. It was just as well she'd mentioned his wife. It had been as effective at cooling his ardour as slapping his face.

It was something to remember. If he ever did look as though he was going to cross the line again she need only mention his late wife and he'd pull away from her with a look on his face as though he'd been sucking a lemon.

Had he been very much in love? And was he still mourning her? No, that surely didn't tie in with what he'd just said about not respecting or admiring any female before. It sounded more as though the marriage had been an unhappy one.

Gingerly, she wiggled her toes. Welcomed the pain of real, physical injury. Because thinking about him being unhappily married made her very sad. It was a shame if he hadn't got on with his wife. He deserved a wife who made him happy. A wife who appreciated all his finer points. Because, villainous though he looked, he was the most decent man she'd ever met. He hadn't once tried to take advantage of her. And he had been full of remorse when he'd seen what her pride had cost her toes. And when she thought of how swiftly he'd made those bucks who'd been about to torment her disperse...

She heaved a great sigh and sank back into the hay, her eyes closing. He might have admitted to breaking into a building, but that didn't make him a burglar. On the contrary, he'd only broken the law in an attempt to redress a greater wrong. He might not have the strict moral code of the men of the congregation of Stoke-town, and her aunt would most definitely stigmatise him as a villain because of it, but his kind of villainy suited her notion of how a real man should behave.

She must have dozed off, in spite of the pain in her feet, because the next thing she knew he was kneeling over her, shaking her shoulder gently.

'You're exhausted, I know,' he said, with such gentle concern that she heaved another sigh while her insides went all gooey. 'But I must tend to your feet before we turn in for the night. We should eat some supper, too.'

She struggled to sit up, pushing her hair from her face as it flopped into her eyes for the umpteenth time that day. He knelt at her feet, holding a wet handkerchief just above the surface of her skin, as though loath to cause her pain.

And though he looked nothing like a hero out of a fairytale, though he had no armour and had put his horse up for security, at that moment she had the strange fancy that he was very like a knight in shining armour, kneeling at the feet of his lady.

Which just went to show how tired and out of sorts she was.

'Don't worry about hurting me,' she said. 'I shall grit my teeth and think of— Oh! Ow!'

'Sorry, sorry,' he said, over and over again as he dabbed at her blisters.

'I wish I had a comb,' she said, through teeth suitably gritted. 'Then I could tidy my hair.'

'You are bothered about your *hair*? When your feet are in this state?'

'I was trying to distract myself from my feet by thinking about something that *would* normally bother me. Trying to think of what my usual routine would be as I prepare for bed of a night. My maid would brush my hair out for me, then plait it out of the way...'

But not last night. No, last night she'd had to rely on Aunt Charity's rather rough ministrations. Because she'd said there was no need to make her maid undergo the rigours of a journey as far as Bath. Even though Bessy had said to Aunt Charity that she wouldn't mind at all, and had later admitted to Prudence that she thought it would be rather exciting to travel all that way and see a place that had once been so fashionable.

Why hadn't she seen how suspicious it was for her aunt to appear suddenly so concerned over the welfare of a servant? Why hadn't she smelled a rat when Aunt Charity had said it would be better to hire a new maid in Bath—one who'd know all about the local shops and so forth?

Because she couldn't possibly have guessed that Aunt Charity had been determined to isolate her—that was why. So that there wouldn't be any witnesses to the crime she was planning.

Prudence sucked in a sharp breath. It was worse than simply taking advantage of the opportunity that being housed in that funny little attic in The Bull last night had provided. Aunt Charity and that awful man she'd married had made sure there wouldn't be any witnesses to what she now saw was a premeditated crime.

'Did I hurt you?'

'What? No. I was…' She shivered. 'I was thinking about my maid, Bessy.' She paused. Up to now she'd been too busy just surviving to face what her aunt had tried to do. But her mind had been steadily clearing all day. Or perhaps the pain of Gregory tending to her feet was waking her up to the unpleasant truth.

'I'm afraid you will have to make do with my clumsy efforts tonight,' he said. Then reached up and twined a curl round one finger. 'Though it seems a kind of sacrilege to confine all this russet glory in braids.'

'Russet glory!' She snorted derisively. 'I never took you for a weaver of fustian.'

'I am not. Not a weaver of anything.' He leaned back on his heels. His eyes seemed to be glazed. 'But surely you know that your hair is glorious?'

The look in his eyes made her breath hitch in her throat. Made her heart skip and dance and her tummy clench as though she was flying high on a garden swing.

Oh, Lord, but she wanted him to kiss her. Out of all the men who'd paid court to her—or rather to her money—none had ever made her want to throw propriety to the winds. And he hadn't even *been* paying court to her. He'd been alternately grumpy and insulting and dictatorial all day. And yet… She sighed. He'd also rescued her from an ostler and a group of bucks, forgiven her for pushing him out of his gig and throwing a rock at him. Even made a clumsy sort of jest of the rock-throwing thing.

A smile tugged at her lips as she thought of that moment.

'So you accept the compliment now?'

'What? What compliment?'

'The one I made about your hair,' he breathed, raising the hank that he'd wound round his hand to his face and inhaling deeply.

'My hair?'

Why was he so obsessed with her hair? It must look dreadful, rioting all down her back and all over her face. A visible reminder of her 'wayward nature', Aunt Charity had always said. It was why she had to plait it, and smooth it, and keep it hidden away.

He looked at her sharply. 'If not that, then why were you smiling in that particular way?'

'I didn't know I was smiling in any particular way. And for your information I was thinking of something else entirely.'

'Oh?' His face sort of closed up. He let her hair fall from his fingers and bent to dab at her feet again.

Good heavens, she'd offended him. Who'd have thought that a man who looked so tough could have such delicate sensibilities? But then she hadn't been very tactful, had she? To tell him she'd been thinking of something else when he'd been trying to pay her compliments.

'I was thinking,' she said hastily, in an effort to make amends, 'of how funny you were, searching about for rocks for me to throw.'

He shrugged one shoulder, but didn't raise his head.

'How very forbearing you have been, considering the abuse you've suffered on my account.'

He laid her feet down gently in the hay. 'That is all I can do for them for now,' he said, and scooted back.

Looked at his hands. Cleared his throat. Scooted another foot away.

Which was both a good thing and a bad. Good in that he was determined to prevent another scene from developing in which their mouths ended up scant inches apart. Bad in that... Well, in that he was determined to prevent another scene from developing in which they would be tempted to kiss.

No, no, it was a *good* thing he wasn't the kind of man to attempt to take advantage of the situation. They were going to have to spend the night together in this barn, after all. And if they started kissing, who knew how it would end?

Yes, it was a jolly good job he was maintaining some distance between them.

It would have been even better if she'd been the one to do so.

'We had better eat our supper before the light grows too dim to see what we're putting in our mouths,' he said, opening his valise and taking out what was left of the provisions they'd bought in Tadburne Market.

'We know exactly what we have for supper,' she said wearily. 'About two ounces of cheese and the heel of a loaf. Between the two of us.'

'If it were only a few months later,' he said, spreading the brown paper in which their meagre rations had been wrapped on the hay at her side, 'I might have found strawberries growing by the stream.'

'Strawberries don't grow by streams,' she retorted as he flicked open a penknife and cut both the cheese and the crust precisely in half. 'They only grow in carefully tended beds. Where they have to be protected from frosts over winter with heaps of straw. Which is why they're called *straw*berries.'

He raised his head and gave her a level look. 'Blackberries, then. You cannot deny that blackberries thrive in the wild.' He picked up the sheet of brown paper and its neatly divided contents and placed them on her lap.

From which he'd have to pluck his own meal. One morsel at a time.

She felt her cheeks heating at the prospect of his hand straying over her lap. Felt very conscious that her legs were totally bare beneath her skirts.

She picked up her slice of cheese and nibbled at it. What had they been talking about? Oh, yes blackberries.

'Some form of fruit would certainly be welcome with this cheese.'

'And with the bread,' he added. 'It's very dry.'

'Stale, I think is the word for which you are searching,' she said, having tried it. 'But then, what can you expect for what we paid?'

No wonder the baker had let them have so much for so little. She'd been so proud of her skills at haggling. But they weren't so great, were they? This bread was clearly left over from the day before.

'I had a drink at the stream,' he said, after swallowing the last of his share of their supper. 'So I am not too thirsty. But what about you?'

'I think I can just about manage to get the bread down. Though what we really need is a pat of butter to put on it. And then about a gallon of tea to wash it down.'

'This will not do,' he growled. And then, before she had any inkling of what he meant to do, he'd swept the brown paper to one side, hauled her up into his arms and was carrying her across the barn.

'What are you doing?'

And what was *she* doing? She should by rights be struggling. Or at least demanding that he put her down. Not sort of sagging into him and marvelling at the strength of his muscular arms.

'I'm taking you down to the stream so that you can have a drink. And dip your feet into the water. I don't know why I didn't think of it before,' he said crossly. 'I must be all about in my head. Dipping a handkerchief in the stream and then dabbing at your blisters...' he sneered.

'I daresay you were attempting to observe the proprieties,' she said kindly. 'For this isn't at all proper, is it? Carting me about like a sack of grain?'

'Proper? There has been nothing "proper" about our relationship from the moment I stretched my foot out in bed this morning and found you at the other end of it.'

Naked, at that, he could have added.

In the gathering dusk he strode down the field in the direction of the water she could hear babbling along its channel. Without giving the slightest indication that he was doing anything out of the ordinary. He wasn't even getting out of breath.

Whereas her own lungs were behaving most erratically. As was her heart.

'And what we're about to do is highly *im*proper, Prudence, in case you need reminding.'

She looked at his face, and then at the stream, in bewilderment.

'Watching me bathe my feet in the stream? You think *that* is improper conduct?'

'No,' he said abruptly, and then set her down on a low part of the bank, from where she could dangle her feet into the water with ease. 'It's not the bathing that's improper. It's what is going to happen after I carry you back to the barn.'

'What?' she asked, breathless with excitement.

No, not excitement. At least it shouldn't be excitement. It should be maidenly modesty. Outraged virtue. Anything but excitement.

'What is going to happen after you carry me back to the barn?'

'We are going to have to spend the night together,' he bit out. He rubbed his hand over the crown of his head. 'All night. And, since it promises to be a cold one, probably clinging to each other for warmth.'

'We don't need to cling,' she pointed out, since the prospect appeared to be disturbing him so much. 'Hay is very good at keeping a body warm. I can remember sleeping in a barn a couple of times when I was very little and we were on the march. Papa made me a sort of little nest of it.'

He gave her a hard look. 'If you were still a little girl that might work. But you are a full-grown woman And there isn't all that much hay, Prudence. It is more than likely we *will* end up seeking each other's warmth. And, unlike last night, which neither of us can remember, I have a feeling we are going to recall every single minute of tonight. You will know you have slept with a man. You will never be able to look anyone in the eye and claim to be innocent. Tonight, Prudence, is the night that your reputation really will be well and truly ruined.'

Chapter Nine

'Oh, my goodness!' said Prudence as her feet slid into the ice-cold water. She didn't know whether it was the shock of it, or something else, but suddenly everything had become clear. 'That was what they were after.'

'What *who* was after? *What* was it they were after?'

'You know,' she said, shuddering at the sting of the water on her raw feet. 'My aunt and that man she married.'

'I don't follow,' he said, sitting down on the bank beside her.

'No, well…' she said wearily. 'That's because I haven't told you everything.' But there wasn't any point in keeping her revelation to herself. He was in it with her now—or would be after tonight—up to his neck.

'I told you I was due to come into an inheritance?'

'Yes.'

'Well, it is not totally without stipulations. The money comes from my grandfather, you see, and he was livid, apparently, when Mama ran off with Papa. He'd already refused consent to their marriage—not only because they hadn't known each other for five minutes, but also because Papa was a soldier. A man who saw nothing wrong with drinking alcohol, or gambling, or any number of things that Grandpapa regarded as dreadful sins.

'Not that Papa was a dreadful sinner—I won't have you thinking that,' she explained hastily. 'It was just Grandpapa was so terribly rigid in his views. Anyway, he cut Mama out of his will. But then when I was born, and Mama wrote to inform him of the event, he put me in it instead. *She* was still disinherited, but he said that it wasn't right to visit the sins of the fathers on the children. And just in case I turned out to be as great a sinner as either of them, there was this…stipulation.

'The money wasn't to come direct to me upon his death but was to be held in trust. Either until I married *"a man of standing"*, I think was the exact term. Or, if I hadn't married such a paragon by the time I was twenty-five, then I could have it without strings, to use however I wish, but only if I am found to be *"of spotless reputation"*.'

'In other words,' he said slowly, 'all your aunt had to do was blacken your name and…'

'Yes. Mama's portion—or rather mine, since Mama didn't feature in the will at all, and I never had any brothers or sisters who lived more than a few days— would go directly to Aunt Charity.'

'Villainous,' he hissed.

'Yes,' she agreed, drawing her feet out of the water and pulling her knees up to her chin.

Wrapping her arms round her lower legs, she gazed across the stream to the ploughed fields on the opposite bank, blinking determinedly whenever the chill breeze stung her raw flesh.

'And it isn't just what happened this morning. Or last night. Aunt Charity and I have been at war, subtly, for years. I can see it all now...'

She shook her head, the furrows blurring as tears misted her vision.

'I thought she was just a cold, strict sort of woman, and I made allowances for the way she was because I could sort of understand how she might resent me for being thrust upon her when she obviously hadn't a maternal bone in her body. But I think it was worse than that. Of late I've felt as though she has been doubling her efforts to make me feel bad about myself. Always harping on about my *"falling short"*, as she termed it. And punishing me for the slightest fault.'

She turned to him and searched his face for his reaction.

'But what if it wasn't that at all? What if she was trying to make everyone think I was a terrible sinner? So that she'd have the excuse to say I didn't fulfil the terms of the will?'

He opened his mouth to say something, but thoughts were tumbling into her head so fast she simply had to let them out.

'It's true that at one time—about the time Papa died and I knew I was never going to get away from her—I was...well, a bit of a handful. No, I must be honest. I was downright rebellious for a while. I told her I hated her and everything she stood for. But as it drew nearer to my birthday nothing seemed to bother me so much. Only a few more months, I thought, and then I will be free. Only a few more weeks, now...'

She shook her head.

'But she still looked at me as though I was a problem

she had to work out rather than a real person… Oh, I'm not explaining it terribly well, am I?'

'No,' he said thoughtfully, 'I think I see only too well.' He sighed. 'For I have been guilty of seeing my young cousin Hugo in that light,' he said.

He plucked at some strands of grass. Tossed them into the stream and watched them float downstream.

'I have shown him scant sympathy whenever he comes to me with his troubles. The last time I refused to bail him out of his difficulties he accused me of having a mind like a ledger. Of not understanding what ordinary people have to go through. And he was right. I *did* regard him as nothing more than a financial drain. And an intolerable nuisance.'

'Yes, but you wouldn't have gone out of your way to destroy him, would you? You're not that kind of man.'

He reached out and touched her arm, just briefly, as though her declaration of faith in him had meant something to him.

'I didn't think my aunt was that kind of person, either. But her husband…' She shuddered. 'I wouldn't put anything past him. As soon as they married there stopped being any money for the things I'd taken for granted before. It started with fewer trips to the dressmaker. When I questioned him he accused me of vanity. And since I already thought he was a terribly pious and unpleasant sort of man I just thought he was trying to *improve* me. But then there were things like… Oh, he wouldn't let me have a fire in my room unless it was actually snowing outside. That sort of thing. And I'm sure there isn't anywhere in the Bible that says you have to go cold to prove how virtuous you are.'

He drew in a sharp breath. 'It is possible that he has

squandered your inheritance—have you thought of that? And this is his attempt to cover it up?'

She thought for a bit. Then shook her head. 'If it is, he's gone a very strange way about covering anything up. Surely my disappearance will eventually cause no end of talk? Especially since it looks as though they mean to explain it away by accusing me of improper conduct,' she finished bitterly.

'And me,' he growled. 'If anyone asks where you have gone, they will drag my name into it.'

'I don't see how they can. They don't know it,' she pointed out.

'*I* will know it,' he growled. 'I will know that some-where people are accusing me of…debauching an innocent. Well, your aunt and uncle picked the wrong man to play the villain of the piece. I won't let them get away with it.'

'Good,' she said, turning to gaze up at him. 'Because you are not a villain. Not at all.'

He might look like one, with his bruised face, his harsh expression, and his dishevelled and muddied clothing. But she knew how he'd come by the mud, and the bruises. At the time he'd told her about his adventure in the mill she'd half suspected he might have made some of it up, to try and impress her. But that was before he'd rescued her from those drunken bucks simply by looking at them with that murderous gleam in his eyes. Before he'd carried her to this stream just so she could soothe her feet in its ice-cold water. And had listened to her as though her opinions had merit.

'So far as I'm concerned,' she said, reaching up to touch the deep groove between his brows, 'they picked the *right* man.'

'What?' His eyes, which had been glaring off into the distance as though he was plotting a fitting revenge on her guardians, focussed on her in bewilderment.

'I know that you will put all to rights, somehow—won't you?' For that was what he did. 'Or at least you will do your very best.'

'How can you possibly know that?' He fidgeted and turned his head away.

'Because that is the kind of man you are. Completely upright.' And not in the way the male members of Stoketown Chapel were upright. Not one of them would break into a warehouse at dead of night to steal a set of false ledgers in order to uncover a fraud. They'd be too scared of what other people would think of their actions.

She might have been mistaken, because it was growing too dark now to see clearly, but she rather thought her last comment might have caused him to blush.

'Time to turn in for the night,' he said gruffly. Then bent to put his arms around her and got to his feet.

Just as before, the ease with which he carried her filled her with admiration. Admiration spiced with a series of totally feminine responses. Because this time he was carrying her to a bed they were going to be sharing.

As though he shared the tenor of her thoughts, he came to a complete halt just before entering the barn and stared into the gloom at the far end. Where they were about to make a bed in the pile of hay.

'This is going to be damned awkward,' he grated, before turning sideways to slide through the drunken excuse for a barn door.

And then he stopped again.

And cleared his throat.

Though she could scarcely hear it over the thunder of her heartbeat.

'Right, this is what we're going to do,' he said. 'I'm going to use my valise for a pillow, then spread my jacket over some of the hay. That is if you don't mind taking it off.' He glanced down at the row of buttons, then at her face, then into the gloom again, his jaw tightening.

'I don't mind at all,' she said. In fact excitement fizzed through her at the prospect of undressing in front of him. Even if it was only his jacket he'd asked her to remove. And she would still be wearing her modest kerseymere gown. 'Hay is very prickly,' she added hastily. 'It is a very sensible notion to use your jacket as a barrier.'

'Sensible,' he repeated, suddenly breaking into a stride that took them all the way to the back of the barn. 'I will use my coat to cover us, as another barrier against the hay. I shall pull it over the top of us both.'

'A very practical notion,' she said.

One of his eyebrows shot up. 'Really?' He pulled it down. 'I mean, naturally. Eminently practical. So,' he said, 'you will remove my jacket while I will divide up the hay, and so forth, to make our bed.'

Our bed. The words sent a flush to her cheeks. And, by the feel of it, to other parts she ought never to mention.

'I give you fair warning,' he said gruffly, 'that if it gets really cold, in spite of all the hay, I shall put my arms around you and hold you close.'

Her heart skipped a beat. But that beat sank to her pelvis, where it set up a low, insistent throb.

'Will you?' Was that really her voice? All low and husky and breathy?

'Yes. But I swear, on my honour, that I shall do nothing more.'

'I know.' She sighed.

'How can you possibly know?'

'I have told you already—I know what kind of man you are.' And she wasn't sure why she'd forgotten it, even for those few exhilarating seconds when he'd been standing there talking about taking her to bed. Wishful thinking, she supposed.

'How can you? We only met this morning. Can you stand for a few moments if I set you down?'

'Yes,' she said. 'And that question only goes to prove what I was saying. You are still going out of your way to tend to my comfort. A lot of men wouldn't bother. They wouldn't try to reassure me that my virtue would remain unsullied, either. In fact, I think a lot of men—' most men, from what she'd seen of masculine conduct so far '—would turn this situation to their own advantage.'

'Oh?' He bent to pick up his valise and held it before him like a shield while she unbuttoned the jacket he'd lent her. As she slid it from her arms he turned swiftly and buried the valise under a mound of hay.

'Yes, indeed,' she said as he turned back and took the jacket from her outstretched hand. He dropped it onto the makeshift mattress quickly, as though it was burning his fingers.

'I have told you all about my fortune,' she said. 'Other men have paid court to me to get their hands on it. You could, at any time today, have started to pressure me into marrying you under the pretext of saving my reputation, and then the money would have been yours. As my husband. But you haven't.'

'Perhaps I am not a marrying kind of man—had you thought of that?'

'No. For one thing you have looked at me once or twice as though you were thinking about kissing me. And you said that thing about my hair.'

'Hmmph,' he said, swinging her into his arms again and setting her down gently onto the makeshift bed.

'For another,' she said as he reared back and began stripping off his coat. 'You have already been married.'

'Perhaps that is what has put me off ever getting married again,' he said bitterly, before coming down beside her and whisking the coat over them both.

'Is it?' She watched through lazily lowered lids as he reached for the hay, pulling bunches of it up and over them until it really did feel as though they were lying in a sort of nest. 'You looked so unhappy when you mentioned your wife. I wondered…'

'Wondered what?' He lay down, finally, next to her, though he kept his arms rigidly at his side.

'Well, *why* you looked so unhappy. You pulled a sort of face.'

'Pulled a face? I *never* pull faces.'

'Well, you did. And it wasn't the sort of expression a widower makes who loved his wife and misses her. It looked as though…'

He made a low growling kind of noise, as though warning her not to proceed any further. She ignored it.

'And anyway, now you have as good as admitted that you weren't happy. What went wrong?'

He sighed. 'I never speak of my wife,' he grunted. 'She and I… We…'

Somewhere close by an owl hooted.

Gregory folded his arms across his chest.

She rolled onto her side and curled up a bit. Just until her knee touched his leg.

Which was warm. And solid.

'There was never any *we*,' he said, with evident irritation. 'The match was arranged by our families. I thought she was happy with it. She seemed happy with it. And I was…content to go along with the arrangement. She was pretty. *Very* pretty, if you must know. Which I thought was better than being saddled with a woman I would struggle to bed.'

Somehow it seemed rather brazen to be snuggling up to him, hoping he might snuggle up to her, while he was talking about having marital relations. She stealthily straightened her leg so that her knee was no longer nudging his thigh.

But she hadn't been stealthy enough.

'If you didn't want the sordid details,' he snapped, 'you shouldn't have pressed me for the confession.'

She hadn't pressed. Not really. But perhaps it was the strangeness of the day, the enforced intimacy they'd shared and were still sharing, that made him feel compelled to tell her all about it. Or the fact that they were lying in the dark, in a barn, feeling extremely awkward, and it was better to talk of something completely unrelated to themselves.

Besides, if he truly hadn't spoken of his miserable marriage ever, to anyone, he probably needed to unburden himself. He'd obviously never felt close enough, or safe enough, with anyone to do so.

She reached out until she found his hand in the dark, and clasped her fingers round it.

'I didn't mean to pry,' she said. 'But if you want to talk about it…'

He gripped her hand hard.

'She didn't like me touching her in bed,' he grated. 'She would never have curled into me the way you have just done, or held my hand, or smoothed my brow when I frowned. Or hugged me because she was pleased to see me.'

The poor man. She ran the fingers of her other hand over his. Squeezed it. The poor, lonely man. No wonder his face had settled into a permanently severe expression. No wonder he glowered at people in such a way that they kept their distance. He must find it easier to keep people away than let them get close enough to hurt him. As his wife had done.

'I was only seventeen when I married her. Not very experienced. And she, of course, was a virgin. It wasn't… The consummation wasn't entirely a pleasant experience for her. When she was reluctant to allow me to return to her bed I tried to be understanding. I thought I ought to give her time to become accustomed.' He gave a bitter laugh. 'And then she confessed she was with child.'

It sounded as though he was grinding his teeth.

'My father congratulated me for ensuring the succession so swiftly. It was about the only time he ever seemed pleased with me. But the irony was that it wasn't mine. The baby she was carrying. It couldn't possibly have been mine. And I was furious. All those months, while I'd been trying to be considerate, she'd been…'

'Oh.' It sounded such a feeble thing to say. But, really, what could she say to a confession like that?

'When she died I struggled to feel anything apart

from relief. You think that was wicked, don't you? That I was relieved I wasn't going to have to bring up some other man's get as my own? Or to face mockery by admitting she'd cuckolded me within six months of marriage?'

'She... Oh, no. The baby died as well?'

'The pregnancy killed her. That's what the doctor said. Something to do with her heart. I wasn't exactly in a frame of mind to take it in. My father had not long since died as well, you see. I'd just...stepped into his shoes.'

She heard him swallow.

'Later, I did feel sorry about the baby. And that was when the guilt started to creep in. I kept remembering standing by her graveside, feeling as though a huge burden had rolled off my shoulders. How all the problems I'd thought I had were being buried with her. How could I regard a child as a burden? As a problem? That wasn't right. It wouldn't have been the child's fault. You, of all people, must know it isn't right to inflict upon a child the feelings you have for its parents.'

'No,' she whispered. 'It isn't. But you wouldn't have done. I *know* you wouldn't.'

'You can't possibly know that,' he grated. 'Hell, I certainly couldn't.'

'I *do* know,' she said, raising his clenched fist to her mouth and kissing the grazed knuckles. 'You might have struggled to be kind to the child, but you would have tried. Otherwise you wouldn't have experienced any guilt over the way you felt when it died. You would have just shrugged your shoulders and walked away. You are a *good* man,' she said. 'And you deserved to have a wife who appreciated just how good and kind you are. A wife who would have at least tried to make you happy. A wife who wanted you to touch her. Give her children. None of what happened was your fault.'

He shifted in the hay beside her and gave a sort of disgruntled huff. Then he rolled onto his side, so that he was facing away from her. She might have thought he was putting an end to their conversation and establishing some distance between them if it hadn't been for the fact that he kept tight hold of her hand, so that as he rolled the movement tugged her up against his back. Just as though he wanted to drape her over himself like a human blanket.

She snuggled closer. For he'd made it clear he hadn't been rejecting her. It had been pride that had made him turn away, she was sure. Men didn't like appearing weak, and he probably regretted spilling all those secrets he'd kept hidden for years. He'd made himself vulnerable to her. Because he trusted her. Or thought she'd understand what rejection of that sort felt like after the way her own aunt had betrayed her.

Yes, if any two people knew what betrayal felt like it was them.

She hugged his waist, wishing there was something she could do to ease his pain. To let him know that she didn't think any less of him for struggling the way he had in the coldness of his arranged marriage, and with his feelings about the way it had ended.

And suddenly it occurred to her that there was one obvious way to do both.

'Do you know what?' she said. 'You *still* deserve a wife who wants to make you happy. Who appreciates how good and kind you are. Who wants you to touch her and give her children. And, what's more, I rather think *I'd* like to be that woman.'

She raised herself up on one elbow so that she could look down into his face. Not that she could see it clearly, in their gloomy corner of the barn. But she certainly felt his entire body tense.

'Are you saying,' he said repressively, 'that you have fallen in love with me? After just one day?'

'Oh, no,' she admitted. 'But I think I very easily could. I've resisted the thought of marriage before, because I couldn't see the point of exchanging one sort of prison for another. I just kept thinking I'd only have to put up with living in Aunt Charity's house for a limited time and then I'd be free. But I don't think marriage to you would feel like a prison at all. You don't seem to want to change me into someone else. You quite like me as I am, don't you?'

She hurried on, because now she'd started she might as well get it all out into the open.

'And I wouldn't even mind handing my fortune into your keeping, if we ever get our hands on it. I'd feel as if you'd earned the right to it. I'm sure you would put it to good use. Could you not do with an injection of capital into whatever business you are in? If you don't mind me saying so, you don't seem to be all that plump in the pocket, or you wouldn't have fallen into such difficulties today, would you?'

'You…you don't know what you are saying,' he hissed, rolling over onto his back so he could look up at her. And then, probably because he couldn't, he reached up to touch her face.

Then snatched it back.

She smiled to herself in the dark.

'I've already told you I wouldn't mind you touching me,' she said gently. 'The way a man touches his wife. In fact,' she admitted daringly, 'I think I would like it very much.'

'And I repeat: you don't know what you are saying.'

'Not…not entirely, no. But I do know that I couldn't lie next to any other man, the way I am lying here with you, and feel like this.'

There was a beat of silence before he said, in a voice that was scarce more than a whisper, 'Like what?'

'All sort of tingly and warm. As…as if something very wonderful is about to happen. Something to do with your lips. And your chest.' She reached between them and laid her hand on his chest, where she could feel his heart beating a rapid tattoo. 'And your legs.' She ran her bare foot up and down his calf. 'I have the strangest urge to wrap myself all around you like a vine.'

'It's the enforced intimacy—that's what it is,' he grated. 'We've been thrown together in unusual circumstances and you're feeling…grateful to me. Attracted, too, I don't doubt. Just as I'm attracted to you. Extremely so.'

Her heart leapt.

'Though I feel I should warn you that it might well be due to some after-effect of the drug they gave us.'

Her heart plummeted.

'And once this is over…'

No, no, it wasn't just because she'd unwittingly swallowed a sleeping draught. The only reason their enforced intimacy had made her admire him so was because all the tests they'd faced had proved what he was really like, beneath the harsh exterior.

'I will still feel like this tomorrow—I'm sure I will.'

'Prudence, Prudence…' He did reach up to cup her face then. 'God, whoever gave you such an inappropriate name? Practically begging a man to make love to you is the least prudent thing an innocent girl like you could do.'

'I haven't begged you to make love to me,' she protested, her pride stung. 'I was speaking in a hypothetical way, about marriage. *You* were the one who leap-frogged over the practicalities and went straight to the wedding night.'

'How can I help thinking about the wedding night when you're lying here half-naked and talking of wrapping yourself around me like a vine?' He pulled her down so that she was sprawled half over his body. Then, just to make sure she knew what he was talking about, he shifted slightly, so that his pelvis made contact with her hip. 'Can you not feel what you do to me?'

Oh, yes, she could feel it. She'd spent her early childhood following the drum. She'd learned a whole lot more about what went on between men and women than sheltered girls her age would have known.

'So you *do* want me, then? It isn't just me feeling like this?'

'Of course I want you,' he growled. 'I've wanted you ever since the moment you sat up in bed this morning and gave me an eyeful of your breasts!'

'But…you threw me out of your room.'

'I thought you were trying to entrap me. I thought…' He groaned. 'I don't know what I thought.' He ran his hands up and down her back. 'But I…' He hauled her close and breathed in raggedly. Clasped the back of her head to his throat.

He was trembling.

'Prudence, I beg of you, don't tempt me any more. You have placed your trust in me. Told me you think I am an upright, honest man. And it's true that all my life I have prided myself on doing the right thing. Even when I knew my wife had committed adultery I refused to sink to her level. But right now I am so close to behaving like the worst kind of scoundrel. It's bad enough that people will be accusing me of taking your innocence. If I do so in fact I will have become the very villain they sought to make of me.'

'No, you won't,' she protested. 'But I understand what you're saying. And you're right.' She sighed. 'If we sin together tonight we would *have* to marry.'

She didn't want it to come to that. She didn't want him to regard her as an obligation. She didn't want him to wake up in the morning feeling that he had no choice but to marry her because he'd ruined her reputation.

She supposed it would have to be enough to know that he wanted her. Wanted her enough to tremble and spear his fingers into her hair, to run his hand to the upper curve of her bottom before snatching it back. To know that the fierce attraction wasn't one-sided.

She snuggled into his embrace. 'We should just go to sleep, then.'

He made a strange kind of strangled sound. 'Sleep? How do you expect me to sleep *now*?'

'I don't know,' she said, yawning sleepily. 'But I don't think I'm going to be able to keep my eyes open for much longer. I'm exhausted. Aren't you?'

He muttered something under his breath that she didn't quite catch. By the tone of his voice, it wasn't anything particularly pleasant. So she didn't ask him what it was. She just closed her eyes and surrendered to the bliss of being held in his arms.

Chapter Ten

Technically, this was the second night he'd slept with a woman—but since last night he hadn't known anything about it, it felt like the first.

It was the first time he'd been aware of her generous curves pressing into his side. The first time he'd breathed in the scent of her hair and rubbed his cheek against the soft profusion of her curls. The first time she'd tucked her poor little ice-cold feet between his legs, seeking warmth—and inadvertently creating it in his own loins.

He ground his teeth at the effort it took to keep completely still, when what he wanted was to roll over and flatten her beneath him.

No—no, he didn't! To do anything of the sort would be worse than anything that had befallen her thus far. She trusted him. Had told him she would even trust him with her fortune, her future, before curling up at his side and trusting him with her very virtue.

He bit back a groan. She'd told him she thought he was upright, when the truth was that the only upright part of him was the very part that wanted to betray her.

Not that he *would* betray her. Whatever it cost him in terms of comfort, tonight he wouldn't do that.

He wasn't an idiot. Later, when she learned the truth about him, he needed to be able to remind her that he *had* been true to her—in this if in nothing else.

Someone up there, he mused, looking at the stars peeping through a gap in the roof, must be laughing at him. Because the first time he'd ever strayed from the narrow confines of his life—from the straight and narrow, if you wanted to put it like that—was the first and only time a woman had placed such faith in him. The first time that he had even cared about a woman's opinion of him, come to that.

Heaven help him, now she was sliding her cold little hand round his waist. It was just as he'd predicted. The temperature had plummeted once the sun had gone down. The fact that he could see all those stars through the barn roof meant that the sky had stayed as clear as it had been all day. There might even be a touch of ground frost by morning. He'd think about frost. Or snow. Or ice. Anything cold. To take his mind off the way she was squirming closer to him in her sleep, seeking the warmth of his body.

It probably didn't help that he'd slept so deeply the night before. It meant that now he didn't feel in the least drowsy. Right, then… Since he was wide awake, he might as well turn the sleepless hours to good account. He would consider Prudence's future, rather than what he wanted to do with her now. The satisfaction he'd gain from bringing down the pair of villains who'd cheated her and dragged him into their plot.

There. That was better. Considering the cold, relentless march of justice was a much more sensible way to spend the night than revelling in the way all her trusting softness felt in his arms. Or savouring the scent of her body mingled with the scent of warmed hay.

Damn. That had only worked for—what?—less than ten seconds?

It was going to be a very long night.

But at some point he must have drifted off. Because the next thing he knew he was being woken, for the second day in a row, by a voice raised in anger.

This time when he opened his eyes it was to see a ruddy-faced man pointing a gun in his face, rather than merely a woman threatening him with a bony finger.

'Do you realise,' he said coldly, 'how dangerous it is to point a gun at someone?'

At his side, Prudence gasped, and stiffened in his hold.

'Don't be frightened,' he said, remembering that it was the second time in as many days that she'd been shocked awake, too. 'He won't shoot us.'

'Oh, won't I?' said the man with the gun.

'No. There are laws preventing such things.'

'I can do what I like on my own land,' said the man with the gun, belligerently. 'Since you got no right to be 'ere.'

'No, perhaps not,' admitted Gregory, for he had very little patience with people who trespassed on his own land.

'Ain't no perhaps about it! I don't hold with vagrants making free with decent folk's property.'

'Oh, but we're not vagrants,' said Prudence, sitting up and pushing her wildly tousled hair out of her eyes.

The farmer—for he had to assume that was this man's status, since he'd claimed they were trespassing on his land—glowered at her. 'Thieves, then. On the run from the law I 'spect.'

'We are no such thing,' said Gregory, sitting up and putting his arm round Prudence's shoulders. It said something about how frightened she was that she shrank into his side and clutched at his shirt front. 'In fact the very opposite. We have been robbed.'

'Oh-ar?' The farmer sneered at them.

'Yes. You see, this young lady's guardians formed a plot to rob her of her inheritance. They drugged us both and abandoned her in my bed, then made off with all her belongings. And then,' he said, rubbing his hand over his head in what was probably a vain attempt to remove all traces of hay. 'Then I was robbed, too—of my purse. And I had to leave my horse and gig at an inn as surety. Which is why we are cutting across country on foot to…'

He floundered to a halt. It probably wasn't a good idea to name the property to which they were heading, or give any hint that it belonged to him, or the man might guess who he was. And then the tale of what had befallen him this past few days would be all over the county in no time.

He'd be a laughing stock.

'A likely tale,' the farmer said. 'Do you take me for an idiot? Come on—up you get,' he said, jerking the gun in an up and down motion. 'We'll see what Jeffers has to say about this.'

Jeffers? Oh, no. He couldn't risk being hauled up before the local magistrate. He'd had the wretched man over to dine once or twice when he'd been staying down here before.

'Oh, no, please—there is no need for that,' said Prudence plaintively. Then she elbowed him in the ribs. 'I don't know why you needed to make up such a silly story, darling.'

Darling? He turned to stare at her.

'The truth is…' She clasped her hands at her chest and gazed up at the man with the gun earnestly. 'We are runaway lovers.'

'Well, I dunno if that ain't as bad,' said the farmer. Although he did lower his gun just a touch.

'I know—you must think we are wicked. But we are so very much in love. And my guardians are so strict. And, yes, it is rather shocking of us to defy them all, but we haven't broken a single law. Except perhaps for trespassing on your land. And if only we could pay for spending the night in your barn we would. But, you see, we *did* get robbed. That part of Gregory's story is true. So we haven't a penny between us. However, we are perfectly happy to work for you for an hour or so to repay you for spending the night here. Aren't we, darling?'

She turned and gave him a look loaded with meaning.

'Work?' The farmer tucked his gun under his arm and gave them a speculative look.

'Well,' said Prudence. 'I'm sure you are a very busy man. Farms don't run themselves, do they? And wouldn't it be better to make us pay for our stay here than waste time running to fetch the local constable?'

'Ar…' said the farmer, scratching his chin. 'There is that. And I can tell from yer voice that yer a lady. No beggarwoman I ever knew of spoke like you. Even though you *are* dressed like that.' His eyes flicked over her rumpled dress, down to her bare feet. And narrowed.

'You ain't used to walking nowheres, either, are yer?'

Was Gregory imagining it, or did the farmer look as though he was starting to feel sorry for her?

'No,' she said plaintively, shaking her head.

He was. The farmer was definitely looking sorry for her. But then the state of her feet was enough to melt the hardest of hearts.

'You'd best get up to the house, then, miss,' said the farmer, albeit rather gruffly, 'and get them feet seen to.'

'Oh, that's very kind of you, but—'

'This 'ere chap of yourn can do some chores to pay for flattening what's left of my hay.'

'Oh, but—'

'He's right, P... *darling*.' He glared at her warningly, hoping she'd get his hint not to reveal their names. Though she'd already called him Gregory, hadn't she?

Thank goodness she didn't know any of his other names, or they might all have come tumbling out.

'Let me do some work while you get your blisters seen to. They robbed us in the night, you see,' he informed the farmer. 'At the last inn. Took all our luggage. My poor love has no stockings to wear and—'

'I don't want to hear about that sort of thing,' said the farmer, taking a shocked step back at the mention of Prudence's undergarments. 'What I do want to know is what kind of work you can do. Don't want you blundering about causing damage as I'll have to clear up after.'

'I have done a bit of work about the stables,' he admitted, after only the briefest of pauses while he searched frantically for some skill he possessed which might be of use to a farmer.

The farmer glowered at him. Then at Prudence. 'Run off with yer groom, have yer?' He clucked his tongue. 'Well, ain't none of my business, I s'pose. Too late to do anything about it now, anyhow.' He glanced meaningfully at the crushed hay, at the way Gregory's arm stayed protectively round Prudence's shoulder, and the way she leaned into him, one hand resting trustingly against his chest.

'Come on, you,' he said, pointing a stubby, gnarled finger at Gregory. 'Let's see what yer made of.'

The farmer's voice was loaded with contempt. He might have some sympathy for Prudence, but he'd obviously cast Gregory in the role of evil seducer. For the second time in as many days he was being accused of the one thing he *hadn't* done.

The only difference this morning was that he now heartily wished he had.

Prudence wiped round her eggy plate with a crust of bread, fresh from the oven, and sighed with contentment.

''Tis good to see you have a hearty appetite,' said the farmer's wife, whose name was Madge. She had taken one look at Prudence's feet, thrown her hands up in horror, and then gone all motherly.

'Well, this is such good food,' said Prudence, with a sigh. Madge had heaped her plate with bacon, fried eggs and mushrooms. 'We hardly ate a thing yesterday.'

And she wasn't sure when she might be eating anything again. Gregory—for she couldn't help thinking of him by his first name after spending the night in his arms—had said they weren't far from his aunt's place and was assuming they would be welcome. But she wasn't banking on it. Aunts, she had discovered, could be extremely unpredictable.

'Now, you must let me help with the dishes,' she said. 'Or something.'

''Tain't fitting for a fine lady such as yerself to ruin her hands with dishes,' said Madge.

'I'm not a fine lady. I'm just…' She didn't know exactly how to describe herself. 'When I was a girl…' She decided to explain as much as she could. 'We travelled all over the place. Papa was a soldier, you see. So Mama and I had to learn how to do all sorts of chores. I can kill a chicken, and milk a goat, and bake bread.'

'Ain't no call for you to go killing none of our chickens,' Madge protested.

'No, of course not, I just—'

'Very well, m'dear. You can do the dishes.' She frowned. ''Twill make it look as though I kept you busy, anyhow, won't it? If Peter comes back in sudden-like.'

'Thank you,' said Prudence meekly.

She was more than willing to let Madge think she was grateful to be spared the prospect of falling foul of her bad-tempered husband if that was what it took to help her overcome her scruples at having a guest do menial work.

The moment Prudence finished the dishes Madge urged her back to the kitchen table.

'Here, you eat a bit of this,' she said, spooning jam onto another thick slice of bread and butter. 'That varmint had no business dragging a lady such as you out into the wilds with no more'n the clothes on your back, and starving you besides.'

'It wasn't his fault—really it wasn't,' she protested, before taking a bite of bread and jam.

But she knew she'd made Madge think it was, by being tight-lipped in response to all her very natural questions. Madge must think she was having second thoughts, or was ashamed of having been so impetuous, or something.

She was just wondering if she could come up with a story that would clear Gregory's reputation, when the flavour of the jam exploded into her mouth.

'Oh, goodness,' she moaned. 'But this jam is good.'

'Last year's strawberries,' said Madge proudly.

'I dreamed about strawberries last night,' she admitted.

'Well, you can take a pot of this jam, then.'

'Oh, no, she can't!'

Prudence saw that the doorway, in which the door had been standing open, was now full of the farmer and Gregory. A distinctly grimy, damp, dishevelled and irritated Gregory.

'She's nobbut a hussy, running off with her groom. Should have put her to work—not filled her with jam what's meant for the market next week.'

''Tweren't meant for no market. That was from a jar I'd already opened!'

As the farmer and his wife launched into a heated argument Gregory jerked his head at her, indicating that she should get up and leave. Which she was only too glad to do.

'Thank you so much for seeing to my feet,' she said, edging past Madge just as she was taking a breath in preparation for slinging another pithy remark at her husband. 'One day you must give me the receipt for that ointment.'

Gregory shot her a look of disbelief, as though he couldn't imagine ever coming anywhere near this farm again.

The farmer, who'd glanced at Prudence's feet when she spoke of them, was now glaring at Madge in a very similar fashion.

'Where'd she get those stockings?'

'From me, of course, you cloth-head,' said Madge.

'Ain't it enough I caught the pair of them trespassing on our land but you must give 'em the food from our table and the very clothes off our back?'

Prudence had just reached the doorway, and Gregory's side, when Madge darted up to her.

'Here,' she said, pressing the remains of the loaf and the opened jar of jam into her hands in defiance of her husband, who was positively swelling with indignation.

'My kitchen,' said Madge, whirling back to him. 'My jam. I made it. And you swore I could do what I wanted with the money I make from it.'

'Ar, but I didn't mean for you to—'

They didn't wait to hear what the farmer hadn't meant for Madge to do with her jam, but took off as fast as they could go.

'What a charming scene of rustic marital bliss,' said Gregory with heavy sarcasm as they made for the barn. 'No wonder he came out here in a mood to shoot something.'

'Here,' said Prudence, thrusting the loaf and the crock of jam at him. 'You are clearly one of those men who wake in a bad mood and need something to eat before you are fit company.'

'It is no longer first thing in the morning,' he replied, taking the bread and ripping off a hunk. 'And it is all very well for you to complain of my mood when you have clearly been treated like a queen in that farmhouse kitchen while *I*,' he said, dipping the bread into the open jam pot, 'have been mucking out the cow byre.'

She wrinkled her nose. 'I thought I could smell something.'

He glowered at her.

'I hope you washed your hands.'

His glower deepened. 'I washed not only my hands but my boots, my breeches and my hair,' he said with his mouth full. 'Under the pump.'

'Oh.' Well, that explained why his hair was wet. 'I did the breakfast dishes,' she put in, hoping to placate him.

'Mrs Grumpy Farmer was clearly a decent sort of woman. Mr Grumpy Farmer did nothing but complain and berate me every time he came to check on my progress. And as for the disgusting state of that byre…' He shuddered expressively. 'No wonder he didn't want to clean it out himself.'

'Oh, dear. Well, I'm very sorry. Perhaps I shouldn't have volunteered our services to Mr Grumpy Farmer with the Gun. I just thought it would be better than having to explain ourselves to the local law. When you started telling him what had happened to us it all sounded so implausible that I could see exactly why he wasn't believing a word of it. Indeed, had I not lived through it I wouldn't have believed a word of it myself.'

'Hmmph,' he said, spraying crumbs down the front of his waistcoat as he stomped across the barn to the mound of hay they'd slept on the previous night.

'Um…' she said, shifting from one foot to the other. 'I can see how much you want your breakfast, but I really don't want to linger here any longer than we have to. Do you?'

'Your point?' He raised one eyebrow at her in a way that expressed many things at once. All of them negative.

'Well, you're clearly going to need both your hands to deal with your bread and jam. So you won't have one free to carry your valise. I was going to suggest I carry it, so we can make a start.' She bent to pick it up. 'It's not very heavy,' she said with some relief.

'And it does have some of your things in it,' he said, with a funny sort of glint in his eye.

'Does it? What—?' She suddenly had a vivid recollection of tossing her stays aside as she'd fled from his room. There were stockings, too. She hadn't stopped to pull them on. And he'd put at least one of them in his pocket. But—why? It wasn't as if they could be of any use to him. And he'd already proved that having only one stocking was of absolutely no use to her, either.

Sometimes men were a complete mystery.

'Come on, then,' he said, turning and heading out of the barn, leaving her to trot behind him with his luggage.

She supposed he was getting his own back on her for getting a decent breakfast while he'd been mucking out a cow byre. Because it certainly wasn't like him to behave in such an ungentlemanly fashion

Not that she could complain, though, could she? She'd offered to carry it, after all. And even if he'd argued that it was his job, as a big strong man, to do so, she would only have pointed out that she was perfectly capable of carrying a small bag for a short while. In a way he was paying her a compliment by taking her at her word and letting her do as she'd suggested.

Or so he would say if she dared say anything derogatory about the way he was striding ahead, enjoying the bread and jam, while she trotted behind him with the luggage.

They walked along in simmering silence past various farm buildings, heading for the track she could see winding across the fields, while he demolished the bread. When the last crust was gone he frowned into the jam pot, then stuck his finger in and swirled it round to get at the very last traces. When his finger was sufficiently loaded, he raised it to his mouth and sucked it clean.

Prudence promptly forgot why she'd been irritated with him as she watched him half close his eyes in bliss. When he set about doing something he did it with total concentration. To the exclusion of everything else.

As if to prove her right, the moment he'd wiped the jar completely clean he set it aside on the top bar of the stile they'd just reached and turned to her with a smile.

'I'll carry that now,' he said, holding out his hand for the valise.

She handed it over without a word of protest. What would be the point? And, judging by the twinkle in his eye, he knew exactly what arguments had been going through her head while he'd been breaking his fast.

He tossed the valise over the stile, then stepped up onto the first rung and swung one leg over the top. When he was safely on the other side he leaned back and reached for her hand to help her over. Since she'd just mounted the lower step his movement brought their faces to within inches of each other. And she couldn't help noticing he had a smear of jam on his lower lip.

'You have…um…' she began, reaching out one finger to wipe the jam from his mouth.

He moved really swiftly, catching her hand and stilling it. And looked at her in a considering sort of way, as though wondering what to make of her. Why didn't he want her touching his face? Well, then, she wouldn't do so. But when she went to pull her hand back his hold on it tightened. And the look in his eyes went sort of slumberous. And then he pulled her hand right up to his mouth, dipped his head, and sucked her forefinger inside.

He swirled his tongue round her finger and her knees went weak. She pitched forward, bracing herself against the top of the stile with her free hand.

He released her finger from his mouth and looked at her. In a steady sort of way that seemed to dare her to do what she wanted. So she did. She leaned forward and pressed her lips to his. He tasted of jam. And fresh bread. And outdoors. And man.

She reached for him and clung as hard as she could with the stile between them. And they kissed and kissed and kissed.

When they finished her legs were shaking so much that the stile might as well have been a sheer brick wall. There was no way she was going to be able to get over it.

As though he knew how she felt, Gregory got onto the lower step, leaned over and grasped her round the waist, then lifted her right over as though she weighed next to nothing.

She landed on his side of the stile, breathless and shaky, flush with the solid mass of his body. And yearning for another kiss.

He steadied her, and gently but firmly pushed her away. 'We need to keep going.' Then he turned to pick up his valise. 'Come on,' he said, holding out his hand to her.

Which filled her with relief. He might have pushed her away, but at least he was prepared to hold her hand. It was like last night. The way he'd turned over, yet kept hold of her hand to let her know he wasn't rejecting her. So she put her hand in his. And noticed, for the first time, that Mr Grumpy Farmer lived on the prettiest farm she'd ever seen. There were primroses on the banks. Little white clouds scudding across the blue sky. Madge's stockings were of thick, serviceable cotton which cushioned her feet from her shoes so that they no longer caused her agony with every step. And the scent of green growing things was almost managing to overpower the rather unpleasant odour emanating from Gregory's general vicinity.

All in all, she didn't think she'd ever felt quite so happy.

Until, that was, she darted a look up at Gregory's face. For *he* didn't look as though he was wallowing in the memory of strawberry kisses over the stile, or indeed enjoying walking through the countryside in any way at all. He certainly didn't look as though he was thanking his lucky stars he'd fallen in with a wealthy girl who'd proposed marriage to him the night before.

On the contrary. Gregory looked the way a man might look if he was on his way to the scaffold.

A cold hand squeezed at her stomach.

She'd thought that last night in the barn, when he'd told her about his marriage, it had meant that they were becoming close. Which was why she'd blurted out the suggestion that they should marry. But he hadn't agreed, had he? Just because he'd kissed her, that didn't mean he wanted to go as far as marrying her, did it? She'd gone and jumped in with both feet again, as Aunt Charity would say, the way she always did. The way her mother always had.

A man like him couldn't possibly want a girl like her for a wife, could he? How could she have forgotten that she'd made an exhibition of herself by singing in the market place? Or that she'd very nearly killed him by throwing that bit of rock? Men didn't generally marry women whose behaviour they couldn't predict. Let alone women who might accidentally kill them if there were any loose rocks to hand.

'You don't want to marry me at all, do you?'

Her stomach cramped again. She'd made a total fool of herself. Here she'd been, assuming he must be dreaming about how he could invest her money to expand his business, whatever it was, but the truth was he hadn't actually said yes. And now she'd gone and kissed him, assuming he was as keen on the idea as she was.

'Last night, when you told me about your marriage, I thought… Oh, how silly of me.' It was all much clearer this morning. 'You were trying to explain why you didn't wish to marry again, weren't you? And I…'

'Hmm? What?' He turned and stared at her as though he'd completely forgotten she was there.

She wrenched her hand from his. 'I am sure we can come up with some other way out of our predicament.'

Even though she had kissed him. What was a kiss, after all? Men were always trying to snatch kisses—especially from girls who practically threw themselves into their arms. Even if they appeared to enjoy the kiss it didn't mean they actually wanted to *marry* the girl they'd been kissing. Men with less honour than him would make the most of the opportunity to have carnal relations with a girl if she was silly enough to indicate she was willing before he put a ring on her finger.

'You don't need to go to the lengths of marrying me,' she said.

What was the matter with her? he wondered. Why had she suddenly changed her mind about marrying him?

He grabbed her hand back and held it tightly. 'There *is* no other way out of our "predicament", as you put it, apart from marriage. No way at all.'

He'd gone over it time and time again. Although Prudence was so far removed from him socially that everyone would describe it as a *mésalliance*, he was going to have to marry her. Oh, not to avoid scandal. But because after that kiss there was no way he was going to let her go. And because he was almost certain she'd never agree to be his mistress.

If he offered her carte blanche, even though it was something he'd never offered any other woman, he couldn't see Prudence taking it as a compliment. In fact she was more likely to take such a proposition as an insult. She might even feel so insulted she'd never forgive him. And he couldn't risk that. She was going to be upset enough as it was once they reached Bramley Park, where he would no longer be able to hide his true identity from her.

But he wanted Prudence.

And he was going to have Prudence.

That was all there was to it.

Chapter Eleven

Prudence's fingers were going numb. Once or twice she'd been on the verge of complaining about the way he was crushing them, but she'd been afraid he might let go altogether. And at least while he was holding her hand she had *some* connection with him.

He hadn't spoken a word since telling her that there was no way out of their predicament but marriage. He'd never been what you'd call a chatty sort of man, but since then he'd become downright distant.

He was also walking slower and slower, dragging his feet, as though he was trying to put off reaching their destination for as long as possible. The only conclusion she could draw was that he was having serious second thoughts about marrying her. It was one thing admitting he wanted to bed her. But in the cold light of day perhaps he was starting to wonder if marrying her to get what he wanted was going a step too far.

Which was perfectly understandable, given the grief his last marriage had brought him. Especially since he hadn't known her long enough to be sure she would take her marriage vows seriously.

'There,' he said grimly as they crested a rise. 'That's Bramley Park.'

He came to a complete standstill, gazing down at a substantial park spread out on the slopes of the next valley. A high stone wall divided the neatly landscaped grounds from the rougher grazing land on which they stood. There was so much parkland she couldn't even see the house it surrounded.

'That is where your aunt lives?'

He nodded.

'She must be a wealthy woman.' Only wealthy people had houses stuck in the middle of so much land, with high stone walls to keep ordinary people out.

'Not really.'

'Oh? But—'

'Come on,' he said impatiently, veering to the left and tugging her after him down the slope towards the wall which bisected the lower part of the valley.

At length, they came to a section where a couple of gnarled trees grew close to the wall, their branches arching over the top.

'I should have asked,' he said, turning to her with a wary expression. 'Are you any good at climbing trees?'

'Actually,' she replied with a proud toss of her head, 'I am *very* good at climbing trees.' At least she had been as a girl. You couldn't grow up on the fringes of the army without learning all sorts of things that decently brought up girls really shouldn't. Or so Aunt Charity had frequently complained.

'Is there *anything* you cannot do?'

He'd said it with a smile. A rather fond sort of smile, she thought. Or was she just looking for signs that he liked her well enough to think that marrying her wouldn't be a total disaster? He might just as well be the kind of man to cover his doubts and fears by putting on a brave face.

'I believe,' she said, pushing back the waves of insecurity that had been surging over her ever since she'd kissed him, and he hadn't been willing to kiss her again, 'in rising to any challenge. Or at least that is what Mama used to say. Whenever things were hard, she'd say we mustn't look upon them as stumbling blocks in our way, but as stepping stones across troubled waters.'

'And what would she have said about walls that block our paths? That we should climb them?'

She was about to say yes, when something stopped her. 'I don't know about that. I mean, that wall was put there to keep people out, wasn't it? And I'm starting to get a horrid feeling that we may be…um…breaking in.'

He'd already admitted he didn't scruple to break into places when it suited him. He was one of those men who thought the end justified the means. Not that he was a bad man. Just a bit of a rogue, as Papa had been.

'We've already had a farmer threatening us with his gun this morning. What if some gamekeeper mistakes us for poachers? It is just the sort of thing that would happen, the way my luck has been running recently.'

'I can promise you faithfully that we won't be mistaken for poachers once we get over that wall,' he replied, drawing back his arm and tossing the valise over it. 'And, what's more, one cannot break into property that one owns oneself.'

'You are trying to tell me that the estate that lies beyond that wall belongs to *you*?' She eyed his clothing, then his black eye and his grazed knuckles dubiously. 'I thought you said it was your aunt's?'

'I said my aunt lives there,' he replied, planting his fists on his hips. 'Prudence, never say you've been judging me by my appearance?'

He ran his eyes pointedly from the crown of her tousled head to the soles of her shoes, via the jacket she'd borrowed from him, which came almost to her knees, and the stockings she'd borrowed from the farmer's wife, which were sagging round her ankles. Then he flicked his eyes back to her face. Which felt sticky with jam and was probably grimy.

'That's a fair point,' she admitted. 'To look at me nobody would ever suspect I was an heiress, would they? But just explain one thing, if you wouldn't mind? If this is your property, then why are we about to climb over the wall when there must be a perfectly good front gate?'

'Because it would take us the best part of an hour to walk all the way round to the main gate. And your feet have suffered enough abuse already.'

'You want to spare my feet? Oh.' She felt mean now, for suspecting his behaviour to be shifty. 'Then, thank you.'

'Don't thank me just yet,' he said, eyeing the tree, the height of the wall, and then her again. 'I really should have taken into consideration how hard it will be for you to climb up that tree in skirts.'

The very last thing she would do was admit that she hadn't climbed any trees for a considerable time.

'I will go first,' he said. 'And help you up.'

He strode up to the tree. Put his fists on his hips and frowned. Which puzzled her, for a moment, since there was a gnarly knot at a perfect height from which to commence his climb. But then she worked out that he must be considering it from *her* perspective.

'I am sure I will be able to manage,' she assured him. 'This tree has lots of handholds and footholds,'

'Footholds?' He looked from her to the tree, then back to her again, his expression rather blank.

'Yes,' she said, pointing to the stubby projection left behind from where a branch had snapped off years before.

'Ah, yes. Indeed.' He rubbed his hands together. Stayed exactly where he was.

'What is the problem?' What had he seen that she hadn't considered?

'The problem... Well,' he said, 'it is merely that I have never climbed this tree before.'

Oh, how sweet of him to warn her that he wasn't going to be able to point out the best route up it.

'There's no need to worry. Although I haven't climbed a tree since I was a girl, this one looks remarkably easy. Even hampered as I am by skirts.'

'Well, that's good. Yes. Very good.'

A determined look came over his face. He stepped up to the tree. Set one foot on the knot she'd just pointed out. Looked further up the trunk. As though he had no idea what to do next.

'Do you know?' she said with a touch of amusement. 'If I didn't know better, I'd think you've never climbed *any* tree before—never mind that one.'

His shoulders stiffened. Oh, dear, she shouldn't have teased him. Some men could take it, and some men couldn't. Funny, but she'd thought he was the type who could. He'd been remarkably forgiving so far, about all sorts of things she'd done to him.

Without a word he reached up for the most obvious handhold, then scrambled very clumsily up to the first branch thick enough to bear his weight. With only the minimum of cursing he pulled himself up and onto it, swinging one leg over so that he sat astride.

Then he turned and grinned down at her. 'Nothing to it!'

She gasped. 'I was only joking before, but it's true, isn't it? You never *have* climbed a tree, have you?'

He gave an insouciant shrug. 'Well, no. But I always suspected that if other boys could do it I could.'

'What kind of boy never climbed trees?'

'One whose parents were terrified of some harm befalling him and had him watched over night and day,' he replied.

'Oh. That sounds—' Very restricting. And a total contrast to her own childhood. Compared with her life in Stoketown, it had taken on a rosy hue in her memory. But, if she looked at it honestly, it must have been a very precarious sort of existence.

'I suppose,' she said thoughtfully, 'that is what parents do. Even mine—I mean, since they couldn't protect me from actual danger, they did what they could to stop me from being afraid by making light of all the upheavals and privations of army life. Treating it all—in front of me, at least—as though it was all some grand adventure.'

'Which is why nothing scares you now?'

'Well, I wouldn't say that,' she countered. Right this minute she was, if not exactly scared, certainly very wary of climbing up to join him. Because she'd suddenly become very aware that learning to climb trees was not the kind of activity that should have formed part of her education, if there were even some boys, like Gregory, who hadn't been allowed to do it. And also, more to the point, that when she'd been a girl she hadn't cared about showing off her legs.

'Come on,' he said, leaning down and holding out his hand to her. 'Up you get.'

'Wait a minute,' she said. 'I need to take some precautionary measures.'

She hitched up her gown and her petticoat as high as she dared, then reached between her legs and pulled the bunched material from behind through to the front, forming a sort of shortened, baggy set of breeches. It was the best she could do. She only hoped nobody came up over the rise and saw her display of legs bare to the thigh. With one hand clutching her skirts, and her face on fire, she set her foot on the knot she'd shown him earlier, took his hand, and let him haul her up onto the branch next to him.

'What a pity it is that ladies' fashions demand they cover their legs so completely,' he said, running his eyes over hers.

'Impractical, too,' she said with a nonchalant toss of her head, since it was impossible to blush any hotter. 'When a lady decides she needs to climb a tree, breeches would make it far easier.'

He grinned at her again, then shuffled along the branch to the top of the wall, slid across it, and dropped down into the shrubbery that grew right up to the base of the wall on the other side. He turned to her and held out his arms.

'All you need to do is slide to the edge and drop down. I'll catch you,' he said.

All she had to do? In a gown that was hitched almost to her waist?

'It's all very well for you. You *are* wearing breeches.'

Which protected his vulnerable parts. It was no joke, shuffling over a crumbling brick wall when shielded only by a cotton chemise and a bit of kerseymere, since his jacket was trailing uselessly behind her.

But at last she was right at the edge of the wall, her legs dangling down into the park. With Gregory standing below, a wide grin on his face.

'Enjoying the view?' she asked tartly.

'Immensely,' he said without a trace of shame. 'You have very beautiful legs. Even those hideous stockings cannot disguise how very shapely they are.'

'You really shouldn't be staring,' she scolded.

'I would be mad not to.'

'I should slap your face.'

'You will have to come down here first to reach it.'

So she jumped.

And he caught her. And steadied her. And then held on to her elbows for far longer than was necessary. And what with all the talk of legs, and the heated look in his eyes, somehow she didn't wish to slap his face any longer.

'Prudence...' he breathed. 'Prudence, about us getting married...'

Her heart sank. She'd already worked out that he didn't really want to marry her. That he was probably thinking of ways to let her down gently.

'I've already told you—you don't have to,' she said, nobly letting him off the hook. If he didn't want to marry her she wasn't going to force his hand. 'It was just a silly idea I had. I could—'

'No. You couldn't. I won't let you go—do you hear me?'

And then, to her complete surprise, he hauled her

all the way into his arms and kissed her. Savagely. The way she'd always suspected a man with a face as harsh as his could kiss.

Yes! Yes, yes, yes, yes, *yes*. It was heavenly. No question this time about who had initiated the kiss. Though of course she kissed him back for all she was worth.

'Oh, Gregory…' She sighed when he broke away. 'That was lovely.'

He reared back, an expression of astonishment on his face. 'Yes, it was.'

All the pleasurable feelings humming through her dropped through the soles of her feet.

'Didn't you expect to like it? After our last kiss I thought— Oh! Did I do something wrong? Was that it?' She tried to pull away from him.

But he held on to her tightly, refusing to release her from the circle of his arms.

'How could you have done anything wrong?' He shook his head in a sort of daze. 'You kissed me back.'

'Well, then, what was wrong with it?'

'Nothing was wrong with it. That was what was so surprising. Prudence…' He shifted from one foot to another. Took a deep breath. 'I never really saw the point to kissing—that's all. There are more…interesting parts of a woman I've always wanted to pay attention to, you see. But your mouth…'

He looked at her lips again. In the way he'd done before. The way that made them tingle, and part, and wait expectantly for the touch of his lips.

'Your mouth is worth…' He cocked his head to one side. 'Savouring—yes, that is the word. I would never feel as though I was wasting my time, no matter how long you wanted to kiss me.'

He cradled her face with one hand, then bent his head slowly, as if they had all the time in the world. This time he kissed her in a far less savage manner, as though—yes, that was just what it felt like—as though he was *savouring* her.

And she savoured him right back. Pressed herself as close to him as she could. Slid her hands inside his coat and wound her arms round his slender, hard waist. Raised one foot and ran it up and down the back of his booted calf. Feeling all the while as though her body was bursting into song.

'Oh, Gregory,' she moaned into his mouth when he paused to take a breath. 'Oh, please don't stop.'

'I must,' he growled against her lips. 'I thought I could kiss you for ever, but the truth is that I'm starting to find it hard not to throw you down behind the bushes and ravish you.'

'I don't think I'd care,' she admitted. 'I know I should, but somehow—'

'No. Don't say it. Don't tempt me.' He closed his eyes as though in anguish and rested his forehead against hers.

'Oh, very well,' she grumbled. 'I suppose you are right.' After all, she didn't really want her first time to take place out of doors, on the ground, did she?

'Come on, then,' he said with a sort of gentle determination. He took her hand. 'Let's get you into the house, while we can both still walk, and set things in train to make our union respectable.'

He picked up the valise and headed for a gap in the rather overgrown shrubbery.

'Gregory,' she said, when he let go of her hand for a moment to raise the branch of an overhanging beech sapling so that she could pass. 'Can I ask you something?'

He blinked. Visibly braced himself. 'You may ask me anything,' he said.

'Well, I'm sorry if you think I'm prying, but I simply cannot understand how it is your wife went with someone else. If you kissed her the way you just kissed me...' She blushed, suddenly realising that this was one of those topics properly brought up girls didn't mention.

'I told you—my wife hated intimacy of any sort. With me, that is. I never managed more than a peck on the cheek.'

Good grief. The woman must have been a complete imbecile. If only she'd let him kiss her, thoroughly, he would have made her feel gloriously wonderful. Although he'd only been a stripling when he'd been married. Perhaps he hadn't yet learned how to kiss like that.

How had he learned to kiss like that?

'You kissed other women, then, didn't you?' she blurted, after turning over the thought for a while. 'I mean, you have been a widower for a very long time. I suppose you've had a few...er...liaisons?'

He froze in his tracks. Turned and glanced over his shoulder at her. 'I've had more than a few "liaisons", Prudence, and you may as well hear about them now. But understand this.' He turned and looked her straight in the eye. 'I was angry. Bitter. I'd stayed true to my marriage vows while she...' His mouth twisted. 'Can you imagine how it felt to know I'd been faithful to a faithless wife?' He seized her hand. 'Just think how you felt the moment you knew that your aunt and uncle— the people you relied on to guard your welfare—had conspired to rob and humiliate you.'

'Yes, I think I see.'

'Do you? Then you will understand my burning need to make up for lost time. Why I bedded as many women as I could. Why I never risked feeling anything approaching affection for any of them. Why I made sure they knew exactly what their purpose was. Which was why I never kissed them the way I just kissed you. I may have kissed their hands in flirtation, or used my mouth or my tongue on sensitive parts of their bodies to arouse and inflame them...or—' He broke off, looking exasperated. 'Good God, Prudence, how do you manage to get me to tell you things like this?'

'I only asked you about kissing,' she pointed out. 'I didn't force you to tell me anything about your... liaisons.' Even though what he'd said had helped her understand him better. 'You could have just told me to mind my own business.'

'For some reason I don't seem to be able to tell you any such thing,' he growled, before turning his back on her and stalking off through the undergrowth.

She had to break into a trot to keep up with him. But neither the fact that he was walking so quickly nor the grumpy way he'd spoken to her could cast her down very much. For one thing, the confidence with which he was striding through the undergrowth proved that he was very familiar with the layout of the grounds. Which laid to rest her fear that they might be trespassing. For another, she couldn't help being pleased that he couldn't keep things from her. Last night's confidences might have been due to some after-effect of the drug. But there was no trace of it left in either of them today. If he couldn't keep anything from her, then it was because somehow she'd got under his guard.

She smiled. He was the kind of man who wasn't used to sharing confidences with anyone, but he couldn't hold back from her—not with his thoughts, or his kisses. After only knowing her for just over a day. Which made her feel very powerful, in a uniquely feminine way.

She was still smiling when they emerged, blinking, onto a massive swathe of lawn on which sheep were grazing. On its far side sat a very neat little box of a house, in the Palladian style, two storeys high. Or perhaps not so little. She counted seven windows across the top floor.

She turned to look at Gregory, who'd come to a complete standstill. He caught her enquiring look and glowered at her.

'This is it,' he said. 'God help me.'

'Whatever do you mean? Gregory, what *is* the matter?'

A muscle in his jaw clenched, as though he was biting back some unpalatable truth. Whatever could there be inside that house which had the power to make him look so reluctant to enter it? The dragon of an aunt? Surely she couldn't have too much influence over him, since he claimed to own the house? Unless he'd fallen on hard times and the woman held some financial power over him? Well, that wouldn't matter once they were married—unless she was the kind of old harpy who would make him feel bad about marrying an heiress.

'You'll soon find out,' he said grimly. Then seized her hand in his and set off for the house once more.

'Please don't worry,' she panted, for he was walking so fast now he'd clearly made up his mind to beard the dragon in her den that she was having to trot to keep up with him. 'Whatever is worrying you, I know you can deal with it. You can deal with anything.'

'I hope to God you're right,' he muttered.

He took a deep breath, like a man about to dive from a high cliff into murky water, then strode up the front steps and rapped on the door.

'Prudence,' he said, turning to her, a tortured expression on his face. 'Perhaps I should have warned you before we got here that—' He broke off at the distinct sound of footsteps approaching from the other side of the door. 'Too late,' he said, shutting his mouth with a snap on whatever it was he'd wanted to warn her of.

Never mind. Whatever it was, she could weather it. If she'd managed to survive this past two nightmarish days, she could weather anything.

But then, as the door swung open, something very strange happened to Gregory. He sort of…closed up. It was as though he had deliberately wiped all expression from his face, turning into a hard, distant, cold man she couldn't imagine ever climbing trees with a grin. He looked just like the man she'd first seen in The Bull—the man from whom everyone had kept their distance. And, even though she was still holding his hand, she got the feeling he'd gone somewhere very far away inside.

A soberly dressed man opened the door and goggled at the sight of them. Which was hardly surprising. Not many people looking as scruffy as they did would have the effrontery to knock on the front door of a house like this. But Gregory didn't bat an eyelid.

'Good morning, Perkins,' he said. 'Something amiss?'

'No, Your Grace,' said the flabbergasted butler.

Your Grace? Why was the butler addressing Gregory as 'Your Grace'?

'Of course not, Your Grace. It is just—' The butler pulled himself together, opened the door wider and stepped aside. 'We were not expecting you for another day or so.'

Gregory raised one eyebrow in a way that had the butler shrinking in stature.

'Your rooms are in readiness, of course,' he said.

'And for my guest?'

The butler's eyes slid briefly across Prudence. 'I am sure it will take Mrs Hoskins but a moment to have something suitable prepared for the young person.'

Gregory inclined his head in an almost regal manner. Then walked into the house in a way she'd never seen him walk before. As though he owned the place. Well, he'd told her he did. It was just that until this very second she hadn't really, truly believed it.

And there was something else she was finding hard to believe as well.

'Why,' she whispered as he tugged her into the spacious hall, 'is the butler calling you Your Grace?'

'Because, Miss Carstairs,' he said, in what sounded to her like an apologetic manner. 'I am afraid that I am a duke.'

Chapter Twelve

'A *duke*?'

No. It would be easier to believe he was a highwayman and that this house was a den filled to bursting with his criminal associates than that.

But then why else would the butler have addressed him as 'Your Grace'?

'This is Miss Carstairs, Perkins,' said Gregory—or whoever he was—to the butler, handing him his valise. 'My fiancée.'

'Your—?' The butler's face paled. His lips moved soundlessly, his jaw wagging up and down as though words failed him.

She knew how he felt, having just sustained as great a shock herself. Which made her realise her own mouth had sagged open on her hearing Gregory claim to be a duke.

She shut it with a snap.

'Fiancée,' Gregory repeated slowly, as though addressing an imbecile.

'If you say so, Your Grace,' said the butler, looking distinctly unimpressed. 'I mean…' he added swiftly, when Gregory raised one eyebrow in that way he had—a way, she now saw, that was due to his being a duke. A duke who wasn't used to having butlers, let alone stray females, dare to express a view that ran counter to his own. 'Congratulations, Your Grace,' said the butler, inclining his head in the slightest of bows whilst refraining from looking in her direction.

'Miss Carstairs and I fell among thieves on the road,' said Gregory. Or whatever she was now supposed to call him.

'Hence our rather dishevelled appearance.' He waved his hand in a vague gesture encompassing them both.

'I shall send for Dr Crabbe at once, Your Grace,' said the butler, his eyes fixed on the cuts and bruises on his employer's face.

Marks that she'd come to regard as an integral part of him. But which were not, to judge by the butler's expression of horror, by any means typical.

'Oh, no need for that. I am sure Mrs Hoskins can supply a poultice, or some soothing ointment of some sort that will suffice. And, while we are on the subject of ointment, Miss Carstairs will need some for her feet.'

'Her feet?' The butler, reduced to repeating his master's words in a strained manner, glanced down at her feet, and then to the staircase, from the direction of which came the sound of a slamming door.

A slender youth, in very natty dress, appeared on the landing and began to jog down the stairs, whistling cheerfully.

Until he caught sight of the three of them standing by the open front door. Which had him coming to an abrupt halt, mid-whistle.

'Halstead!'

Since the youth was staring at Gregory, Prudence

could only suppose that Halstead must be his real name. Or his title. Aristocrats always had a handful of each.

'The devil!'

'Language, Hugo,' said Gregory—or Halstead—or whoever he was. Though at least she could surmise that this youth was the Hugo with whom Gregory had suspected she'd done some sort of deal when they'd first met.

'Language be damned,' said Hugo, reaching for the banister rail to steady himself. 'You didn't last the full week. I've won.'

Won? Won what?

'Extenuating circumstances,' said Gregory, waving a languid hand in her direction. He spoke in a bored drawl. As though he was completely unmoved by the shock afflicting everyone else in the hallway, which he'd caused by strolling through the front door and announcing both his rank and his betrothal.

'No such thing,' said the youth, folding his arms across his chest. 'Ain't you always telling me that there's never any excuse for outrunning the constable? That if you only have a little backbone, or willpower, or a modicum of intelligence…'

'Not here,' muttered Gregory—she had to think of him by some name, and that was the one she'd grown used to. And if he hadn't wanted her to use it he should jolly well not have let her do so! 'We will repair to the morning room,' he said, taking her elbow firmly to steer her across the hall. 'While we await refreshments.' He gave the butler a pointed look.

The butler flinched. 'Her Ladyship is in the morning room, taking tea,' he said, glancing at Prudence, then back at Gregory, in ill-concealed horror.

'Ah,' said Gregory, coming to a full stop.

'No point in trying to keep anything from Lady Mixby,' said Hugo cheerfully, jogging down the rest of the stairs. 'Since the person she is currently entertaining to tea is a most interesting cove who claims you sent him here. By the name of Bodkin.'

Bodkin? Wasn't that the name of the man with whom he'd told her he'd broken into a mill? Making it sound as if he was some sort of…Robin Hood, or something. Going about righting wrongs. Now this Hugo person was making it sound as though it was a great jest. Coupled with his first remark, about not lasting a week and not winning, it sounded suspiciously as though Gregory had gone to the factory in the course of trying to win some kind of wager.

Now all those things he'd said about what she had been doing in his bed made perfect sense. He'd thought that Hugo was doing all in his power to make him lose whatever wager they had agreed upon.

'This way,' said Gregory, steering her across the hall with the grip he still had on her elbow.

She put up no resistance. She didn't have the strength. It had all seeped out through what felt like a great crack, somewhere deep inside her, where once her trust in Gregory had resided. She hadn't even felt this stunned when she'd discovered that Aunt Charity, who'd appeared to be a pillar of society, had turned into a criminal overnight. Into a person she didn't really know at all.

Because she'd never actually *liked* Aunt Charity, try as hard as she might.

But she'd started to look upon this man who was ushering her across the hall as a bit of a hero.

Now it turned out he was someone else—some*thing*

else—entirely. A duke. A duke who'd been so bored with his dull existence that he'd put on rough clothes and changed his name in order to win a bet.

The butler leaped ahead of them to open the door to a room that was flooded with sunshine. Three people were sitting there.

A young man, wearing clothes that were so plain and so coarse that he just had to be Mr Bodkin, was perched on the very edge of a hard-backed chair, his hands braced on his knees as though ready to take flight at the slightest alarm. There was also a bracket-faced woman at a table under the window, tucking into a plate of cakes and sandwiches, a teacup at her elbow. And on one of the sofas placed on either side of the fire sat a plump little woman wearing lavender satin and a frivolous lace cap of white.

The plump woman uttered a piercing shriek when she saw them, and clapped her hand to her ample bosom.

Mr Bodkin started to his feet, took half a pace in their direction, then halted, saying, 'Mr Willingale…?'

The bracket-faced lady froze, a sandwich halfway to her mouth.

'Mr Willingale!' said the plainly dressed young man again, this time with more certainty. 'It *is* you. Thank heaven. I was that worrit when I got here and you hadn't arrived. I was sure summat bad must have happened to you.'

'I told you there was no need to worry,' said Hugo, sauntering into the room and closing the door firmly behind him. 'I told you we weren't expecting Halstead until the end of the week.'

'Halstead?' Mr Bodkin frowned. 'Who's Halstead?'

'I am,' said Gregory.

'But you told me you was Mr Willingale,' said Mr Bodkin, looking as bewildered as Prudence felt.

'Well, he ain't,' said Hugo firmly. 'He's Halstead. Duke of.'

So she wasn't the only person he'd lied to about his identity. It should have been of some consolation. Why wasn't it?

The youth in homespun glowered at Hugo. 'Beggin' Yer Lordship's pardon, but I know what he said.'

Hugo was a *lordship*? Well, naturally! If Gregory was a duke all his relatives were bound to be lords and ladies, too.

'Never mind that for now,' said Gregory firmly, as the two younger men squared up to each other. 'Miss Carstairs is in dire need of tea and a seat by the fire. Miss Carstairs,' he said, addressing the plump lady on the sofa, 'is my fiancée, Lady Mixby.'

The lady in lavender uttered another little shriek, though this time she clapped both hands together instead of clasping her chest as though she'd suffered a severe shock.

'Oh, how wonderful! You are going to marry again. At last! Come here, dear,' she said to Prudence. 'And tell me all about yourself.'

Gregory held up his hand repressively. 'You are not to pelter her with questions. None of you. Miss Carstairs has been through a terrible ordeal.'

And it wasn't over yet. This had all the hallmarks of being a continuation of the nightmare that had started when she'd woken stark naked in bed with a stranger. Since then nothing and nobody had been what they seemed.

'Oh, my dear, how selfish of me,' said Lady Mixby.

'You do look somewhat…*distrait*,' she said, kindly choosing the most tactful way to describe her dirty, dishevelled appearance. 'Come and sit here on the sofa,' she said patting the cushion beside her. 'Benderby!' She waved at the bracket-faced lady. 'Ring for more hot water and cake.'

Benderby put down her sandwich, went to the bell-pull and tugged on it. Prudence collapsed onto the sofa opposite the one occupied by Lady Mixby. Gregory sat down beside her. And took her hand.

What with being in a room full of titled people—not to mention Mr Bodkin—all of whom were already shocked by her appearance, she didn't have the nerve to create a scene by tugging it free. The only way to express her confusion and resentment was to let it lie limp and unresponsive in his.

Bodkin stomped across the room until he was standing right in front of the sofa, glaring down at them. 'Why does he keep saying you're a duke?'

'Because,' said Gregory calmly, 'that is what I am. The Duke of Halstead.'

'You're not!'

'I am afraid,' he said, apologising for his rank for the second time that day, 'that I am.' He gave her hand a slight squeeze, as though including her in the apology.

She didn't return the pressure.

'I am the Duke of Halstead,' said Gregory. 'The owner of Wragley's. To whom you wrote.'

'But you *can't* be! I mean we—' Bodkin clenched his fists, which were grazed about the knuckles, just like Gregory's. As if he'd thought the same thing as her, he glanced down at them.

'Yes, I do recall the incident,' said Gregory. 'Though

why you think that precludes me from being the Duke of Halstead, I fail to comprehend.' He leaned back and crossed one leg over the other.

'Well, because dukes don't go visiting mills and getting into fist fights with the foreman, that's why.'

'Is that so?'

Gregory drawled the words, looking down his nose at the poor man. Even though Bodkin was standing over them. But then he'd managed to look down his nose at *her* when she'd been kneeling over him in the lane, hadn't he? And now she knew how he'd managed it. He'd clearly spent his entire life looking down from a lofty height on the rest of the human race.

'Bodkin has been keeping us vastly entertained with his tales of how you and he broke into your own factory at dead of night and had to fight your way out,' said Hugo with glee. 'Lord, but I'd have given a monkey to have seen it!'

His *own* factory? Of course it was his own factory. He didn't work for anyone as any sort of investigator.

He was a duke.

'You would first have had to be in possession of a monkey,' said Gregory scathingly.

'I don't see why you need to bring monkeys into it,' Lady Mixby complained. 'As well as talk of brawling with common persons. No offence, Mr Bodkin. I am sure you are a very worthy person in your way, and I have found your company most refreshing, but for Halstead to declare he means to have a new duchess is far more interesting!' She waved one dimpled hand in Prudence's direction. 'For him to perform such a volte-face will rock society to its very foundations.'

It certainly would if they knew where she'd come from and how they'd met.

'We were not speaking of real monkeys, Lady Mixby,' said Gregory witheringly, 'but a sum of money. Vulgar persons describe it that way.'

'Halstead, I know I owe you a great deal,' said Lady Mixby, her face flushing. 'But I must really protest at *anyone* using vulgarity in my drawing room.'

'Bravely said, Aunt,' he said icily. 'I beg your pardon, Aunt, Miss Benderby, Miss Carstairs.'

'Never mind begging everyone's pardon,' said Hugo, going to stand behind Lady Mixby's sofa and placing his hands on its back. 'We're *all* of us dying of curiosity. Oh, and I had to let Lady Mixby in on the nature of our wager once Bodkin turned up, so you don't need to go into why you went haring off to Manchester under an alias, without your valet or groom.'

Well, that was what *he* thought. Prudence most definitely wanted to know the *exact* terms of the wager.

'No,' continued Hugo, 'what *we* want to know is how you came to acquire a fiancée who looks like a gypsy when everyone knows you'd rather cut off your right arm than ever marry again.'

So that was why Lady Mixby had said society was going to be rocked to its foundations. Well, she'd known about his reluctance to marry again. Because he'd confided in her. But she'd never suspected it was common knowledge. That put a different complexion on things entirely.

Gregory gave him a look that should have frozen the blood in his veins. 'I'll thank you to keep a civil tongue in your head,' he growled.

She supposed she should be grateful that he was trying to defend her but, really, who could blame Hugo for speaking of her this way when it was obvious they'd never have crossed paths if he hadn't been engaged in trying to win some sort of wager?

At that moment there was a knock at the door and the butler came in with a tea tray.

'Better bring a decanter of something stronger,' suggested Hugo as the butler deposited the tray on a table beside Prudence's sofa. 'Tea may suffice for this wench, but my poor old cousin looks decidedly in need of something more restorative.'

So did she.

'Ale,' said Gregory to the butler. 'If this young scapegrace must start drinking at such an early hour I would rather keep him away from anything too strong. Since I have good reason to know he does not have the head for it.'

'That was uncalled for,' said Hugo sulkily once the butler had gone off on his errand. 'Raking me down in front of the servants.'

'Would you kindly pour the tea, Lady Mixby?' said Gregory, ignoring Hugo. He'd been studiously ignoring her, too. He must know she was shocked, and felt betrayed and insecure. But he was explaining himself to the others. His family. As if he suspected them of thinking she was some terrible catastrophe that had befallen him and he needed to reassure them that he hadn't lost his mind.

Though if he gave her an opportunity to express any opinion at all she'd prove that she was, and he had.

'I feel sure we would all benefit from a cup.'

'I know I certainly would,' Lady Mixby muttered as

she lifted the lid to examine the state of the brew in the teapot. 'Milk and sugar?'

Lady Mixby plunged into the ritual of the tea tray with such determination that Prudence could only follow her lead. Though she felt rather like a marionette having her strings pulled as she responded mechanically to the familiar routine.

The one good thing to come out of it was that as Lady Mixby held out the cup of tea she'd poured, milked and sugared for her, it gave her the perfect excuse for wresting her hand from Gregory's. Though her hand was trembling so much that the cup rattled in its saucer with a sound like chattering teeth.

'Miss Carstairs,' said Gregory, reaching out to take the cup and saucer from her trembling fingers. 'I fear this has all been rather too much for you. I think you should go to a guest room and have a lie-down. A bath. A change of clothes. And something to eat and drink in peace.'

'Oh, what a good idea,' said Lady Mixby, leaping to her feet.

That did it. He might have said all the right things, but deep down he was ashamed of her. Just as Aunt Charity had felt shamed by having to house her, the product of a runaway match. Aunt Charity had spent years failing to make her acceptable to her congregation and the community of Stoketown. And in the end had just kept her out of sight as much as possible.

And this was how it had started. By sending Prudence to her room whenever there was company she wanted to impress.

'If you think for one moment,' said Prudence, snatching the teaspoon from the saucer as he took it away, so she could use it to emphasise her point, 'that I am going to let you shuffle me out of the way so that you can explain your behaviour over the last two days to everyone else and leave me in the dark, then you have another think coming!'

Gregory reached out and confiscated the teaspoon, then tossed it to the tea tray, where it landed with a tinkle amongst the china.

'You are overwrought,' he said repressively.

'Is that so surprising? I *trusted* you! I thought you were a decent, hard-working man. A man who'd set out to right wrongs and defend the helpless. Instead you are the kind of man who makes the kind of wagers that result in fist fights and falling into bed with strange women! I trusted you with my virtue, and with my money—'

Lady Mixby gasped and fell back to the sofa, her hands clasped to her bosom.

But Prudence was beyond caring. She'd sat there listening to him account for himself with growing resentment. She couldn't hold it in any longer.

'And now I find out that I don't even know your name!'

'Well, that at least is easily rectified. My name is Charles Gregory Jamison Willingale, Seventh Duke of Halstead. I think we can gloss over the lesser titles for now.'

'Oh, you do, do you?'

How could he sit there and calmly reel off a list of names whilst completely sidestepping the real issue? Which was that he'd deceived her. *Deliberately* deceived her.

'And as for explaining myself to everyone else...' He

glanced from Hugo to Bodkin with a sort of chilling hauteur that made him look even more like a stranger than ever. 'I have no intention of doing any such thing.'

'Oh, I say—that is dashed unfair!'

Gregory held up his hand to silence the outburst from his indignant young cousin. 'No,' he said. 'What would be unfair would be to divulge anything to anyone before I have done so to my fiancée. She, of course, must take precedence over anything you feel I owe you, Hugo. Or indeed you, Lady Mixby.'

'Of course, of course,' said Lady Mixby, nodding her head whilst clasping and unclasping her hands.

'We will all adjourn until dinner.' He got to his feet. 'Which will give Miss Carstairs and I a chance to bathe and change and generally refresh ourselves.'

Hugo wrinkled his nose. 'Come to mention it, you *do* smell rather ripe.'

When she made no move from the sofa, His Grace the Seventh Duke of Wherever-it-was extended his hand to urge her to her feet. But she had finally reached the stage where, had she been a bottle of ginger beer, her top would have popped off under the pressure building up inside from constant shaking.

'Will you *stop*,' said Prudence, batting away his hand, 'calling me Miss Carstairs? And telling everyone I am your fiancée. When obviously I can never be anything of the sort!'

Dukes didn't marry nobodies. Especially not nobodies they'd only known five minutes.

He didn't even have the grace to flinch. Clearly all the grace he had was in his inherited title.

'Overwrought,' said the man who had first appeared to be a villain, had then for a few magical hours looked to her like the answer to all her prayers, but who now turned out to be a duke. 'I can understand that the discovery you are about to become a duchess has come as a shock. But once you have had a lie-down and composed yourself you will see that—'

'Don't talk to me in that beastly manner. And *don't*—' she swatted his hand away again '—order me about.'

She was just taking a breath to unburden herself in regard to her sense of injustice when there came another knock at the door. This time it was a plain, practical-looking woman dressed all in black who came in.

'Excellent timing, Mrs Hoskins,' said Gregory smoothly, taking Prudence's elbow in a vice-like grip and lifting her to her feet. 'Miss Carstairs, as you can see, is in dire need of a change of clothes and a bath. As am I,' he said with a grimace of distaste. 'Miss Carstairs,' he said, giving her a level look. 'I will speak with you again at dinner.'

'*Dinner!* You intend to leave me in this state until dinner?'

'We keep country hours at Bramley Park,' he said. 'You will only have to wait until four of the clock. It will take you at least that long to bathe and change and,' he said, in the same steely tone he'd used on Hugo, 'to calm down.'

Calm down? *Calm down!* She'd give him 'calm down'. How dared he talk to her in that insufferably arrogant way? As though she was in need of a set-down?

'You can take your hands off me,' she hissed, wrenching her arm out of his grip. 'And think yourself lucky I am too well-bred to slap your face for your... impertinence!'

Lady Mixby gasped. Pressed both hands to her flushed face this time.

Prudence stuck her nose in the air and stalked from the room.

Chapter Thirteen

Prudence was well on her way up the stairs before realising she had no idea where she was going. She would have to slow down and wait for Mrs Hoskins, or she'd risk looking like an idiot.

As well as feeling like one.

For what kind of idiot proposed to a man she'd only known for two days? A man she'd met, moreover, in bed? And stark naked at that.

Her feet stumbled and slowed of their own accord, which gave Mrs Hoskins a chance to catch up with her.

'It's just along this way, miss,' she panted, indicating the left branch of the upper landing. 'I hope it's to your liking.'

Prudence hoped she'd made an appropriate response, because it certainly wouldn't be this woman's fault if it wasn't. But in the event, when she saw the room, it was almost enough to make her burst into tears. Because it was simply magnificent. The most beautifully decorated, perfectly proportioned room she'd ever had for her sole use.

To start with, everything matched. There were velvet

curtains in various shades of green all over the place, chairs with spindly gilt legs upholstered in toning shades of satin, and a mostly green carpet that looked as soft as moss. Clearly each item of furniture, each square yard of velvet and satin, had been purchased specifically to enhance the beauty of this one room.

It cast her own little room in her aunt's house in Stoketown completely in the shade. And *that* room had totally intimidated her when she'd first seen it. It had made all the rough-and-ready billets in which her parents had lived seem like hovels.

'Is something amiss? Would you prefer to have a room at the back of the house? It will not have such a fine view, but it would get less sunlight,' said Mrs Hoskins.

The housekeeper looked so concerned Prudence made a determined effort to pull herself together. She *could* step into this room. They wouldn't have had the carpet put on the floor if they weren't prepared to let people walk on it. True, they couldn't have imagined anyone with such mucky shoes ever setting foot up here, but she could remove them. She was at least wearing stockings today, even if they were borrowed and rather too large. So her feet wouldn't leave a trail of blood-stains behind.

'Oh, no—no need to prepare another room. Thank you,' she said, toeing off her shoes.

The chances were that all the rooms in this house were equally grand. Apart from perhaps the servants' quarters. And it would look extremely odd if she asked to have a look at *them*.

'This room is lovely. It is just a bit...' Her lower lip quivered. The truth was, the way Gregory had or-

dered her up here had reminded her far too much of
the way Aunt Charity had always sent her to her room.
When she'd 'answered back'. When she'd been supposed to 'think about what she'd done'. When her aunt
had wanted some peace and quiet. When visitors had
come. He'd told her to calm down and tidy herself up,
as though he didn't think she was fit to stay in the same
room as a duke's family. Not that she was going to admit
that to Mrs Hoskins.

'I mean, after all that has happened this last few
days, I...' Her breath hitched in her throat. It was as if
her self-esteem was being crushed by a velvet brocade
fist. How could a girl like her have had the temerity to
propose marriage to a duke? Even the curtains were
sneering.

A *duke*!

She wrapped her arms round her middle, where a peculiar swirling sensation had started up. Not only had
she proposed to him, but she'd thrown a rock at him.
Knocked him right down and made him bleed.

That had to be against the law—assaulting a duke.
Might it even count as treason?

Her hand stole to her throat as she thought of the
punishment meted out for treason. Which she deserved,
didn't she? Since she'd been so adamant that her aunt
and uncle should be brought to justice for merely drug-
ging him!

'Oh, you poor lass,' said Mrs Hoskins, slipping a
firm hand under her elbow. 'You look nigh to fainting
away. What a terrible time you've had, to be sure. And
you such a fine lady, I'll be bound—else His Grace
would never be making you his duchess.'

Fine lady? She wasn't *any* kind of lady. She was an

army brat. That was what Aunt Charity had called her. The disgraceful result of a runaway match. And if she wasn't good enough for Aunt Charity how could she be good enough for a duke?

'You'll feel better for a warm bath and a nice lie-down,' said the housekeeper as she drew her into the terrifyingly opulent room. 'Milly and Sam will be bringing up the bath and some hot water, and then Milly will stay to help you bathe,' she said, steering Prudence towards the bed.

'No!' Prudence recoiled from the smooth satin coverlet and the starched white lacy pillows in horror. 'I mean, I don't think I should sit on the bed to wait, do you?' She indicated her clothes. 'I slept in a barn last night. I shouldn't want to dirty the coverlets.'

'A barn, was it?' Mrs Hoskins's eyebrows shot up her forehead and almost disappeared under the rim of her cap.

Oh, no. Now it would be all over the servants' hall that their duke had spent the night in a barn. He'd be livid with her. If he wasn't already. It was hard to tell now he'd taken to wearing that wooden mask instead of his normal face.

'Well, then, how about you come along over to the window seat and rest yourself there while your bath is made ready? The covers wash well if so be that you do make a mark on them,' she said soothingly. 'Not that I think it is at all likely,' she added.

'Yes, very well,' said Prudence, feeling like the worst sort of impostor as Mrs Hoskins led her across the room.

No wonder he'd been so angry to find her next to him in bed that first night. No wonder he'd raved about plots and schemes and kept on asking if Hugo had put her up to it. She sank down shakily onto the seat and buried her face in her hands. *That* was why he'd taken her up in his gig. He'd been trying to find out whether Hugo was cheating.

She knew the lengths to which men would go in order to win wagers. Over the most ridiculous stakes, too. It made no difference whether they'd staked the services of a beautiful mistress or a tin whistle—it was proving that they were 'better', in some ridiculous manner, than the man with whom they'd made the wager, and that was what counted. That was why he'd asked all those questions. It hadn't been chivalry. It hadn't been concern for her at all. No, it had been indignation at what he had perceived as an attempt to make him lose.

If they hadn't lost his purse he would no doubt have dropped her off somewhere once he'd satisfied himself that she really didn't know either who he was or anything at all about Hugo. Only he *had* lost his purse. And his horse and gig.

And then, to cap it all, she'd asked him to marry her.

A bustle in the room made her drop her hands and look up. A male servant had deposited a hip bath on a towel before the fireplace, and a maid was pouring water into it from a can of steaming water.

'Now, Milly,' Mrs Hoskins was saying sternly. 'You are not to pepper His Grace's intended with a lot of impertinent questions. She's been through a terrible ordeal, as anyone can see.'

Both Milly and Sam darted a glance to where she was sitting, trembling and probably ashen-faced because she'd realised what she'd done, and adopted similarly sympathetic expressions.

Which made her cringe. If they only knew how outrageously she'd behaved they'd be sorely tempted to eject her from the property. As swiftly as possible. Which made her wish she wasn't sitting quite so close to the convenient mode of exit a window might afford a brace of scandalised servants.

'I'll leave you with Milly now,' said Mrs Hoskins. 'She's not what you're used to, I'm sure, but she's a good girl.' Mrs Hoskins shot the blushing maid a stern, meaningful look before bustling out of the room, taking the male servant with her.

Milly dropped a curtsey. 'Sam will be bringing up some more hot water shortly,' she said. 'But don't you worry he'll come in here a-gawping at you, for I shan't let him. He'll leave it at the door. So if you want to get started…?'

She must look dreadful for everyone to be so insistent on getting her into a bath. And she probably smelled dreadful, too, since she'd not had an opportunity to bathe or change her clothes for a couple of days.

'I would like to get out of this dress and get clean,' she admitted. Though no amount of bathing and tidying was going to change who she was underneath. 'But I don't have anything to change into.'

'Oh, Mrs Hoskins explained about your luggage getting stolen. It must have been that frightening!' Milly's eyes were round, in a mix of horror and fascination. 'Thank goodness His Grace was at hand to rescue you and bring you here.'

Was *that* the story circulating around the servants' hall? Typical! Men would do anything to save face. He'd rather let people think he'd been doing something akin to rescuing a damsel in distress than for anyone to suspect that what he'd really been doing was…was…going to any lengths to win some stupid wager.

'Mrs Hoskins will be bringing you my Sunday best, miss,' said Milly as she unlaced Prudence's gown and helped her out of her chemise.

The girl said nothing about her lack of corset, or the coarse weave of her stockings, though she couldn't help wrinkling her nose as she rolled the whole lot into a bundle and took it over to the door, where she dropped it on the one patch of board that wasn't covered by expensive carpet. She wouldn't be a bit surprised to learn they were going straight to the bonfire, rather than the laundry.

Prudence stepped into the bath and sat down, hugging her knees to her chest.

'I do hope you like the gown,' said Milly. 'I know it won't be what you're used to, but Mrs Hoskins insisted, since I'm nearer to you in size than anyone else here.'

Prudence had a short but horrible vision of trying to make do with one of Lady Mixby's gowns.

'I'm very grateful to you for lending it to me,' said Prudence with complete honesty. Even a servant's Sunday best was far better than what she'd been wearing.

'Oh, I ain't lending it! His Grace is going to buy it off me. For five guineas—can you imagine? Why, I'll be able to get three new gowns, a bonnet and gloves for that. I mean,' she added, going red in the face, 'I beg pardon, my lady. I forgot I'm not supposed to gabble on. Mrs Hoskins said as how you're used to having a properly trained ladies' maid, and how I was to mind my tongue, but as usual it's run away with me. There I go again!'

Why was it that everyone kept talking about what

she was 'used to'? How did they *know* what she was used to? Nobody had asked. They just kept assuming she must be a fine lady, because only a fine lady would be entitled to marry a duke.

And she'd done nothing to correct their assumptions, had she? Because she didn't want anyone thinking she was a designing hussy who'd got her claws into their duke while he was travelling about the country under the name of Willingale, dressed like some kind of tradesman.

'His Grace is going to have Mrs Bennet—that's our village dressmaker—come and bring you some fresh things in the morning, and measure you up for whatever else you may need,' said Milly, vigorously soaping a washcloth. 'Shall I do your back first, my lady? Or your hair?'

'Oh, my hair,' she said. If she could make her hair look tidy she might feel more able to go downstairs when it was time to face all those titled people again. Aunt Charity had always said it made her look as wild and immodest as her mother had actually been. She'd always made her braid it and cover it under caps and bonnets. 'I can manage the rest myself, but my hair has always been a bit wild,' she said as Milly handed over the washcloth. 'Do you have a really strong comb you can lend me? Or perhaps we should just cut out the worst of the tangles.'

'If we do then you need not worry that it will show. I might be a bit of a gabster, but I'm good with hair. Done all my sisters' in my time, I have.'

'Well, that's good to know.'

And it was good to have the help of a maid again, too. A maid who didn't seem to mind being a maid, at that. Milly was taking her time massaging her scalp, and it felt absolutely wonderful.

So wonderful that she actually closed her eyes and started to relax. And as she did so her spirit began to revive. Just as it always had whenever she'd been sent to her room to 'think about what she'd done'. She'd never managed to stay cowed and guilty for long after one of her aunt's rebukes. Because as she'd thought about whatever it was that was supposed to be unforgivably immodest, or vulgar, or sinful, she'd remembered how often her mother or father had done or said the very same thing. And she had refused to betray them by being ashamed of behaviour they would consider perfectly normal.

She didn't fit in with Aunt Charity and her circle—that was what it amounted to. Any more than she'd fit in with a duke and *his* circle.

So there was no point in allowing herself to be intimidated by the luxurious surroundings, or the titles his family bore. Any more than she'd allowed herself to be beaten down by Aunt Charity's pious homilies. She'd soon learned that no matter how hard she tried to fit in, she'd never measure up. Because of who her parents were. And so she'd stopped trying.

And she wasn't going to start tying herself up in knots trying to fit in here, either. She was done with being intimidated. Gregory had no right to make her feel foolish, or guilty, or out of her depth. If dukes didn't want people to assume they were ordinary men, then they had no business going around under false identities.

They had no right making out they were heroes, either. Why, if there had been any rescuing going on, she'd done her fair share. Who'd had the idea of singing for food money so that he hadn't needed to pawn his watch, which was probably a priceless family heirloom? And whose quick thinking had saved him from being hauled up before the local magistrate by Mr Grumpy Farmer?

The moment Milly finished rinsing her hair she surged out of the tub on a wave of indignation. She hadn't been able to rebel very successfully against Aunt Charity because she'd only been a girl. But she was a woman now. And over the last couple of days she'd discovered that she was well able to overcome whatever fate threw in her path.

And that included deceitful dukes!

'Hand me that towel,' she said imperiously to Milly. 'And bring me those clothes.'

She was not going to let him hide her away up here as though she was something to be ashamed of.

'Where are you going?' cried Milly when she walked to the door and flung it open the moment she was dressed.

'I need to have a few words with G...His Grace,' she said, since she had no wish to offend the servants by referring to their lord and master by the name he'd given her. After all, her quarrel was with *him*, not them.

'Oh, no, my lady, you cannot disturb His Grace just now,' said Milly in horror. 'He will be in his bath. He had Sam and me fetch the water for yours first, so he's bound to be a few minutes behind. And what with Sam having no experience as a valet, even if His Grace is out of his bath I shouldn't think he'll be ready to receive anyone.'

'I don't care,' she said, clenching her fists. After all, it wasn't as if she hadn't seen it all before, was it?

Though admittedly not wet.

A rather scandalous vision popped into her head of all those rippling muscles with soapsuds sliding slowly over them.

'Oh, please, my lady,' wailed Milly, bursting the vision, and with it all the soapsuds. 'Don't go out yet!'

Prudence whirled round to see Milly wringing her hands.

'I don't want no one to see you with your hair like that.'

As Milly pointed to her head Prudence realised she still had a towel wrapped round her wet hair.

'They'll all say I can't get you presentable,' Milly continued. 'Let alone I haven't treated your blisters yet. They'll say I ain't up to the job. And then I won't be your maid no more. And I did so long to be your maid. And go to London and dress you for balls and such.'

Prudence wasn't ever going to go to London—not as the Duchess of Halstead anyway. The very idea was preposterous. She'd thought she was going to be marrying the rather hard-up and ordinary Mr Willingale—a man who made his living somehow by righting wrongs and sticking up for the underdog. Not a duke who went about the countryside in disguise as a means to alleviate his boredom. For he'd admitted he'd been leading a dull life, hadn't he?

But she did thank heaven that Milly had had the courage to speak her mind. If she'd gone barging into the Duke's room while she was so angry with him that she'd forgotten she had her hair wrapped in a towel she would have definitely embarrassed herself. Oh, yes, she could just see him lounging back in his tub, looking

down his imperious nose at her, while she stood over
him screeching her complaints.

'That's a good point, Milly,' she acknowledged.
'Thank you.' And she meant it. It was going to be much
better to marshal her arguments so that she could break
off their betrothal in a dignified manner. 'You had better dry and style my hair so that I shall look my best
when I next speak to *His Grace*.'

'I shall run and fetch a comb and some scissors,' said
Milly with evident relief. 'I won't be but a twinkling.'

'I will put some ointment on my feet while I'm waiting,' said Prudence, going to the dressing table on which
Mrs Hoskins had placed the pot.

The minute she'd gone Prudence plonked herself
down and plunged her fingers into the pot of green-
ish salve. Right, then. She'd use the time until Milly
had made her presentable enough to appear in public to prepare a speech in which she'd explain that she
couldn't marry Gregory, not now she knew who and
what he really was.

But she hadn't come up with anything much before
Milly returned with the scissors. And also a maid with
a tea tray. And Lady Mixby.

'I hope you don't think of this as an intrusion,' said
Lady Mixby. 'I just thought I would check that you
have everything you need. Particularly that cup of tea
you didn't drink downstairs. And just one or two little
sandwiches and cakes, since you looked close to fainting. There is nothing worse, I find, than a hot bath if
one is already a touch light-headed.'

There was nothing Prudence could do but say thank
you.

Lady Mixby beamed at her. Then went across to the

little table on which the maid had set down the tea tray. 'I shall just pour you a cup and bring it to the dressing table while Milly makes a start on your hair. And then you can sip it and nibble at these few dainties while she works. Oh,' she said, setting the cup on the dressing table. 'I see Mrs Hoskins has found you a gown. I hope you don't mind that it appears to be dreadfully behind the fashion.'

Milly pulled her lips together and carried on doggedly combing out Prudence's tangles.

'Oh, no, I am very grateful for the dress. It is lovely to be in something clean and respectable again.'

Which was the absolute truth. Milly's Sunday best had turned out to be a rather lovely gown of mossy green wool, with a demure neckline and long sleeves. Since it was exactly the sort of thing she was used to wearing, it made her feel much more like herself instead of some kind of impostor creeping in where she had no right to be and pretending to be something she wasn't.

Milly flashed her a grateful look in the mirror as Lady Mixby went to the window seat.

'I am sure it must be,' said Lady Mixby, hitching herself up onto the cushions 'I cannot tell you how shocked I was to see you and Halstead standing on the threshold of my drawing room looking like a pair of gypsies. Oh, but only for a moment. For then, you see, I recalled the Hilliard portrait of the First Duke. And saw that Halstead wanted only a pearl earring and a lace ruff and he would have passed for an Elizabethan privateer.'

He would, at that.

'Though I hear he has shaved now,' Lady Mixby continued, 'which is a great pity. He looked dangerously attractive with that hint of a beard.' She sighed.

'Milly, are you sure you should be using the scissors quite so freely? Poor Miss Carstairs will not have any hair left at this rate.'

'I have given Milly leave to do what is necessary,' Prudence explained when Milly's nimble fingers stilled for a second. 'It is much kinder for her to cut out the worst of the knots than attempt to remove them with the comb.'

'Well, if you are sure…'

'Oh, yes. It has been several days since I've had use of a comb, you see, and my hair has always been difficult to manage, even with regular brushing.'

Prudence had only refused to have it cut before out of a perverse determination to thwart Aunt Charity. She wouldn't mind having it all cut off now, while Milly was at it. Only just as she opened her mouth to make the suggestion she recalled the look in Gregory's eyes as he'd wound one curl round his finger. One curl of what he had called 'russet glory'.

'Several days! How perfectly frightful,' Lady Mixby was saying. 'And what kind of thief would steal a lady's comb? My goodness—what wickedness there is in the world. You must have a macaroon,' she said, hopping to her feet, going to the tea table and putting one on a plate. And then adding a couple more dainties and bringing them across.

'There. Three cakes. I was just saying to Benderby this morning how things go in threes. First Hugo came to visit, which he only does when he is quite rolled up. And then that strange Mr Bodkin person arrived, in possession of Halstead's ring. His very own signet ring, which was handed down from the First Duke—the one

I told you he resembles so nearly. Or would if he would only keep the beard and get himself a pearl earring.'

She sighed wistfully, giving Prudence the impression she had a rather romantical notion of pirates. Or Elizabethans. Or possibly both.

'That set us all in a bustle, as you can imagine. If dear Hugo hadn't been here I should have been quite terrified,' she said, absentmindedly popping the macaroon she'd fetched for Prudence into her own mouth. 'But he took charge in the most masterful way, considering his age, taking Mr Bodkin aside and getting the whole story from him before explaining it to me. At least, he explained *some* things, which all sounded highly improbable—but then when gentlemen go off in pursuit of some wager they often get tangled up with the most extraordinary company.'

Prudence was about to agree, since she'd had pretty much the same thought earlier, but Lady Mixby hadn't even paused to take breath.

'Why, you only have to think of cock pits and boxing saloons and places of that nature. Not that I have ever been in one. Nor would I wish to. They sound perfectly frightful.'

While Lady Mixby was giving a delicate little shudder at the thought of what might go on in a boxing saloon, Prudence took the opportunity to inject a word or two of her own.

'So Hugo told you all about the wager, did he?' She said it as though she knew all about it, hoping that Lady Mixby would enlighten her without her having to admit she was almost completely in the dark.

'Incredible, isn't it?' Lady Mixby's eyes widened. She leaned forward in a conspiratorial fashion. 'I would never have believed it of Halstead, had he not arrived here today without his valet and groom, looking so very unlike himself. Though, come to think of it, now I've seen his resemblance to the First Duke—who was little more than a pirate, really—I can believe him to be getting up to any amount of mischief. Not that I am implying he has done anything that is not fitting to his station in life.'

She looked at Prudence guiltily.

'*Has* he? Oh,' she added, before Prudence had a chance to draw breath. 'Not that I would blame you if you had done something you ought not... The way he looked just now, I can see exactly how it might be that you couldn't resist him. Though I would not have thought anything of the sort had you not said that about trusting him with your virtue. Oh, dear—how I do rattle on. I have ever been thus. It is why I never *took*, as a girl—why I never married. No rational man could have put up with me—that is what my father always said.'

'I'm sure that is not true,' said Prudence faintly, in the pause that came while Lady Mixby was popping a second fancy cake into her mouth.

'Dear girl,' she said, flicking crumbs from her skirt onto the expensive carpet. 'It is such a sweet thing of you to say, but the truth is we were all as poor as church mice in spite of our name. Such is the way of the world. Girls with plain faces only get proposals if they have a dowry large enough to make up for it. Whereas the veriest drabs will have oodles of men paying them court if they have money to back them,' she said with a shrug.

She was in blithe ignorance of the way she'd just plunged a knife into Prudence's already sensitised heart. Because she *did* have money, didn't she? Could that be why Gregory had tacitly accepted her proposal, in spite of the discrepancy in their rank? After all, the men in Aunt Charity's congregation had suddenly started looking at her differently once it had become common knowledge that she was heiress to the Biddlestone fortune.

Was Gregory really as mercenary as the men of Stoketown?

'But let us not dwell on the past,' said Lady Mixby, sighing and clasping her pudgy hands together. 'I am so looking forward to hearing all about how you met Halstead and how you came to fall in love. I know you don't need to remind me,' she said, raising her hand in the air as though in surrender. 'Not a word about any of it until we are all together after dinner. Speaking of which,' she said, getting to her feet, 'I should really go and get changed. Or should I?' she said, just as she reached the door. 'Would it be terribly tactless of me to dress up when you have nothing decent to wear? Halstead himself is borrowing the Sunday clothes of the under-gardener, who is the only one of the male staff with broad enough shoulders to have a shirt that would fit. I shall ask Benderby. Such a treasure, you know. I can always rely on her to come up with a practical solution.'

The room seemed very, very quiet once Lady Mixby had left. Prudence had never come across anyone with the ability to speak continuously without pausing for breath before. Or with the tendency to flit from one subject to another like a butterfly.

How on earth could Gregory have led her to believe for one minute that Lady Mixby was a dragon? She was the very opposite. It almost seemed wrong to describe her as an aunt at all. In fact she'd been so welcoming that she'd completely dispelled the slightly oppressive atmosphere of the room. It no longer felt as though the furnishings had been expressly designed to depress the pretensions of impostors, but rather to enfold any weary guest in a sumptuous sort of embrace.

The only trouble was that now Lady Mixby had told her that one of Gregory's ancestors had been an Elizabethan pirate she couldn't help picturing him with a pearl earring and a rapier in his hand. So instead of arming herself with a quiver full of clever remarks with which to confound him, she now spent the time before dinner imagining him engaged in various nefarious pursuits. The most frequent of which imaginings involved him mounted on a black horse, holding up a stagecoach at midnight. Though the one of him lounging back in his bathtub, naked apart from some strategically placed soapsuds, came a close second.

By the time she was ready, physically, to go downstairs, she was no more prepared to cross swords with His Grace the Duke of Halstead than poor betwattled Lady Mixby would ever be.

Chapter Fourteen

'Miss Carstairs, how very much better you look,' said Gregory when she entered the dining room.

Prudence couldn't help raising one hand to her hair and flushing self-consciously. Did he really like the way she looked in this gown, with her hair neatly brushed, braided, and coiled on the top of her head?

His eyes followed the movement of her hand. He must have seen she was blushing, but his expression remained completely impassive. How different he was now from the man he'd been in that barn, when he'd described her hair as russet glory and trembled with the force of the desire he said he'd felt for her. This Gregory was a complete enigma. It was as if, the moment they'd set foot in Bramley Park, he'd deliberately snuffed out the man she'd come to know.

So how could she care so much about what he might be thinking? How could she long for him to find her as attractive as she found him, seeing him for the first time closely shaved and in a full set of clean clothes—even if they did belong to a humble gardener?

Bother Lady Mixby for putting that vision of him

with a pearl earring into her mind. Though, to be fair, she'd come up with that vision of soapsuds slithering over his naked masculine musculature all by herself.

Well, it was no use having visions of that sort. Because they were weakening her resolve to put an end to a betrothal which should never have begun.

She drew on every ounce of pride she possessed, and said, 'Thank you,' in as calm a voice as she could muster. 'The maid you sent was very proficient. It is entirely due to her,' she couldn't resist adding, 'that I no longer look as though I've been dragged through a hedge backwards.'

'You have never looked as though you had been dragged through a hedge backwards,' he said, in a manner that must have looked to everyone else like gallantry. 'Not even after you spent the night sleeping in hay.'

'Sleeping in hay?' Hugo, who'd leapt to his feet, was grinning. 'I heard a rumour that you spent last night in a barn, Halstead. And now you have confirmed it.' He rubbed his hands together in glee. 'I can't wait to hear how all this came about.'

'Come, let me place you at my right hand, Miss Carstairs,' said the Duke, ignoring Hugo as he led her to the rather small square table standing in the very centre of the room.

Hugo took the chair at his left without being asked.

'As you can see,' said Gregory witheringly. 'We are dining informally tonight.'

'I thought it for the best,' said Lady Mixby. 'All things considered.'

'Yes, but *some* of us have managed not to forget our manners,' he replied, as Mr Bodkin held out a chair for Benderby.

Hugo shot Gregory a look loaded with resentment, but didn't get to his feet. Really, he was a very badly behaved boy. He put her in mind of one of the subalterns once under her father's command, who'd come from a good family and had resented taking orders from men he regarded as his social inferiors. It had been insecurity, she'd overheard her father explain to her mother, that had made the lad so spiky and awkward, not any deep-seated malice. And once he'd proved his worth in battle his manners had greatly improved. What a pity there was no battle that Hugo could fight—that would knock some sense into him.

Benderby gave the butler a slight nod once they were all seated more or less where they wished, and he in turn marshalled Sam, his footman, into action.

'I do hope the meal will meet with your approval,' said Lady Mixby anxiously.

'I am sure it will,' said Gregory. 'Since Mrs Hoskins was not expecting us today, we can hardly expect her to have prepared anything fancy, can we?'

The housekeeper would have had a jolly good try, though. Having the Duke turn up out of the blue must have created a state bordering on panic below stairs.

'The cook here is excellent,' put in Hugo. 'I can vouch for that.'

'No doubt,' said the Duke. 'Since you have been availing yourself of his services for the past se'ennight.'

'Only five nights, in point of fact,' said Hugo smugly.

'Thank you, Hugo,' said Gregory repressively. 'There is no need to dwell on that just now. Is the soup to your liking, Miss Carstairs?' he asked, turning to her.

'The soup? You want to talk about the *soup*?'

He gave her a look that was almost as quelling as the

one he'd directed at Hugo. It made her want to seize the tureen and upend it over his head. But she wasn't going to allow him to goad her into that kind of behaviour.

'The soup is delicious,' she said, satisfying herself with imagining it dripping down his clothes.

The Duke of Halstead—for now that he was speaking in that odiously pompous manner she couldn't think of him as anything less—turned to Mr Bodkin.

'And you, Mr Bodkin? Everything is to your satisfaction, I trust?'

Mr Bodkin mumbled something indistinguishable, his face glowing an even deeper shade of red than it had been when Gregory had commended his manners while criticising Hugo's.

The poor man. As well as feeling out of place, he must now feel out of his depth, with all the undercurrents swirling between the diners seated at this table.

Lady Mixby tried to lighten the atmosphere by launching into typical dinner table conversation. But since it was mostly about people Prudence had never heard of, and events she'd never considered before, it only had the effect of making her feel a strong kinship with Mr Bodkin. And although she knew that they couldn't possibly talk about anything very confidential or meaningful in front of the servants, every time a new dish came to the table she grew more and more tempted to empty the contents over the Duke's head. Which in turn reinforced her earlier fears that she didn't belong here. Because what kind of woman would empty the soup tureen over the head of a duke?

But at length the servants stopped scurrying to and fro, ceased depositing fresh courses on the table and whisking away the old ones. Sam deftly removed the cloth and Perkins brought in a decanter of port on a silver salver. Lady Mixby stood up, signalling that it was time for the ladies to withdraw to…wherever it was that ladies went in this house. Prudence would just have to follow Lady Mixby and Benderby, who'd also risen from her place.

As she got to her feet Mr Bodkin shot her a look bordering on panic. She could heartily sympathise with his reluctance to be left to the tender mercies of Gregory and Hugo. At least while she'd been at table he hadn't been the only one feeling like a fish out of water.

Hugo had been wriggling in his seat like a schoolboy waiting to be let out of lessons for some time. He was evidently itching to have Gregory to himself so they could settle up over their wager.

As the men rose to their feet, she wondered whether she could breach protocol by inviting Mr Bodkin to join the ladies. She was just about to suggest it when Gregory picked up the decanter and made for the door which Perkins was holding open.

'Hi, where are you going with that?' Hugo objected.

'The morning room,' said Gregory. 'We shall all be more comfortable there.'

'*I* shan't,' said Hugo.

'Hugo,' Gregory growled. 'I told you I was not going to discuss…anything with you before I had explained it all to Miss Carstairs.'

'Yes, but—'

'The sooner we get it all out into the open the better,' said Gregory implacably. 'Lady Mixby, you will forgive us if just this once we break with tradition and accompany you to the morning room, won't you?'

'Of course,' she said at once. 'I am positively agog

with curiosity.' She flushed. 'Not that I... I mean of course I'm sure it is none of my business, but... Oh, do come along, Hugo!' She turned a beseeching look in his direction. 'Nothing so exciting has happened in this family for an age. I, for one, cannot wait to hear Halstead's account of how he met Miss Carstairs, and if he says he wishes to give it in the morning room then I see no reason why we shouldn't all go there at once.'

'Miss Carstairs?'

He was actually deigning to ask her opinion?

'It is well past time you explained yourself,' she said. Her patience had been stretched thinner and thinner the longer the meal had dragged on, and it wasn't going to take much for it to snap altogether. 'And if you call me Miss Carstairs once more, in that odiously pompous way, it won't be *tradition* that will be broken!'

'I say, Miss Carstairs,' said Hugo. 'I think I am beginning to like you.'

It was all she could do to resist the urge to poke out her tongue at him. He was the kind of boy who dragged everyone down to his level.

Fortunately Lady Mixby took her arm before she could poke out her tongue, or hurl any dishes, or slap anyone's face.

'I know you recall the way to the morning room, but let me get you settled into a comfortable chair—not too close to the fire, but out of any draught,' she said, leading her across the hall and into the reception room she'd been in earlier that day.

It was no longer flooded with light. The sun had moved round to shine through the windows in a different part of the house, leaving the whole room rather gloomy, in spite of the fire crackling in the grate. She wondered that the ladies chose to withdraw to *this* room in the evenings, and why they called it the morning room if it was used at other times of the day.

'Rather than have you all bombarding me with questions,' said Gregory, once they'd all taken seats in various parts of the room that Prudence thought ought more properly to be called the...the sitting room. Or the ladies' parlour. Or something that actually described the fact that ladies used it at many times of the day. 'I have decided it would be better for me to relate my story in my own words.'

Typical. *Everything* had to be his own way.

'But before I begin it occurs to me that it would be rather ungentlemanly of us to sit here drinking our port while you ladies go without refreshment. So I wonder if you would care to join us. Just this once? While we are dispensing with tradition?'

'Oh!' Lady Mixby's face lit up. 'How novel. Yes, I should *love* to try a glass of port.'

'Miss Benderby?'

'I'll not refuse, Your Grace.'

He opened his mouth, as though to ask Prudence if she'd like a glass of port, and then paused. Was he recalling her objection to him calling her Miss Carstairs in that odious manner? Was it too much to hope he was actually considering her feelings?

She turned to Lady Mixby. 'I have never tried it, either, Lady Mixby,' she said, 'and I'm not sure if I should.'

'I am sure it cannot be wrong, since His Grace has suggested it,' said Lady Mixby, making Prudence grind her teeth.

'You can have tea, if you would prefer it,' said *His*

Grace. 'I shall have to ring for more glasses anyway. I can easily ask them to bring a pot and cups while they're at it.'

'I will light the candles while we're waiting,' said Benderby, getting to her feet. 'Then the servants will have no excuse to come knocking on the door without us sending for them.'

'Oh, what a good idea,' said Lady Mixby. 'This room is always so gloomy in the afternoons. It will look so much more cheerful with some light.'

So why do you sit here, then? Prudence wanted to ask, but didn't. It would only show her up as someone who didn't understand the way the upper classes lived and made use of their houses.

As Benderby went round lighting the candles and drawing the curtains Prudence succumbed to the temptation to try a glass of port. She had a feeling that a cup of tea wasn't going to be enough to sustain her through the rest of the evening. She was going to have to sit and listen to Gregory explaining away the reasons he'd allowed an impertinent nobody to inveigle him into a betrothal. Oh, why hadn't she asked to speak to him in private earlier? They could now be explaining that it had all been a mistake. That she'd had no idea who he was when she'd proposed. That she was doing her best to put things right.

Perkins arrived, and Gregory ordered him to bring three more glasses.

'And will that be all, Your Grace?' Perkins glanced round the room, his eyes resting briefly on the lit candles, the drawn curtains, and the full coal scuttle sitting on the hearth by the blazing fire.

'We shall ring if we require anything else,' said Gregory firmly.

Which left Perkins in no doubt that he had better not return to this room without that summons.

'I shall begin by explaining,' said Gregory to Prudence as he brought her a glass and poured just half an inch of the rich blood-red liquid into it from his decanter, 'why I told you my name is Willingale and not about my title.' He paused, his lips tightening for a second. 'I suspect that by now you have worked out that some of what I have been doing over this past week is on account of a wager I made with Hugo.'

Prudence nodded. Her feelings were so turbulent she couldn't have formed a sensible response even had she wanted to.

'Hugo is not only my nearest male relative, but my heir,' he said, sauntering across to where Hugo was lounging on an armchair and pouring a generous measure into the glass Hugo was holding out ready. 'Therefore I make him a quarterly allowance. Which he considers insufficient.'

Hugo snorted and pulled a face.

'We were having one of our regular discussions, during the course of which Hugo accused me of being miserly...'

Lady Mixby gasped. 'Oh, Hugo, how could you? Halstead is the most generous of men. You know very well he gave me a home here, saying it was so that I could look after the property which would otherwise remain empty and neglected. And he gives me a simply huge allowance. It is supposed to be for the household bills, which everyone knows his man of business settles in full because I haven't the ability to look after a…a cushion! I'm that scatterbrained. I'd only get into a scrape if I was obliged to balance the accounts, if ever I was given any to balance—which I must own I haven't.'

She paused with a frown as her speech became too tangled even for her to follow herself.

'Yes, yes, he's always been very generous to *you*,' said Hugo, as Gregory took her glass and gave her twice the amount he'd poured for Prudence. 'But he don't understand what it's like being on the Town these days. If he'd only increase my allowance I wouldn't have to keep going to him to bail me out.'

'And I repeat,' Gregory said wearily, arriving at the chair upon which Benderby was sitting and filling her glass to the brim. 'Until you learn a little sense, and stop allowing yourself to be gulled by a lot of Captain Sharps, raising your allowance will only serve to line their pockets.'

'And *I* repeat,' said Hugo, as Gregory went to the sideboard to fetch another glass. '*Anyone* can be gulled when first on the Town. It has happened to lots of my friends. So I said to him,' he said, turning to Prudence, 'that I'd like to see him exist on what he allows me out in the real world, without an army of servants at his bidding to smooth his way.'

'And I replied that not only could I exist,' said Gregory, taking the port to where the mill worker was perched on the edge of an upright chair by the window, 'I could also make myself useful—which is something Hugo has never even attempted to be.'

'Well, you can see how it was,' said Hugo to Prudence. 'He sat there behind his desk, looking down his nose at me, when he has never had any notion of what it's like to manage on a limited income, let alone have dealings with ordinary people on equal terms. So I challenged him to do it. To live for just *one week* like an ordinary man, on what he'd expect me to live on, without being obliged either to pawn something or ending up in the roundhouse.'

So *that* was why he'd been so reluctant to pawn his watch. And had been prepared to muck out a cow byre rather than risk being taken to the local magistrate. It would have meant losing the wager.

Prudence felt as if she'd been hit in the stomach by an icy fist. She'd made a fool of herself. Had sung in public and been molested by drunks because she'd thought he looked upset at the prospect of having to pawn that watch. How *could* he have let her do that?

'In my arrogance,' he said, 'I accepted. Not only to survive for one week on Hugo's terms but to achieve something useful, which I'd already stated I could do. The letter from *you*, Mr Bodkin, was lying on my desk. I had already decided to investigate your complaint. But with Hugo's challenge ringing in my ears I vowed to go in person to Wragley's and put right what was wrong, rather than just sending an agent.'

'What?' Mr Bodkin got to his feet, sloshing port over the back of his hand. 'You came up to Wragley's, pretending to be someone you're not, and goaded me into getting into a fight with my foreman, so's I lost my job and my home, because of some stupid wager?'

'Not exactly,' said Gregory. 'I *had* come to investigate the claims you'd made, and I was never pretending to be someone I'm not. My family name *is* Willingale. I just omitted to inform you of the titles I possess.'

'Aye, but—'

'I know, I know…' Gregory raised his hands in a placatory gesture. 'The foreman turned you out of your job and your home. But I did tell you, did I not, that if that happened you should come here and the Duke himself would make it all right? That if you handed the ring I gave you as a token to the lady who lived here she would take you in and house you until such time as the Duke could reinstate you?'

'Aye, but—' He rubbed the back of his hand with his other cuff.

'And I shall not only reinstate you, but will promote you to foreman, since I have excellent reason to know I can trust you to fulfil the role with complete integrity.'

Bodkin sat down abruptly. 'I never thought to... I mean, thank you, Mr Will... I mean, Your Grace,' he stammered, attempting to get to his feet again. And then sinking straight back down again under the weight of his sudden, unexpected elevation to factory foreman.

'I have already sent a letter of dismissal to Bigstone,' said Gregory. 'Though that is a mere formality.'

'Hold on a minute,' said Prudence. 'A formality? Don't you have to give a reason for dismissing one of your workers?'

There was a rustle of clothing as everyone turned to look at her as though wondering who'd spoken. Yes, they'd all forgotten she was there, so interested had they been in hearing about Gregory's determination to win his stupid wager with Hugo.

'Isn't it a gross abuse of your rank simply to turn a man off on a whim?'

'But it isn't a whim,' said Gregory, looking thoroughly perplexed. 'I have just told you—we found proof that he had not only been cheating me, but had abused his own power over the workers under him.'

'So you write one letter, explaining nothing, and—
poof! He's out on his ear. Is that how you normally op-
erate? Trampling over lesser beings as though they are
of no consequence?'

'She has a point, Halstead,' said Hugo. 'You do tend
to snap your fingers and expect everything to fall into
place.'

'It comes of being descended from a pirate, I expect,'
put in Lady Mixby.

Benderby glanced at Lady Mixby's empty port glass
with a shake of her head, while Hugo barked out a laugh

'Yes, there have been times when you have looked as
though you'd have loved to tell me to walk the plank,'
said Hugo.

'I beg your pardon?' Gregory turned to Hugo and
raised one eyebrow in a way that somehow expressed
a sort of disdainful astonishment.

Hugo wasn't a bit cowed. 'Oh, don't bother to deny
it,' he said. 'You've wished you could be rid of me many
a time. You've told me to my face I'm just a drain on
your resources...'

Prudence remembered Gregory confessing something of the sort to her. And her reaction then: that he
wasn't really bad enough to do anything of the sort.

'And if it wasn't for the fact that my existence has
spared you from having to marry again,' Hugo continued, 'you'd wash your hands of me...'

That jolted her right back to her own dilemma.
Which was how to extricate themselves from a betrothal
she was becoming increasingly convinced he couldn't
possibly want.

'No, I would not,' said Gregory. 'I may find you extremely tiresome, but I would *never* wish any harm to

come to you.' He glanced at Prudence, as though recalling the very same conversation. 'Hugo…' He sighed. 'I have only ever wanted you to learn habits of economy because of the immense responsibilities you will have to carry. Hundreds of people's welfare will be in your hands. You will not wish to let them down.'

Hugo winced. 'I'm sick of hearing about duty and responsibility and not letting the family down. Especially since, as Lady Mixby has just pointed out, our ancestors got away with being pirates. Or leading armies into mad battles. Or offering up their womenfolk to the King for a mistress. All of which would be considered scandalous these days, apart from going into battle— but, since as an only son I'm too precious to risk having my blood spilled on foreign soil, apparently I cannot even make my mark that way.' He sat back and folded his arms across his chest.

Gregory blinked. 'So that accounts for your freakish starts, does it? The notoriety of our ancestors? Combined with the frustration of being constricted and robbed of any real challenge?' He paused, seeming to gather himself together. 'Much as I hate to admit it, I think I can see what you mean. For something of the sort went through my mind when you issued your wager. How, I wondered, would I have fared on a battlefield, like the Fifth Duke? Or on a voyage of discovery, like the First? When, as you had so recently pointed out, I had never been permitted out of doors without a retinue of servants to smooth my path.'

Something jogged Prudence's memory, too. Gregory confiding that he'd never climbed a tree as a boy. And then his clumsy attempt to do so. And then the look of utter triumph blazing from his face when he not only scaled it, but helped her up and over the wall, too.

She took a sip of her port as she mulled this over. She could see, she supposed, why he'd felt he had to prove himself, if he'd been so coddled and cosseted all his life. She could see how tempting it must have been to take up Hugo's wager. She only had to think of the way he'd reacted to her own challenge to think of other ways to deal with the loss of their transport. He'd not only taken her up on it, but raised the stakes—the way he'd done with Hugo.

It was simply part of his nature to rise to any challenge. And master it.

It was part of what made her admire him so much.

Not that it excused him for allowing her to believe he was the kind of man she could marry, when he clearly wasn't. Girls with an upbringing like hers didn't marry dukes. She didn't know how to move in the elevated circles to which he belonged. Why, she couldn't even join in the kind of conversations he held over a dinner table. Let alone penetrate the mystery of why a room was called a morning room when people used it in the evenings.

Prudence must have made some kind of sound, expressing her turmoil, because he turned to look at her, a question in his eyes. She was just lifting her chin to stare him down when Lady Mixby startled everyone.

'And of course you were already in low spirits,' she observed. 'With it being the anniversary of Millicent's death.'

He whirled on her, a look of complete shock on his face. Quickly concealed. So quickly that Prudence was probably the only person in the room who noticed.

'I recall it being close to Easter, you see...' Lady Mixby was carrying on, blithely unaware of having provoked such a strong reaction in a man who was trying so hard not to show any. 'I was bitterly disappointed at having to go into black gloves just when I was hoping to start enjoying all the pleasures of the season. I dare say that every time Easter comes round your mind gets jogged by little things that throw you right back to that terrible time. The daffodils coming into bloom, for instance. I can never see daffodils bobbing in the breeze but I think of that churchyard, and how sunny and cheerful it all looked in spite of the terrible tragedy you'd just suffered. To lose your wife so suddenly, and she so young... Well, you both were...'

She ground to a halt, finally noticing the grim way Gregory was staring at her.

'Oh, dear me. I do beg your pardon. How tactless of me...'

'Not at all,' he said through clenched teeth. 'Your remark was most perceptive. And your memory is perfectly correct. It was at Easter-tide when Millicent passed. The very date that Hugo came to me. A day I always wonder whether—'

The Duke of Halstead—Prudence *must* get used to calling him that, since she could never allow him to be anything more to her—stalked away from them all. Twitched the curtains aside and stared out of the window for a moment. Lowered his head. Raised it, took a deep breath, and turned round.

'And so I decided,' he said, raising his chin with a touch of defiance. 'To find out, once and for all, whether I was worthy of the name Willingale, or whether I was merely a shadow of a man. An apparition created by the brilliance of my title blazing over a great mound of wealth. Hugo had offered me the perfect way to find out. Because, as he's already pointed out, I could never seriously consider joining a regiment and fighting in a battle, nor sailing away to India on a merchantman— not with all the obligations I have. But I thought that perhaps my estates could do very well without me for just one week.'

Prudence recalled the things he'd told her about his wife and how she'd made him feel. And then she thought of Hugo blundering in, in the completely insensitive way that young men do, and challenging him when he had already been questioning himself.

Her heart went out to him. Beneath the pompous exterior he'd adopted since coming here and taking up his role as Duke was a man who was painfully aware of his own faults and failings. Even the way he had just spoken made him sound more like the Gregory she'd known before they'd come to Bramley Park and he'd turned into the self-contained Duke of Halstead.

She still felt hurt by his deception, but she could see why he'd set out on what had been far more than just a silly wager between two bored, titled gentlemen. He'd wanted to prove himself.

'Well, now you know,' said Hugo with a smile of triumph. 'Because you *couldn't* last a week on your own with only the resources available to me. So I've won.'

'On the contrary,' Gregory drawled quietly. 'I could very easily have stayed out the full week if I'd thought fulfilling the terms of the wager I had with you was the most important consideration. But by that time it wasn't.'

'It's all very well saying that *now*—' said Hugo.

Prudence's heart began to flutter. Because Gregory had turned to her and was looking at her in exactly the same way he'd looked at her when he'd kissed her, that second time, in the shrubbery.

'You can say whatever you like, Hugo,' said Gregory, without taking his eyes from her. 'I have nothing to prove to myself or anyone else any longer.'

Chapter Fifteen

Her heart plummeted. She'd so hoped he'd been going to say he'd decided she was more important than winning the wager. Instead he'd more or less said that nobody's feelings mattered but his own.

'I have learned a lot of things during the course of this week,' he said, turning to Hugo. 'That I am every bit as resilient and inventive as any of my ancestors. I got myself to Wragley's in disguise, located the false ledgers, and subsequently fought my way out. And then I extricated Miss Carstairs from the clutches of a pair of villains, survived the consequences of a robbery which left us penniless, and faced down a farmer with a gun.'

'I say, it does sound as though you've had an adventure,' said Hugo, with what looked like a touch of jealousy. 'You should be thanking me.'

'Yes,' he replied, looking a little taken aback. 'I suppose I should.'

'That wasn't what you said before,' Prudence pointed out. 'You practically accused me of being in league with Hugo to make you lose the wager,' she said bitterly.

'What?' Hugo sat up straight. 'You thought I'd stoop to cheating?'

'Well, you did procure that vile creature I hesitate to describe as a horse, and the most broken-down vehicle it has ever been my misfortune to drive. Can you wonder that I thought you were attempting to prevent me from even reaching Wragley's in the first place?'

'Oh, that,' said Hugo with a dismissive wave of his hand. 'That was just in the nature of a jest. You are never seen out on the road except in a spanking rig with the most magnificent horseflesh between the shafts. I thought it would be fun to see you brought down a peg.'

'Hence the clothes, too?'

Hugo grinned, completely unabashed. 'That's it. Though you have to admit the disguise I provided did the job, didn't it? Neither Bodkin nor Miss Carstairs suspected for one minute that you're actually a duke, did they? And you should have seen how inventive I was with reasons for your disappearance from London. Just as the Season was getting started, too. *Everyone* wanted to know where you were.'

'The only person who might have been really worried by my absence,' said Gregory repressively, 'and might have had the gall to demand answers, would have been Jenkins. And I'd already sent him to Ely to make sure I'd have a change of horses at all the posting houses en route. But never mind all that now,' he said, turning to Prudence. 'I admit when we first met I was so fuddled that I couldn't believe anyone but Hugo could be responsible for what was happening to us. And, yes, I was still obsessed with winning at that point. But the moment I knew you really had been the victim of a crime I decided to bring you straight here. Which meant forfeiting the wager.'

Oh. Now he came to mention it, she *did* recall the rather determined look that had flashed across his face when he'd said he was going to bring her here *straight away.*

'Surely you can tell that by the time we reached that barn none of that mattered any more?'

She recalled the way he'd held her all night. He had not only kept her warm, but had made her feel safe. Cherished.

He seized hold of her hands. 'What matters now is the future we can make together.'

A maelstrom of conflicting emotions surged through her—hope, longing, suspicion, fear. They brought tears to her eyes.

'We cannot make a future together.'

It wasn't what he really wanted. Why, Hugo had said he'd rather cut off his arm than marry again.

'What? What are you saying?'

'That I cannot marry you.' She reached inside herself for the little speech she'd prepared. 'We only met because of the sordid, money-grubbing plot hatched by my aunt and that vile man she married—'

'Which I can easily thwart. They cannot very well accuse you of having loose morals once you have married a duke. They wouldn't dare risk the notoriety and expense of challenging your grandfather's bequest with me at your back, either.'

'But I am not,' she said grimly, 'going to marry you.'

'Nonsense—of course you are,' said Gregory.

'There is no "of course" about it,' she snapped.

'Then why on earth did you propose to me?'

There was a gasp from Lady Mixby. And Hugo, who'd been in the act of taking a sip of port, sprayed ruby-red droplets in all directions. But Gregory didn't appear to notice.

'And why do you think I accepted?' he continued, in the teeth of her determination to set him free and the muted sounds of shock emanating from every other person in the room.

Damn Prudence for getting him so worked up that his usual mastery over his emotions, over his actions and speech, had totally deserted him. How could he be standing here with his cousin, his aunt, her companion, and a virtual stranger watching while he blurted out things he'd vowed nobody should ever know?

'But you didn't,' said Prudence, to his complete astonishment, relegating what anyone else in the room might think to a very minor position.

'Yes, I did!'

He cast his mind back. Came up blank.

'That is, I may not have said in plain speech, *Thank you, Prudence, yes, of course I will marry you*, but you knew I'd accepted. I spoke of our marriage the next day as a *fait accompli*. Subsequently I introduced you to everyone in this house as my fiancée. The wedding will follow as a matter of course.'

'It doesn't need to, though.'

She gazed at him in the way she did when she'd made up her mind about something.

'Yes, it does need to,' he said, scrambling for a reason that would reach her. 'I have…er…tarnished your reputation. You admitted as much in front of Lady Mixby.'

'Tarnished—fiddlesticks! Now that I know you are a

duke I'm certain you could dispose of me in some other way than by marrying me.'

'Perhaps I do not wish to dispose of you.'

'Of course you do. You cannot seriously wish to marry a mere Miss Carstairs, from Stoketown. What will everyone say?'

'I do not care what anyone will say. In fact I care so little that I have already sent the notice of our betrothal to the *Gazette*.'

'Well, you will just have to *un*send it, then!' She stamped her foot. 'I mean, send another letter telling them it was a mistake. I'm sure it will catch up with the first before it gets into print. You cannot marry me just because I've admitted, to *one* person, that we spent a night together.'

'And to the other people present. Besides,' he put in swiftly, 'this is not just about restoring your reputation, Prudence. It is about justice. Can't you see what would come of letting people like your guardians think they can go around abusing their position of trust? Or what it would mean if it ever got out that they'd tricked a duke, and that duke had let them get off scot-free?'

He simply could not permit anyone to cross him, or wound those he loved.

'Justice?' She looked pensive. 'Well, I suppose...'

'Obviously,' he plunged in, seizing upon what looked like a weak spot in her defences, 'not only must they return the money they thought to steal from you, but they must also be suitably punished.'

'Punished?' She looked at him rather reproachfully. 'Is that really necessary? Wouldn't depriving them of my money be punishment enough?' She pulled her hands from his. 'If you persist in hounding my aunt she could end up in prison. Which would destroy her. And I'd never forgive myself. Because she isn't a bad person—not really. Until she married Mr Murgatroyd she tried to do her duty by me, even though she found it so hard. And who could blame her? My grandfather left me the money she considered hers.'

'Did he not also leave her a similar sum?'

A frown flickered across her face. 'Well, yes,' she said. 'I suppose he must have done. She was certainly considered well-to-do.'

'But instead of being satisfied with her own inheritance she decided to rob you of yours, too?'

'No... I don't think she did. I think it was Mr Murgatroyd who put the notion in her head.'

'Nevertheless, she went along with it.'

'Isn't a wife supposed to obey her husband?' she shot back.

'In theory. From experience, however, I can testify that it is rarely the case.'

'Well, I'm sure it was in this case. Because Mr Murgatroyd isn't the sort of man a woman *can* disobey.'

'And yet she married him. Even though she was well-to-do. She didn't have to do any such thing. And don't forget I was on the receiving end of her diatribe that morning in The Bull. She put on a performance worthy of Drury Lane. Flung herself into the role of aggrieved guardian of an ungrateful, unruly ward with a gusto that had nothing to do with coercion.'

'Do you *have* to rub it in?' she complained, rubbing at her arms. 'Don't you understand how much it hurts already to know that they could do such a thing to me?'

Of course he understood. Didn't she see that was exactly why he'd spent that sleepless night in the barn, working out ways and means to see the pair of them destroyed? *Utterly* destroyed!

He tried to take her hand again. She hid it behind her back as though she couldn't bear to let him touch her.

'Well anyway,' she said firmly, 'there isn't any point in arguing about something that won't happen. For we will not be getting married.'

'Why do you persist in saying that?' He was starting to feel as if he was standing on quicksand. No matter what argument he put forth to smooth away the obstacles in their path, she persisted in trying to avoid walking down it with him.

'Because we cannot possibly marry.'

'I don't see why.' He'd never gone to such lengths for a woman in his life. He'd forfeited the wager, and he was now sacrificing his pride by standing here arguing with her about what should be a private matter in front of his family. What did she want from him? What more could he do?

'For heaven's sake, I didn't know who you were when I proposed!'

The way he saw it, she knew him better than anyone else ever had. It was only his title he'd hidden from her. Not who he really was.

'I don't know why you are being so stubborn about this,' she complained. 'You told me how much you hated women trying to trap you into marriage.'

'What? When did I say any such thing?'

'Practically the whole of that first day we were together. You accused me of being in league with Aunt Charity to do so.'

'Not in so many words,' he replied uncomfortably, aware that he *might* actually have planted the seeds of doubt in her mind that were bearing such bitter fruit today.

'But it was what you believed.'

'Not for very long,' he pointed out. 'I soon worked out that the plot was against you, not me. And that I was dragged into it purely by chance.'

'Yes, but it infuriated you, nonetheless. Now that I know you are a duke I can see why. And also why you cannot allow this foolish betrothal to stand.'

Foolish? His feelings might sound foolish to her, perhaps. But there were other reasons for the marriage which she must surely appreciate. Since they were all of a practical nature. And she was the most practical female he'd ever met.

'Then may I just remind you of the advantages of letting this betrothal stand? Once we are married I will be able to restore your inheritance—'

'Oh,' she gasped. 'So that is what this is all about. My inheritance!' Her face went white, but her eyes blazed with indignation. 'Yes, you… I remember now…you only started looking on me with interest once I told you about it. You—' She sat down hastily, one hand pressed to her mouth. As though she felt sick.

Not that she could possibly feel as sick as he did.

How could she accuse him of only wanting to marry her to get his hands on her money? How could she ignore everything he'd done for her, everything they'd been through together?

If that was what she thought of him, *really* thought of him, then they didn't have any future, did they?

He stalked to the window and stared out into the blackness. The same blackness that was swirling within him.

'Miss Carstairs, I beg your pardon,' he said, turning to face them all again. His face had turned hard. And his eyes were so cold they might have been chiselled from ice. 'It appears I have been labouring under a misapprehension. Naturally, if you have changed your mind about wishing to marry me, then you have the right to cry off. It is perfectly acceptable since it is an established fact,' he said, with a cynical twist to his mouth, 'that women change their minds as swiftly and unpredictably as the weather changes in spring.'

It felt as though he'd just plunged a dagger into her stomach. For a while there, when they'd been arguing, he'd begun to seem like the Gregory she'd thought she knew.

Now he'd turned back into the Duke of Halstead.

'You need only say the word, Miss Carstairs, to end this farcical betrothal.'

Farcical? Was that how he saw it?

Well, of course he did. She was a nobody. She still couldn't really understand why he'd kept on insisting they had to get married. Everyone knew he never wanted to marry anyone ever again—let alone her. And it was farcical for two people who'd only known each other for such a short time to get married. Especially two people from such different social spheres.

'I shall, of course, ensure you have the means to live comfortably until your own money is restored. After all, if you refuse to go through with the ordeal of marrying me then there is no reason for me to pay heed to your ridiculous plea for clemency for your aunt, is there? Until such time as she releases it, however, you may stay here. Or at one of my other properties, if you prefer.'

What had she done? Insulted him to a point past

bearing—that was what. Because marrying him *wouldn't* have been an ordeal. Not if he hadn't been a duke anyway.

How could she have been such an idiot? Gregory had never given her cause to suspect him of double-dealing. He'd been chivalrous to the point of…of saintliness! Any ordinary man would have washed his hands of her after she'd thrown that rock at him, but what had *he* done? Lent her his coat and bought her breakfast.

Even after she'd insulted him in the worst possible way just now, by accusing him of avarice, he was still going to do all that was necessary to get justice for her, to get her money back and ensure she had somewhere to stay while he was doing it.

But she'd had years of being an obligation already. She couldn't face forcing him to stick by a betrothal he'd considered farcical from the very first.

She opened her mouth to say the words that would end a betrothal that should never have begun.

And hesitated.

There was no consolation at all in telling herself she was about to do the right thing.

But she loved him too much to let him put his head in what he considered to be a noose.

She bowed her head and squeezed her eyes shut. Loved him? How could she have fallen in love in such a short space of time? Why, because she was her mother's daughter, that was why. Her mother—who'd fallen in love with a handsome young officer at the assembly and run away with him before a week was out.

Oh, Lord, but Aunt Charity was right about her. She was the amalgam of all the worst traits of her parents. Not only did she have her mother's impulsiveness, she had inherited a hefty dollop of her father's stubborn pride, too. That was what had made it so hard for her to swallow the discovery that Gregory was a duke. She'd had no qualms about proposing marriage when she'd believed she had the upper hand. When she'd felt as if she was graciously bestowing her hand upon a penniless but worthy suitor. But when he'd turned the tables on her…

She hated having nothing to bring to this union. Becoming a burden again. An obligation. And she'd rather retain at least a sliver of pride than face a lifetime of such humiliation.

She lifted her head and regarded him bleakly.

'Very well,' she said. 'I release you.'

And, just to prove how sensible she could be, she ran from the room.

She ran all the way up the stairs, so that she reached her room out of breath. There she was immediately challenged by the luxurious carpet, which lay, just like his title, directly in her path. She pulled off her worn-down shoes, wishing she could as easily discard her grubby background, then dropped them by the door, wishing it was as simple a matter to dispose of the way they'd met. Or the things she'd said to him just now. Things that had hurt and alienated him.

She ran across the sumptuous carpet and threw herself face-down on the bed. But even there the pristine eiderdown wouldn't give her leave simply to burst into tears. Not until she'd squirmed her way up the bed and got her face into a pillow out of which salt stains would wash could she really let go.

Chapter Sixteen

It was the most selfless and also the most stupid thing she'd ever done.

She could have been his wife. *His wife!*

And now her life stretched out before her as a long, grey, barren vista. Because he wouldn't be a part of it. He was too proud to remain friends with her. Even if he never managed to extract her money from Aunt Charity—because there was every chance Mr Murgatroyd had somehow lost it all anyway—and she became his pensioner, he'd take good care to avoid her. His pride would demand it.

She didn't know how she would bear it.

She'd been alone before. During those long, dreary years with Aunt Charity she'd felt terribly alone. But it would be as nothing compared to the misery of being without him.

She was just reaching for a handkerchief to blot up the tears when the door burst open so forcefully it banged against the wall and bounced back onto the man who stood there, breathing hard and looking as if he was about to commit murder.

'Gregory!' She sat up and swiped at the tears streaming down her face. 'What are you doing in here?'

He stalked across to the bed.

'Firstly, I want to know how much, exactly, you stood to inherit from your grandfather. Since you accused me of wishing to marry you so that I could get my hands on it.'

'I was very wrong to think that,' she said. 'I know now you wouldn't have done anything so underhand. It isn't *you*.'

'How much, Prudence?' He planted his hands on his hips and glowered down at her.

She supposed it didn't matter now. 'It was ten thousand pounds.'

He raised one eyebrow. 'Per year?'

'No. Ten thousand pounds total. In trust.'

He gave a bark of bitter laughter. 'I could drop that amount in one session at White's and not turn a hair. Haven't you taken a good look at this house? Don't you realise it's only one of my smaller properties? So far from London or any of the race courses that I chose it only as a rendezvous for settling up with Hugo? And you heard what Lady Mixby said about me letting her run tame here. What kind of man can afford a profligate widgeon like her for a pensioner, do you suppose?'

She swallowed. It had been bad enough to learn of the discrepancy in their rank. But now...

'My main seat is in Sussex,' he continued. 'It is one of the largest houses in the country. I employ hundreds of servants in my houses, and untold numbers in my factories, mines and farms.'

A cold hollowness opened up inside her. He was *that*

rich? So rich that her ten thousand pounds was like a drop in an ocean? Oh, to think she'd accused him of wanting to gain control of her money. What had seemed like a fortune to a girl born into an army family, then brought up amongst the middle classes, turned out to be small change in the world Gregory inhabited.

So why had he been so determined to stick to a betrothal *she'd* instigated when she couldn't even bring what he'd think of as wealth to the union?

Why, precisely for the reasons he'd given. Because he'd wanted to restore her damaged reputation. And to be in a strong position to bring her guardians to justice. And get her money back *for her*.

All very fine, honourable motives. None of which would have been of any benefit to him.

And she'd flung it all back in his face.

No wonder he'd looked at her with such coldness. No wonder he'd stalked away and turned his back on her. She couldn't have offered him a worse insult if she'd been trying.

'So that's that point dealt with,' he said. 'Secondly, let us discuss your attitude to the wager I had with Hugo. I saw your face when he said one of the conditions was that I was not supposed to pawn anything. What do you suspect me of there?'

She sighed. He was determined to make her eat her words. Even the ones she'd only thought.

'I felt like an idiot for not understanding why you'd been so reluctant to pawn your watch. I thought at the time that it was because it had some sentimental value to you, but now I can see that it meant you losing the wager.'

'I concede,' he said, 'that I was smarting over having to sink to the depths of visiting a pawn shop. But I told you later, didn't I, that I regretted not doing all in my power to bring you here safely? You must know by now that your welfare had become more important than winning a wager that I'd agreed to in a fit of…of temporary insanity?'

She recalled his horror when he'd seen the state of her feet. His words of contrition.

'I know you were sorry you'd let me walk all day with no stockings on,' she conceded, 'once you saw my blisters. But I can't help wondering if you agreed to my suggestion to leave the horse where it was because you were still trying to delay meeting up with Hugo until the agreed time.'

'It was not a deliberate delaying tactic,' he said, coming to stand over her. 'And you know how much I detested that horse. I was downright glad at the prospect of never having to set eyes on it again.'

She didn't like the way he was towering over her.

'You let me sing in the market square,' she pointed out, surging to her feet so she wouldn't feel quite so far beneath him. 'I was accosted by those drunken fops…'

'I didn't *let* you sing in the market square. I couldn't stop you. You even stole my hat to collect the takings.'

They were standing toe to toe now, just the way they had stood when they'd been arguing at the foot of the market cross.

'And don't forget,' he said, pointing his finger at her, 'that this morning I climbed the wall of my own property so you wouldn't have to walk all the way round to the front gate. Is that the act of a man who is trying to delay his return?'

'I suppose not,' she admitted grudgingly. 'But—'

'But nothing. You have no reason to break our betrothal. So I am not going to permit you to do anything so foolish—do you hear me?'

She gaped at him.

'But *why*? I mean, you cannot *possibly* want to marry me.'

'I want to know why you persist in saying that, Prudence. When I have given no indication that that is the case.'

'But... Well...' She twisted the handkerchief between her fingers. '*I* asked *you* to marry me. And you were thinking about it, I do believe, because you wanted to...to bed me,' she finished in a rush, her cheeks heating. 'And then in the morning, when the farmer found us and I sort of embellished our relationship so he wouldn't haul us off for trespass, I can see that you had to go along with it. And then, when we got here, I suppose you felt honour-bound to introduce me as your fiancée since you hadn't found the words to let me down gently.'

'What utter nonsense! If I hadn't wanted to marry you I would have introduced you to my family as a lady under my protection. I am a selfish man, Prudence. Nobody can make me do anything I don't want.'

'What are you saying?' She rubbed her forehead, where a vein was starting to throb.

He strolled to the foot of the bed and propped one shoulder up against the post.

'You do realise,' he said coldly, 'that after this episode you will be completely ruined?'

'Wh...what? Why?'

Was he threatening her? Saying that since she'd refused to marry him he wouldn't help her get her money back? No, no, that couldn't be it. He wouldn't do something so despicable.

Would he?

'Most women would kill to have been in your shoes,' he said. 'Betrothed to me, that is. No matter how the betrothal had come about. Nobody is ever going to believe you cried off. They will say that I jilted you—do you realise that? They will speak of you as my leavings. Is that what you really want?'

'No, of course I don't!' She gasped, sickened by the picture he'd painted of a future of shame. 'But surely you can see it will be even worse for you if we were to marry? I *had* to let you off the hook—can't you understand? If I made you stick to a vow you gave under duress I'd feel as if I was no better than…than…' She shook her head, at a total loss to think of anyone she could imagine doing anything worse than forcing a man into a marriage he didn't really want.

'So you maintain you broke the betrothal for *my* benefit?'

'Yes. You deserve better.'

'Isn't that for me to decide?'

'Well anyway, it's too late now.'

'No, it isn't,' he said. Then he strode back to her side of the bed and dropped down on one knee. 'I can see that I have made you think I am a touch reluctant to enter into the matrimonial state for a second time. So this time round *I* am asking *you*. So you can have no doubt it is what I want. Prudence…' He took hold of her hands. 'Would you do me the very great honour of becoming my wife?'

All the breath whooshed from her lungs, leaving her head spinning.

'You cannot mean that—'

'Why not?'

'Because you said…and Hugo said you'd rather cut off your arm than marry again—that everyone knows it.'

'You are surely not going to base your entire future on what Hugo says?'

'No, but he—'

'Prudence, listen to me,' he said sternly. 'You told me once—do you recall?—that you were reluctant to marry because you wanted to be free. Yet you changed your mind and proposed to me. Why can you not believe that meeting you has changed my view of matrimony, too?'

'But you—'

'Yes, I stood over Millicent's grave and vowed that no woman would have a hold over me ever again. I admit it. And I have never let another woman close. And I *did* gain a reputation in society, which I freely confessed to you, for keeping my numerous *affaires* on a purely physical level. I was determined that no woman would ever reduce me to the state she did.'

'Exactly! Which is why I cannot bear to back you into a corner now. You got all tangled up in my troubles, and now you—'

'Hush.'

He reached up to place one finger against her lips. It was all she could do not to purse them and kiss it.

'Look at me now. I am on my knees, asking you to marry me. I don't *have* to. Last time I *had* to marry a woman chosen for me by my parents. This time I am asking you to marry me because I *want* to.'

Her heart lurched. She wanted to say yes. Oh, how

she wanted to say yes. But all the obstacles that made their union impossible still existed.

'But I'm a nobody!' she wailed. She had a vision of a flock of outraged society matrons pointing their fingers at her and wagging their heads in disapproval if ever she appeared in public on his arm. Then going into a huddle and whispering about how she'd snared poor Gregory. Which would make her look scheming, and him like a pigeon for plucking. 'Worse, I'm the product of a runaway match. I grew up following the drum, for heaven's sake!'

'Yes, I've been thinking about that,' he said, 'and talking to Lady Mixby, who remembers all the old scandals. Your father wouldn't happen to be the same Edmund Carstairs who ran off with a girl he met at an assembly in some out-of-the way place in the north where he was stationed while he was in the militia, would he?'

'Well, yes…' she admitted.

'Then you are from a good family.'

'Not directly. I mean, yes, my *father* was well-born, but once he married my mother he was entirely cut off from them all. And they never acknowledged me. Not even once, both my parents had died. It was the Biddlestones who took me in when I became an orphan.'

Even though they'd done so grudgingly. And ended up betraying her.

'That will not be an obstacle to your social success. Everyone knows what a clutch-fisted man your grandpapa Carstairs is. People will be only too ready to believe he didn't want the expense of bringing you out, if we start rumours to that effect.'

'Why would we do any such thing?'

'To smooth your path, of course. Not that it will need all that much smoothing. For heaven's sake, your Carstairs grandfather is an earl, didn't you know that? The Earl of Sterndale. Which makes you perfectly eligible. The granddaughter of an earl may go anywhere, and marry as high as she pleases.'

'I don't think of myself that way. Not after the way he repudiated me when Papa sent me to him—'

'Yes, but since then your father has died a hero, hasn't he? And even I remember rumours about how your grandfather shut himself away for a week and was as surly as a bear when he came out. I shouldn't be a bit surprised to learn that he will acknowledge you now joyfully. Particularly if you are presented to him as my duchess,' he finished with a cynical twist to his lips. 'So that acknowledging you won't cost him a penny.'

She sucked in a deep, painful breath. Then forced herself to say what had to be said.

'In other words you are going to have to spend the rest of your life making excuses. Explaining me away. I had enough of that with Aunt Charity. And I couldn't bear it if you…' She turned her hands over in his and gripped his. 'I don't want you always to be ashamed of me.'

'Ashamed of you?' His eyes widened in surprise. 'Why should you think I could ever be ashamed of you?'

'Because you already are.'

'No, I'm not.'

'You are. From the very first moment we got here, and your butler practically had an apoplexy at the sight of me, you have been obliged to make all sorts of excuses to explain me away.'

'Perkins is far too good at his job to have anything like an apoplexy,' countered Gregory. 'And anyway, I don't care what servants think.'

'But *I* do. I don't want people whispering about me wheedling my way into your life. Or you being made to feel as though you need to hide anything about my past—which you've just admitted you would have to.'

Gregory's brows drew down. 'For heaven's sake, woman, the only reason I have come up with ways to smooth your path into society is because *you* are making an issue of your past. Nobody else cares or they wouldn't be so keen to see us wed.'

'They...your family...are keen to see us wed?'

'Admittedly Hugo is thinking primarily of himself. Once I start producing my own heirs he thinks he will be free to live as he pleases, instead of having to train to be a duke. And even as I stormed from the room, vowing I'd make you change your mind, Lady Mixby was wittering on about how romantic it was and how she was going to look forward to introducing you to society by means of a grand ball.'

She looked at him then. Really looked at him. With a growing surge of hope swelling in her heart. Because all she could see in his eyes was determination

'So long as you aren't ashamed of me...'

'Never!'

She wished she could believe him. But actions spoke louder than words. 'Then why did you send me to my room the moment we got here?'

'Need I remind you that you were *trembling*? Which you'd never done before. Not even when you were woken by a farmer with a gun. At first I couldn't think why you were so overset. But then I reasoned that if even *I* felt self-conscious, because I smelled of the cow byre and looked like a vagrant, then it must be ten times as bad for you. I was at least among my own family—you were facing a set of strangers. Hugo was being abominably rude, and Lady Mixby was being…' He compressed his lips for a second. 'Lady Mixby. I thought you'd feel better able to deal with them all in a…er…complete set of clean clothes. And naturally you were upset with me, too, for not being completely honest about my identity. I hoped that if you had a chance to calm down you'd be able to see things weren't as black as they seemed. Besides, you needed to get your feet treated,' he finished on a shrug.

Once more she'd misjudged his motives. She'd been so angry, so hurt, when he'd hustled her upstairs, because it had put her in mind of the way she'd been treated by her aunt. She'd assumed he wanted her out of the way, too. Because she had already felt betrayed on discovering he'd been hiding so much from her when she'd thought they'd been so close.

But Gregory had been thinking of her all along. Not only that, but he'd pretty accurately judged how she'd been feeling during that first awkward meeting with his family. Even down to his oblique reference to her lack of decent underwear.

'Oh, you dear, dear man,' she said, reaching out her hand to caress his cheek.

He grabbed at it. 'Shall I take that as a yes?'

Chapter Seventeen

'Oh, Gregory...' She sighed. 'I wish I could say yes— I really do...

He surged to his feet. 'You cannot possibly still be harbouring any doubts, surely?'

'I cannot help having a few,' she protested. 'I mean, when I suggested marriage I thought I had many practical reasons for doing so. Only when we got here they all turned out to be nonsense.'

'What do you mean, nonsense?'

'I have no title, nor even a fortune—not by your standards. I suddenly felt as if I had nothing to bring to our marriage except disgrace. So I couldn't understand why you seemed content to go along with it unless it was because you didn't want to go back on your word, once given. And anyway, had I known at the time you were a duke of course I'd never have been so...so...*forward* as to dare propose in the first place.'

'Which is one of the reasons I didn't tell you,' he said grimly. 'Don't you have any idea what it did for me when you whispered that shy proposal in that barn? To know you were willing to trust your fortune to me, thinking I had nothing? Prudence, nobody has ever thought I was of any account.'

'Of course they have,' she said, frowning. 'You're a *duke*.'

'No,' he groaned. 'You don't understand. Me.' He beat his chest with the flat of his free hand. 'This. The man. You heard Hugo. He said what everyone else thinks. That I am nothing without the title, and the wealth, and the body of servants whose only function is to maintain my dignity. Even my wife—' He stopped, his face contorting with remembered pain. 'You are the only person who has ever seen *me*. Wanted me. Gregory. Just Gregory.'

'But you are not just Gregory, though, are you? Can you not understand why I have felt as though I can't marry you?' She cupped his lean jaw with one hand. 'I wouldn't know how to begin to be a duchess. I'm so ordinary.'

'Not to me, you aren't! You are the only woman I have ever spent an entire day with. The only one I have ever held in my arms all night. The only one I could imagine ever wanting to do either with.'

'Are you sure,' she asked, searching his earnest face, 'that it isn't all because of the extraordinary adventure we've had? That once you get back to your real life you will wake up and realise you were carried away on a tide of…of recklessness, or something? I mean, when I proposed to you, you said I'd have changed my mind by the morning, once it was clear of that drug.'

'My mind is completely clear now,' he said earnestly. 'And I swear I will never grow tired of you, Prudence. Because you have seen *me*. The man I am inside. You looked right past the title—'

'Which was only because I didn't know it was there,' she pointed out.

'Even now you know I have it you would rather I didn't, which is completely astonishing. Do you think I could lightly let such a rare treasure slip through my fingers? A woman who sees me and not the title?'

'But you almost did, though, didn't you? You practically *invited* me to break off the betrothal. Just now.'

'I felt as though you'd ripped my guts out when you did it.'

'I felt as though I'd ripped out my own, too. Especially as you went all cold and hard and didn't seem to care. My only consolation was thinking that if you really didn't care then I'd done the right thing by you.'

'You little fool,' he grated, gripping her shoulders. 'Couldn't you tell it was pride that made me let you go? Pride that made me vow you wouldn't reduce me to grovelling, the way Millicent made me grovel? Not in front of my family anyway. It took me about two minutes to work out that if I could get you alone all I would have to do was kiss you and you would do anything I wanted.' He shook his head, as though in disbelief. 'But the moment I saw you lying there, weeping, I knew that kissing you into submission wasn't the answer. That I needed to break down all the barriers you'd thrown up between us, no matter how much I hurt you in the process.'

'You were a bit ruthless,' she admitted.

'Because I was fighting for *us*,' he said.

And not grovelling. He would never do anything that smacked of grovelling. But then, nor would she.

'And I'm about to be more ruthless still,' he said grimly. 'Because I cannot help thinking that if I'd made you mine in that barn you wouldn't have put me through all this tonight. You wouldn't have dreamed of breaking off the betrothal, no matter how many doubts you might have had about my motives, or my status, or any other damn thing about me. The one time in my life when I have an attack of conscience where a woman is concerned,' he said, shaking his head as though in disbelief, 'and it all blows up in my face!'

And then he swooped, hauling her into his arms and kissing her hungrily.

Oh, if only he'd acted like this, spoken like this, before, she would never have dreamed of breaking off the betrothal. She flung her arms about his neck and kissed him back as well as she was able, given her inexperience.

It appeared to be enough for him, for he plunged his tongue into her mouth and took her experience of kissing to a whole new level. It was as if he wanted to devour her. It was so breathtaking she was going dizzy with it. It felt as though she was falling.

And then she realised she *was* falling—backwards onto the bed.

'I'm done with being a gentleman, Prudence,' he snarled.

'Good…' She sighed as he rained kisses over her face.

'I cannot stand the thought of any other man touching you,' he moaned into her neck. 'I saw it happen, in my mind's eye, the minute you broke our betrothal. Men swarming round you like bees round a honeypot. You're so beautiful,' he said, rearing up and looking down at her as though he'd never really seen a woman before.

He cupped her cheek. His hand was trembling.

'I know I said I would get your inheritance back for you, but I'm not sure I could have done it if you weren't going to be my wife. It would have tempted even more men to court you. And you might have fallen for one of them.'

'I wouldn't. I couldn't. There is nobody for me but you, Gregory.'

His jaw hardened. 'I intend to make sure of that. Tonight will be like a branding. No other man will ever have you after this. You are mine.'

'Yes,' she purred.

But he didn't seem to hear her acquiescence. For he had seized her wrists and pinned her hands high above her head, stretching her out beneath him like a sacrifice.

Her heart was beating so wildly it felt as though it was going to burst through her ribcage. He was going to take her here, now, with all his family downstairs, wondering what was going on. It felt so decadent. So thrilling.

'You do want me, don't you, Prudence? You wouldn't have proposed in the first place if that wasn't so. You wouldn't kiss me back with such enthusiasm if you didn't want me.'

Was that a hint of uncertainty she saw in his eyes? Had Millicent wounded him so deeply that even now he couldn't quite believe that a woman could truly want him?

'Yes, I want you,' she said. Hoping that all the love she felt for him was blazing from her eyes. 'You know I do.'

His hold on her wrists slackened. 'Even though we're not yet married?'

That question made her love him all the more. For

even though he was desperate to brand her he would still stop, right now, if he thought for one second that she had any reluctance at all.

'Even though you're a duke,' she replied.

'You're trembling again,' he said.

'It's excitement,' she panted. 'I know I ought to feel outraged or terrified by your threats to…to ravish me. But I don't want to protest, or struggle. The weight of your body, pinning me down like this, is…'

And then her words ran out. She didn't have enough experience to be able to describe what he was making her feel. But her body told him, arching up to make the contact with his powerful hips even stronger.

There was no longer any uncertainty on his face. It had been replaced by a knowing smile.

'What you are feeling now,' he drawled, 'is nothing to what I'm going to make you feel soon.' He nuzzled at her ear then, nipped at the lobe, then let go of one of her wrists so he could run his hand down her body, as though tracing her shape. It made her hips, her breasts, hunger to experience a similar caress.

She whimpered and writhed beneath him.

He nipped at her lower lip. Flicked his tongue into her mouth, making her open it to grant him access. Ran his hand back down her side and round to her hips. When she wiggled in response, he slid his hand round to her bottom and kneaded it.

He teased and tormented her with skilful caresses and kisses, rousing her to such a pitch that all she could think of was ripping his clothes off. Or hers. Oh, Lord, she needed… Oh, she needed…

She pulled his face to hers so she could kiss him. And

he let go of her other hand so that she could put both arms round his neck and plunge her fingers into his hair.

'Mine,' he breathed into her ear, before capturing her chin, turning her head and plundering her mouth yet again.

'Yes.' She sighed when he paused for breath. 'I think I can really believe it now. Only…'

'Only what?' He tensed. 'What now?'

'Nothing, really. It's just that if you *had* made me yours, that night in the barn, I would have felt as though I was bestowing some great gift upon you. Whereas now…' She glanced round the room. At the velvet hangings, the moulded cornices, the marble mantel, all of which shrieked of his wealth. And made her dreadfully conscious of how little she was worth.

'The reason I didn't make you mine that night is because I didn't want you to have no choice in the matter once you had discovered all there is to know about me. I knew you'd be shocked when you found out I'm a duke. I feared you might think I'd deceived you for some nefarious reason. I wanted you to be able to remember that I'd behaved honourably, in that one way at least, and then you might be able to forgive the rest.'

'Oh, Gregory.' What a selfless thing to have done for her. 'What a pity we cannot return to that night and do it right this time, knowing all there is to know about each other.'

'That,' he said, rolling off her and standing up, 'is an excellent idea. Come on,' he said, grabbing her hand and hauling her to her feet.

'What are you doing?'

'I think you can see perfectly well what I'm doing. I'm taking the quilt off the bed.'

'Why? What for?'

'Because we would both rather our first time together had been out in that barn.'

'Well, yes,' she admitted.

'Well, then, don't just stand there,' he said as he rolled the quilt and slung it over one shoulder. 'Get some blankets,' he said as he grabbed a couple of pillows. 'As many as you can carry.'

'What? But we cannot go all the way back to the barn. Not at this hour of the night.' She considered it. 'Can we?'

'No need,' he said with a wicked grin. 'I have somewhere much better in mind.'

She was so relieved he wasn't going to put off making love to her properly—or should that be *im*properly?— that she asked no more questions. She just set to, stripping down the bed as swiftly as she could.

They stumbled down the main staircase with bundles of bedding in their arms and crossed the hall to a door at the rear as quickly and quietly as they could. Gregory looked totally nonchalant, but Prudence was rather nervous of anyone seeing them and correctly guessing what they were up to. Not half an hour ago she'd broken their betrothal and stormed off upstairs. And then he'd stormed up after her. If he'd…subdued her in private she might have given the excuse that she hadn't had any choice in the matter. But here she was, carrying her fair share of blankets, proving she was as eager as he to behave with a scandalous lack of propriety.

By the time they went out through a door at the back of the house her cheeks—nay, her entire body was flushed with nervous excitement, and her heart was pounding. She was sneaking off into the night to make love to a duke, without being married to him.

She was then going to marry that duke.

She couldn't really believe either. It was like something out of a dream. The fact that it was another clear, moonlit night added to the surreal quality of what she was doing as they crossed a smooth, silvered lawn to a path which plunged them into the darkness of a shrubbery.

This path was wide enough that the branches didn't snag at her hair or her clothes, the way they'd done when he'd led her to the house. Though she was still in almost as much turmoil. That time she'd been worried someone might catch them and accuse them of trespassing. *Again.* This time she just felt…downright naughty. As well as slightly stunned that she was actually doing this. She wasn't the kind of girl who sneaked out into the night to have assignations with men. Not even men she was going to marry. Not that there had been any others. Because she'd always sworn she wouldn't marry anyone. Or at least that was the way she had been thinking ever since Aunt Charity had started trying to matchmake for her.

She shook her head as her thoughts got into a tangle as dense as the shrubbery through which Gregory was leading her.

But it wasn't long before the shrubbery gave way to another lawn, in the centre of which stood a low brick building with a thatched roof. It looked like a tiny one-roomed cottage.

'The summer house,' said Gregory, setting his hand to the door latch.

'A very substantial summer house,' she observed, eyeing the casement windows and the solid oak door.

'Well, it needs to protect the ladies who wish to take the air in summer from the weather we typically get in these parts,' he said, putting his shoulder to the door when it refused to budge. 'Ah...' He sighed in relief as it gave inward, scraping across the somewhat unevenly flagged floor.

She peered inside as he pushed the door wider. There was enough moonlight filtering in for her to be able to pick out a couple of upholstered chairs set under one of the windows, and a table with some straight-backed chairs under another. But what really caught her eye was a little brick arched fireplace, in a nook directly opposite the door.

They were certainly not going to be cold in here overnight. Not once she'd lit the fire, which would only take a minute or two. She found a tinderbox and candles on the mantel shelf, dry kindling in the grate, and plenty of logs in a box on the hearth.

'You see, Prudence?' Gregory came up behind her as she set one of the candlesticks back on the mantel after touching the flame to the kindling, and put his arms round her waist. 'I couldn't manage without you. Not even so far as to the summer house in my own grounds.'

'You have servants to light your fires,' she said, pulling his hands away so she could kneel down on the quilt which he'd spread out on the hearthrug.

'Nobody lights my fires the way you do,' he growled, dropping to his knees beside her.

He draped one arm round her shoulder. It slid to her waist as she leaned forward to peer into the grate and check the kindling. She tried to ignore the way he was stroking her bottom. But it wasn't easy. The flames that licked over the twigs when the paper caught fire were no less greedy than the sensations his hands were stoking in her body. Soon she could no longer be bothered with what was going on in the grate and she knelt back on her heels, turned to him, and lifted her face hopefully.

'Am I allowed to kiss you now, then?' he asked. 'Not too busy with more practical matters?'

He didn't wait for her answer but began to nuzzle at the sensitive spot just below her ear. It sent a shiver right down her spine. A delicious shiver of longing.

'Now, where were we…?' he murmured, placing a kiss on her jaw.

Chapter Eighteen

'Right about here…' She sighed, sliding her arms round his neck and kissing him back. He caught her hard into his chest. Then they surged together, kissing and running their hands over each other as though neither could quite believe this was really happening at last.

And soon that wasn't enough. She just had to tear his shirt from his breeches so she could get at bare skin. Which was all the encouragement he needed to start plucking at the ties at the back of her gown. He undid them with a dexterity clearly gained from frequent practice.

But she didn't care.

'Oh, yes,' she panted when he tumbled her down onto the quilt. 'Oh, God…oh, Gregory,' she moaned as he pulled the front of her bodice down. 'Oh, yes, push that out of the way.' She gasped. And gasped again as he closed his mouth over her breast. She plunged her fingers into his hair once more as he sucked, and licked, and nipped at her.

'I cannot live without you,' he bit out briefly, before

swirling his tongue round one painfully sensitised nipple. 'Don't make me do without you, my sweet love.'

His sweet love? Was she really his sweet love?

'Oh, Gregory,' she sobbed, as tears welled in her eyes.

Something arced between them and then they were kissing frantically. She clawed at his back as he pushed up her skirts. Wrapped one leg round his hips as he ran his hand up the outside of her thigh and kissed her neck again. Her face. The cleft between her breasts.

She was on fire. Burning up with the need that only he could create within her. That only he could assuage.

He raised himself slightly. Slid away so that he could bring his hand between her legs.

'Oh, yes,' she moaned as he delved, and stroked, and pleasured her. 'Yes. Please. Oh…'

Something like a shower of fireworks went off inside her, scattering her in a blaze of sparks across the heavens, before gently drifting her back down to the hearth. Where she discovered he was holding her close, his fingers buried in her hair, his chest heaving as though he'd just been running.

He dropped a kiss on her brow. 'Wait right there,' he said as he got to his feet.

She watched drowsily from between heavy lids as he gathered pillows and blankets, then came back and dropped to his knees beside her.

'Lift your head,' he said, passing her a pillow. She did as she was told without demur, seeing as he was only ministering to her comfort.

'Raise your arms,' he ordered next.

When she did so, he pulled the sleeves down her

arms and off. She raised her hips so that he could remove the gown altogether.

'Now for the stays,' he said. Then checked himself. 'Good God—your other stays are still in my valise. If anyone unpacks for me...'

She tried, and failed, to stifle a giggle.

'Are you laughing at me?'

'I'm sorry. I couldn't help it.'

'You will pay for that, you minx,' he growled.

And deftly removed every last stitch of her clothing with ruthless efficiency. Then he knelt back. And stared at her. For so long that she began to start wondering if she should be worried. Or if she ought to feel shy. A modest, virtuous woman would surely wish to cover herself? In at least a couple of strategic places.

All Prudence wanted to do was preen. Because the way he was drinking in the sight of her, lying naked and ready for him, made her feel like a goddess being worshipped by an acolyte.

'You look so lovely, lying there with the firelight flickering over your body, I cannot decide where to start,' he said at last. 'Should I start at your poor abused toes and work my way up?' He ran one hand along the length of her leg, round and over her hip, up and over one breast, ending by cupping her cheek.

'Or at your hair? Your glorious hair?' He leaned forward and started plucking out the pins.

'Wait, Gregory,' she said, as a thought suddenly struck her. 'I know where you should start.'

'Where? Where do you wish me to begin making love to you?'

She smiled up at him. 'I thought you already had. But, please, my dear, won't you put a couple of logs on the fire before you do anything else? I don't want the fire to go out at a crucial moment and for you to have to stop to get it going again.'

'I can promise you the fire won't go out all night,' he growled.

She didn't think he was talking about the one just getting going in the hearth.

'My practical little wife-to-be,' he said, tending to the fire. 'Always thinking one step ahead. You will be a formidable duchess, you know.'

She didn't really believe him, but she felt far too lazy, too replete in the aftermath of all those fireworks going off inside her, to be bothered to argue.

And she was glad she hadn't when he knelt over her with an intent expression on his face and shrugged out of his jacket. Then his waistcoat. Then his shirt. His chest was as magnificent as she remembered. Only now she had the right to run her hands over it. To follow the dips and hollows, experience the difference in texture between smooth skin and hairy, hard muscles and the soft skin of his nipples. To sit up and kiss the bruises marring his ribs.

He shuddered. Gripped her shoulders and pushed her away. 'Don't,' he grated. 'Not yet. Or I won't be able to keep my promise.'

'But I want to *feel* you,' she complained. 'Taste you.'

'*I* will make *you* feel,' he said, taking hold of her wrists and pinning them above her head.

Again.

'It will be like nothing you have ever felt before,' he vowed, before stopping her mouth with a kiss.

The feel of him on top of her, bare chest to bare breasts, was indeed like nothing she'd ever felt before.

She couldn't help rubbing herself up against him, to increase the wondrous pleasure of it.

He lifted himself off her, keeping her wrists clasped firmly in his hands as he kissed each breast, then her stomach, and then...

If he hadn't been holding her hands so firmly she would have tried to grasp his head and stop him. It wasn't easy to cast off all the morals her aunt had tried to din into her over the past dozen years. And for him to put his mouth *there* simply couldn't be right.

But it felt so good. The way he kissed, then nibbled, then licked...

'Gregory!' she gasped. 'Gregory, that is...' And then her ability to breathe and speak at the same time ceased. All she could do was writhe, and pant, and moan. Those fireworks were going to go off again. She could feel them building, fizzing inside her.

Then Gregory let go of her hands, shifted slightly to one side, and pushed one finger inside her.

She screamed. And went off like a rocket. One single, immense rocket that blotted out every single star twinkling feebly in her night sky.

'Gregory,' she moaned, as she slowly came back together.

'Shh...' He was next to her now, holding her in his arms, stroking her hair, dropping kisses on her brow.

'I don't think,' she panted, 'I can keep on doing this all night.'

He chuckled. 'A short while ago you were claiming you didn't want me to let the fire go out—not even for an instant.'

'I didn't know what I was talking about,' she complained.

To her immense relief he let go of her and sat up. Though she felt perversely disappointed when he then stood up.

Until she saw him undoing his breeches and shucking them off. She held out her arms as he came back to her, clasping them round his back as he lay fully on top of her. At which point a wave of shockingly fierce response had her pressing up against him. It was as though her hips had developed a mind of their own. And her legs, which parted in welcome.

'There, you see,' he said. 'You are still smouldering. You can blaze again. And again.'

Incredibly, it was true. For the feel of him there, hard against her softness, probing insistently every time he flexed his hips against hers, was making the explosive excitement start to grow all over again.

He kissed her, stroked her, licked and nibbled at her throat, her breasts, while his hands kneaded at her bottom. And then he shifted slightly so that he could reach for himself, where he lay between her legs, and rub himself along her wetness. Then he held himself poised, where she was melting and aching for him. And pushed, just a little, so that he was stretching and penetrating her.

She arched up to him—and felt a sting from which she instinctively recoiled.

He followed her down, allowing her no quarter.

Pushed again.

This time there was a searing pain which tore her out of the sensual haze in which she'd been floating.

He stilled. Kissed her cheek when she turned it away from the fire, away from the sight of him looming over her. Kissed her neck. Stroked her damp hair back from her forehead. Then reached between them and began to gently caress the point where they merged.

Unbelievably, the slow burn started up all over again.

She turned her face to look up at him. 'I can't, Gregory. Please, I...'

'You can,' he said. 'You only have to let go.'

Let go? What was she to let go *of*, precisely? He was the one pinning her to the floor. Moving inside her now. Pushing even deeper. Withdrawing. And circling his fingers over a place that seemed to be screaming for him to do it harder.

Harder?

Yes, she wanted more of him. More sensation.

The next time he pushed in she pushed up, against him, to increase the sensation.

'That's it,' he murmured. And kept on murmuring words of encouragement, and praise, and approval as he kept up a gentle, rhythmic thrusting.

Until she didn't want him to be gentle any more. Until she was gripping his buttocks and twisting her hips, clamouring to reach that place he'd already taken her to twice before.

And then she got there. Only this time it was even better because he was there with her. She could feel him pulsing deep inside her as he groaned into her ear. And it was better feeling him drift back down to earth with her, too. Feeling his heart pound against her chest. His breath coming in great, ragged gasps.

For a while they just lay there, getting their breath back, and in Prudence's case watching the firelight sending shadows flickering across the beamed ceiling.

Until he reared up, looked down at her with a smug smile, and said, 'There. You will *have* to marry me now.'

* * *

They slept wrapped in each other's arms until dawn. At which time the light crept in through the curtainless windows and roused Gregory. His breath billowed out like a cloud when he yawned. He reached over to the log box, extracted the last log and tossed it onto the fire.

From somewhere deep beneath the covers Prudence lifted her head and squinted up at him crossly.

'Lie down,' she complained. 'You're making a draught.'

'I'm taking care of you, you ingrate,' he countered happily.

She shifted against him, snuggling closer. 'You are,' she conceded. 'You got up some time in the night to fetch extra blankets, didn't you?'

'All on my own,' he jested. 'Without any help from a servant.'

He felt her smile against his chest.

'I suppose we ought to get back to the house before anyone notices we are missing,' said Prudence.

He snorted. 'Didn't you see the curtains twitching last night? They all know exactly where we went. So...' he rolled on top of her '...you will have to marry me now.'

'You said that last night.'

'I still mean it.'

'So do I,' she said, wrapping her arms round his waist and hugging him hard.

In this position, he approved of hugs. In fact there was a great deal to be said for hugs at any time of day. So long as it was Prudence doing the hugging.

'So you are still of a mind to marry me, in spite of my being a duke?'

'I think I shall have to,' she said. 'Not because of what we did last night. But because I could not bear the thought of life without you. Although,' she said, wriggling rather deliciously before swatting his bottom, 'I am still cross with you for not telling me the truth about your station before we got here. You might have warned me, and then I wouldn't have felt like such a prize idiot.'

'I was too worried about how you might react to broach the subject,' he admitted. Now that he was sure of her, it felt safe to confess many things. 'I'd been trying to think of ways to tell you about my being a duke long before we got here. But… Well, for one thing I wasn't sure you'd believe me. I had visions of you saying that you must have hit me really hard with that rock for me to suddenly start getting delusions of grandeur. Or of you becoming afraid that I was a dangerous lunatic, escaped from some asylum, and trying to run away from me again.

'I couldn't let you go,' he said, dropping a kiss on her brow. 'I needed to keep you near. Actually,' he admitted, with a burn of something that felt like guilt heating his cheeks, 'I'd even considered claiming to get lost and not finding Bramley Park at all just to prolong our time together without the dratted title coming between us.'

'You would really have rather stayed out on the road, facing farmers with guns and eating stale bread that I'd earned by singing, than come back to all this?'

'Without question.'

'But you didn't,' she pointed out, pragmatic as ever.

'I couldn't, in the end.' He sighed. 'On account of your feet. You were in pain, Prudence. And you needed a decent meal and clean clothes. It would have been monstrous to keep you in that state just to preserve the illusion that I was an ordinary man. Besides which, if I'd succumbed to the temptation to put off the moment when you discovered what I really am you might have thought it was because I was still trying to win that wager. And I couldn't have you ever thinking that I'd put something so trivial before your welfare. Whichever path I chose, I risked losing you. I was...' he shuddered '...caught on the horns of a horrible dilemma.'

'Oh...'

She gazed up at him with eyes full of what looked like understanding—at least he hoped it looked like understanding. And appreciation. And love.

'You really are the most darling of men,' she said at last.

'Event though I'm a duke?'

'Yes. Although...'

'What?'

'Well, it's just that I don't want you to ever regret marrying me,' she said.

'I couldn't.'

'Are you sure? When you were so set against marrying? Even more than I was, by the sound of it...'

'That was only because I hadn't met *you*,' he countered, seeing the real anxiety in her lovely brown eyes.

'No, be serious,' she said, swatting his bottom again.

Which he was starting to like.

'I want to be the best wife I can be for you,' she said. 'Only I don't understand how I can do that. I'm certain to let you down...'

'You couldn't! Because you love me. The reason I was so unhappy in my first marriage was because of... Well, you know the way Millicent behaved.'

'Yes, you explained a little of that. It sounded perfectly horrid.'

'It was. And they said *she'd* be the perfect duchess.' He couldn't help grimacing at memories of the pain and humiliation he'd experienced as a young man. 'She couldn't *ever* have been the perfect duchess. For all that she was born with a title and came from a noble family. And she had money—yes, all the things you say you don't have. But she didn't love me. Nor have any of the other women who have made an attempt to lure me into their clutches loved me. They've merely coveted the title. You are the only woman who has loved the man and rejected the title. That *is* what you've done, isn't it?'

He looked at her keenly, wondering even now if she was going to recoil from the duties and status that went with marrying him.

'Well, not *rejected* the title, exactly. It's just that it… it scares me a bit. Well, a lot. I don't know how to be a duchess, Gregory. And you ought to have a wife who can do you proud.'

'I ought to have a wife who can *love* me,' he came back swiftly. 'That's all it will take, Prudence, for you to be my perfect duchess. For you to love me.'

'It's lovely of you to say so, but surely it will mean more than that?'

'Prudence Carstairs,' he said, pretending shock. 'Are you admitting to being afraid of something? You who faced down a farmer with a gun?'

She blushed. And wriggled. Which almost made him abandon their conversation and simply give in to the physical appetite she was arousing. It took a serious effort of will for him to concentrate on what she was saying. But he made himself do so. Because this was important. To her, and therefore to him.

'Physical danger is something I'm used to,' she said dismissively. 'Running the gauntlet of indignant society matrons, all pointing their fingers at me and whispering behind their fans, is quite another matter.'

He took hold of her chin. 'If anyone dares to whisper behind their fan about you, you will simply look down your nose at them the way you did at me when I had the effrontery to try and stop you from singing in public. Remember that? I thought at the time you could have outdone any of the patronesses of Almack's for haughtiness. Even dressed in rags and singing your heart out at the market cross, you looked like a duchess to me.'

'Oh, Gregory...' She sighed, shaking her head. 'You aren't looking at me the way everyone else will. They'll say I'm an upstart. That I smell of the shop.'

'So what if they do? Why should you care about what anyone thinks or says but me? And don't forget,' he murmured into her ear, swirling his tongue round the shell-like whorls for good measure, 'if anyone dares to criticise you, and I find out about it, I will make them rue the day.'

'Would you? Yes, I suppose you would.' She bent her head to give him better access to her ear, and in doing so her neck. 'I shouldn't think anyone would dare do anything much, would they?'

'Of course not. I'm not a man to cross, Prudence. You can trust me to keep you safe...' he paused to apply his mouth to her throat '...and happy.'

'Yes...' she breathed as he reached the spot he'd been seeking and sucked. 'After all, I trusted you with my fortune and my future when I thought you had nothing at all, didn't I? I don't know why I thought you were suddenly someone else the minute I discovered you had a title.'

'I am not anyone else, Prudence. I'm just the man who loves you.'

'And I love you.'

'Thank God,' he breathed. 'I thought you were never going to admit it.'

'But—you knew. Didn't you?'

'No,' he growled. 'You kept me guessing.'

'But you knew.'

'No, I bloody well didn't.' He reared up onto his elbows and glared down at her. 'You have kept me on my toes ever since you ran from that ostler and climbed into my cart. From that moment on I've always been half afraid you would run off and I'd never see you again.'

'Well, I won't, my darling.' She reached up and stroked his cheek. 'My love, I will marry you, and stick to you like a burr for the rest of my days.'

'Thank God,' he breathed again. And lowered himself back down.

Chapter Nineteen

The sun was high in the sky and the fire was nothing more than a pile of embers when they finally emerged from the summer house.

Gregory didn't think he'd ever witnessed a more lovely morning. There had been a heavy dewfall in the night, which made even the dank shrubbery sparkle as though it was bedecked with jewels. The gloss didn't even fade as he caught sight of Hugo, pacing up and down the terrace. Nor even when, upon catching sight of them, he came jogging down the steps and headed across the lawn to intercept them.

'Good morning, Halstead,' said his cousin. 'Miss Carstairs.'

Gregory didn't have to look at Prudence to know she was blushing at being caught outside. Everyone must know they'd spent the night together in the summer house. Especially since she had the quilt wrapped round her shoulders, across which he'd draped his own arm. And with that glorious abundance of hair rioting all down her back she looked thoroughly loved this morning.

'Need a word,' said Hugo, completely unabashed.

What a pity he didn't have the tact to consider sparing her blushes.

'Last night, what with all the…er…fireworks between you two,' he said with a grin, 'we never did get round to settling up.'

'You need to confront me about that *now*? Is the case that urgent?'

Hugo's face fell. 'You must know it is—or I would never have lashed out at you the way I did. Fact is, I was jolly glad to have the excuse to get out of Town and hide away up here.'

'If you had only explained I would have bailed you out, you young idiot. And I shall, of course, settle all your debts—as agreed in the terms of our wager.'

'You'd have bailed me out anyway?' Hugo planted his fists on his hips. 'I wish I'd known that. I would have wagered on something worth having.'

'Such as?'

'A commission with a good regiment. In fact it would probably be to your advantage to get me into one which is serving overseas anyway. Then I won't be able to do your reputation any damage by letting the cat out of the bag about all this.' He waved his arm in a way that encompassed the pair of unmarried lovers and, by implication, the way they'd met. 'Inadvertently, of course,' he said, going slightly pink. 'When I'm in my cups, say.'

Gregory narrowed his eyes and hardened his jaw. 'You have first a more pressing duty to perform.'

'Oh?'

'Yes. I need you to go and procure a licence, so that Miss Carstairs and I can be married as soon as possible. And then to stand as my groomsman.'

'Of course,' said Hugo, standing a bit straighter.

'Only then will I purchase your commission. Not because I fear anything you might inadvertently do to my reputation,' he pointed out, 'but because this past week has taught me that every man deserves a chance to find out what he's made of.'

Hugo whooped with glee, darted forward and kissed Prudence's cheek.

'What was that for?' She tried to clap her hand to the spot where Hugo had kissed her, but he grabbed it and pumped it up and down.

'To thank you for agreeing to marry him. For putting him in such a mellow mood. Welcome to the family, Miss Carstairs,' he said, and then, with another whoop of delight, went haring off back across the lawn in the direction of the stables.

'You don't think badly of me?' he said, after they'd walked a little further across the dew-spangled lawn. 'For agreeing to purchase him a commission? You understand why I did so?'

'Of course.' She smiled up at him. 'In fact I was thinking only last night that it would be the making of him.'

'There—you see.' He smiled down at her. 'We are of one mind already. How can our marriage fail to prosper?'

Prudence could still think of plenty of ways their marriage might fail to prosper. If, for example, she ever decided to find his dictatorial manner objectionable. For he had decided they would get married within two days at the local parish church, had set Lady Mixby to arranging their wedding breakfast, Mrs Bennet the local dressmaker to furnish her with suitable clothing, and Benderby to organise their subsequent departure for London.

All without asking her opinion once.

But since he had made it clear that he needed her at his side every moment of the day, and she had no wish to stir from that position, it was hardly worth mentioning. And anyway, did she really care where they married so long as it was soon? And wasn't a quiet country church preferable to a grand society wedding where a lot of strangers would come to gawp at her?

He was going to have to return to London and take up his responsibilities one day. The longer they put it off, the more nervous she was likely to get about taking her place at his side. Besides, Lady Mixby and the redoubtable Benderby were coming, too. Both of them were in high spirits over the prospect of overseeing her presentation, her first ball as Duchess of Halstead, and the many and varied delights of the subsequent season in London.

It wasn't that she was letting everyone ride roughshod over her. She wasn't. She was just so blissfully happy that she didn't want to do anything to spoil it. And, really, what would be the point of throwing what might amount to a tantrum because her husband was anticipating her every need before she could even voice it?

She would be wise to choose her battles carefully—not rip up at him over every little thing. Or the combination of his autocratic nature and her independent spirit would result in them spending their whole life fighting.

They had been in London for a week before she finally had no choice but to take a stand.

'There—what did I tell you?' he murmured as yet

another doyenne of society bowed to them as their carriages passed in the park. 'Nobody has shown you anything but the greatest respect. Not even your grandfather.'

They'd gone to visit the Earl of Sterndale privately only the day before. And, just as Gregory had predicted, the old man had welcomed her with open arms.

'You have a look of my boy,' he'd said, with the suspicion of a tear in his eye. When she'd bristled with indignation that *his boy* had died without ever having been forgiven, the old man had said, 'Ah, yes, just that look.'

'It must be very gratifying to be always right,' she said now to Gregory. And then, because he'd raised one eyebrow at her, she hastily added, 'Even about your driving. You are managing *these* horses very competently.'

'Baggage,' he responded, though at least the brow had gone down. 'I would defy anyone to make the creature Hugo foisted on me go in a straight line.'

'It may be less cantankerous after having that week's rest at the inn, eating its head off,' she replied, paraphrasing the landlord.

'We will soon find out,' he replied with an evil smile. 'I'm making Hugo a present of it.'

'I wouldn't be a bit surprised if it doesn't make a very good sort of horse for a cavalry officer,' she said. 'It will need very little encouragement to lash out with its hooves, or bite persons who dare to attempt to get near its master.'

'Providing Hugo can persuade it that he *is* its master.'

They both laughed at the vision of Hugo attempting to train the horse, and harmony was restored.

'Good afternoon, Your Grace,' said the butler of the house in Grosvenor Square of which Prudence was now mistress, when they returned later that afternoon. 'Wrothers has informed me that the person you have been expecting from Liverpool is waiting in your study.'

From the way he'd said *'person'*, Bispham clearly did not think much of Gregory's visitor.

She half expected Gregory to tell the butler to dismiss them, as he'd dismissed so many people since their arrival in London. Gregory's secretary appeared to do nothing but turn away people who wished to have an interview with her husband.

Instead, Gregory turned to her with an abstracted air after tossing his gloves into his hat and handing them over.

'You will go to the morning room and take tea with Lady Mixby,' he said sternly. 'I will deal with this.'

He then strode off, leaving her standing in the hall staring after him.

Fuming.

She was not his servant to order about.

'Who is this person, Bishpham?' she asked as she shrugged her furs into his waiting hands.

'I really couldn't say, Your Grace,' he replied. 'But His Grace frequently has to have dealings with all sorts of odd people in the performance of his duties to the Crown.'

'Yes, I suppose so…' she began. Then went rigid as she heard a voice raised in anger. A female voice. An all too recognisable female voice.

All thought of meekly going upstairs to drink tea, as she'd been told, went flying out of the window. She stormed past the butler, across the hall, through the room over which Wrothers presided, and straight through into her husband's inner sanctum.

And she saw that she had not been mistaken.

'Aunt Charity!'

Her aunt was sitting on a hard-backed chair to one side of her husband's desk. He was standing over her, looking particularly intractable. Wrothers was standing in a corner, his arms folded across his chest.

'I told you to let *me* deal with this,' said Gregory upon seeing her.

'Deal with this? *Deal with this?* This is not a "this"— it is a her. I mean, it is my aunt.'

'Oh, Prudence, Prudence… I never meant it,' her aunt wailed.

'Didn't you?' Her heart was thudding uncomfortably high in her throat. As though she was going to be sick.

Gregory came round the table and to her side. 'I told you to let me deal with this,' he repeated, murmuring into her ear. 'This is likely to be an unpleasant interview.'

'I don't understand. Where did you find her? *How* did you find her?'

'Liverpool. And I had people search for her.'

Oh, yes, the moment Bispham had mentioned Liverpool, Gregory's relaxed demeanour had completely disappeared. He had known at that moment exactly who was waiting for him in here.

'Liverpool? What on earth was she doing there, of all places? And why did you have people searching for her?'

'I will explain it all later,' he said, ushering her inexorably towards the door. 'Go and have some tea and—'

'No. Absolutely not. I need to know what is going

on. What she thought she was doing. How she could
have done it.'

'Prudence, will you just do as you are told?'

'No. Not this time.'

He gritted his teeth. 'And here was I, thinking you
were becoming more malleable.'

'Malleable!' She rounded on him with real anger. 'I
lost my virginity in that summer house—not my mind.
The only reason I haven't objected to you giving me orders since then is because you haven't asked me to do
anything I didn't want to.'

'And there was I also thinking I had turned my ti-
gress into a purring kitten with my prowess in bed,' he
said ruefully.

'Well, you thought wrong.'

'Clearly,' he said. And then tipped his head to one
side. He nodded. 'Very well,' he said. 'You may stay.'

May stay? She was just about to protest at his choice
of words when she caught a glimmer in his eye. And a
twitch to his lips.

He was trying not to laugh.

And then she recalled that he had never minded her
standing up to him. Out on the road they'd gone at it
like hammer and tongs on more than one occasion and
he'd never held it against her. In fact she wouldn't be
a bit surprised to discover that it was one of the things
that had made him fall in love with her.

Lifting her chin, she flounced over to another chair
and sat down on it.

Her aunt, who had been watching the murmured
and yet heated interchange warily, now burst into noisy
sobs.

Gregory motioned for Wrothers to leave the room.

He did so, looking mightily relieved. It was Gregory himself who went to the sideboard and poured a glass of brandy. And then strode to her aunt and offered her the glass.

'Oh, Aunt Charity doesn't drink…'

Her aunt was a Methodist. Though not, apparently, a very consistent one. For she snatched at the glass as though at a lifeline and downed half the contents in one go.

Prudence waited in vain for her to cough and splutter. She simply gave a little shiver, then downed the rest like a seasoned toper.

When Prudence looked to Gregory he gave a wry smile, then made a gesture towards Aunt Charity as though to indicate that the lady was all hers.

She could ask whatever questions she liked. Though all she could think for a moment was, *How could you?*

'Perhaps you would like to begin with ascertaining what your aunt was doing in Liverpool?' Gregory suggested.

'You know very well what we were doing in Liverpool,' said Aunt Charity crossly. 'We were leaving the country. It was all Mr Murgatroyd's idea,' she said, turning the empty glass round and round between stiff fingers. 'He said it was the only way to escape the gossip. To start a new life in the New World. He made it sound so…' She shook her head and shut her eyes briefly in what looked like a spasm of pain.

'He had lost all the money in Prudence's trust, I take it?'

Aunt Charity's shoulders slumped. 'He said he was going to triple it. That we would be so wealthy nobody would think it odd for us to leave Stoketown and set up in a nice, fashionable resort somewhere.'

'Why should you want to leave Stoketown?' asked Prudence.

Aunt Charity had been such a committed member of her congregation. So active in all the good works performed in the community.

'Because I couldn't ever hold my head up there. Not after Alfred.'

Alfred? Gregory mouthed at Prudence.

'Her first husband,' said Prudence. 'The one who drank.' She eyed her aunt's empty glass again, wondering if her aunt had been spotless during that period of her past.

'I thought if I married a really, really moral man that it would counteract the shame of having been dragged down by an habitual drunkard.'

So that explained why she'd married Mr Murgatroyd—one of the most moralising, narrow-minded men in the whole congregation.

'Because no matter how many good works I did,' Aunt Charity continued, 'people were never going to forget the…the *degradation*…of my marrying a man who turned out to be the very opposite of what I thought…and now I've done it twice!'

She burst into tears again.

Gregory calmly walked over, took the glass from her hand, replenished it and handed it back. The contents went the same way as the first.

'Mr Murgatroyd promised me he would take me away from it all. That if he could only have some capital he would make us so rich that we could shake the dust of Stoketown from our feet and live like kings. I should have known better than to trust in a handsome face and lying lips,' she finished bitterly.

'What happened to the money?'

'He invested it in a canal. A canal that never got dug. No chance of getting any sort of refund. And with you getting so near to coming of age, and not being the sort we could trust to be discreet about our shame, we had to do something. You wouldn't marry any of the men we knew would have covered it up. So he came up with a new plan.'

'To discredit me? And abandon me?'

'No!' She hunched her shoulders. 'Not at first,' she continued, looking a touch shamefaced. 'We were going to emigrate. All of us. We lied about taking you to Bath, it is true. Our destination was Liverpool all along. We intended to tell you the truth when we got there. But then we stopped at that funny little inn and saw… him…' She gestured to Gregory with her empty glass. 'Mr Murgatroyd said as how he wished to spare me an embarrassing scene at the dockside when we broke the news to you. And asked wouldn't it be better to leave you behind and start our new life without any reminders of the past? Because he was sure if we took you with us you would be bound to do nothing but complain and ruin our fresh start. And now I know I shouldn't have listened, but it was so tempting,' she wailed. 'He could always make me believe anything he said. Oh, what a fool I've been.'

'You left me at that inn because you thought I'd ruin your fresh start? How…how *could* you?'

'Well, it wasn't as if you were going to come to any harm, was it? Mr Murgatroyd made sure *he*—' she waved her empty glass at Gregory again '—was completely insensible before he carried you into the room, and I undressed you. I sat there all night. And the moment he began to stir I made all that commotion and brought crowds of people in before anything untoward could happen. You were never in any danger.'

Aunt Charity had sat there all night? It put a slightly different complexion on things, but still…

'But you just left me there. You abandoned me. What did you think would happen to me?'

Aunt Charity blinked. 'Well, we assumed you would go straight back to Stoketown, of course.'

'And how was I supposed to get there?'

Aunt Charity looked confused. 'Somebody would have told you how to get a seat on the mail.'

'The mail coach?'

'I don't see why not. We left enough money for you to travel swiftly and to tide you over for a good few months until you got on your feet again. Though I see we needn't have bothered,' she ended with a sniff, looking round the study and then at Gregory. 'It's just typical for you to end up with a duke.'

'You left Prudence money?' Gregory was frowning, looking from one woman to the other.

'Yes. Twenty pounds. As you very well know,' she said indignantly. 'It would have come in very handy in our new lives, let me tell you. Quite a sacrifice it was, parting with that amount. But I insisted.'

Prudence pressed one hand to her forehead. She supposed it might be true. That her aunt had left her some money. Aunt Charity would have seen her tuck her reticule under her pillow when she'd brought her that hot milk. She might have put some money in there.

'And all my things? What did you do with those?'

'Your things? Why, I packed them all up neatly and had them sent back to Stoketown by carrier as soon as we arrived in Liverpool. In fact it was while I was doing that that *he* gave me the slip,' she added bitterly. 'He said he was going to see about our berth on the ship, but when I got back to the hotel from the carriers it was to find all his luggage gone.'

Tears streamed down her face unchecked.

'I was afraid to go down to the docks at first, because he'd told me it was a rough, horrid place and that he'd handle things. By the time I'd plucked up the courage, the ship had sailed. And I was left there alone, with no means of paying the bill, since he hadn't left me with *anything*! And I know you sent that young man—' she gestured to the door through which Wrothers had gone '—to hunt me down and bring me to justice, but I have never been so glad to see anyone in my life.'

'It appears,' said Gregory with scorn, 'that rather than own up at once that she had no means to pay her shot your aunt stayed at the inn, racking up a substantial debt.'

'I spent most of my stay there on my knees,' said the tearful older woman. 'Praying for inspiration. Or a miracle. I know it will be hard for you to forgive me, Prudence, for the part I played in all this, but at least you have the satisfaction of knowing that I have already been punished by a higher authority.'

Gregory made a sort of snarling sound. He was looking at Aunt Charity as though he couldn't believe his ears.

'That's true,' Prudence pointed out. 'All the things she did to me have now been done to her. She has been robbed and abandoned. By a man she loved, at that.

So you could say her punishment is greater, since I found *you*.'

She got up and went to him, hands outstretched.

'You are going to ask me to let her off, aren't you?'

She nodded. 'We learned something about giving people a second chance, didn't we? In that barn? The farmer forgave us for literal trespass and spared us both a horrible time trying to explain everything away to the law. Could we not now forgive Aunt Charity for her trespass against us?'

He was still glowering.

'You have already forgiven her, haven't you?'

She nodded. 'Because if it hadn't been for her giving way to Mr Murgatroyd's persuasion we would never have met. Besides, she took me in when nobody else would.'

'Grudgingly, you said.'

'Nevertheless…' She spread her hands wide.

He stepped forward and took them. 'You are the most generous-hearted, lovely creature on God's whole earth. No wonder I love you so much.'

'Then you won't have her prosecuted?'

'How can I when to do so would offend you?'

As he drew her into his arms Aunt Charity collapsed into a fresh spurt of sobbing. Though now, Prudence suspected, they were tears of relief.

'Thankfully,' he said dryly, 'I have no end of properties in which I can stow indigent aunts. Some of them even further from London than Bramley Park.'

'So there are *some* benefits to marrying a duke, after all,' she said with a smile.

'Baggage,' he murmured, pinching her chin. 'You know very well that you adore being married to a duke.'

'Only because I happen to adore the Duke in question,' she countered.

'Long may that continue,' he said.

'Oh, it will,' she vowed, reaching up to kiss his cheek. 'It will.'

* * * * *

If you enjoyed this story, you won't want to miss these other great reads from Annie Burrows:

THE CAPTAIN'S CHRISTMAS BRIDE
A MISTRESS FOR MAJOR BARTLETT
LORD HAVELOCK'S LIST
PORTRAIT OF A SCANDAL
REFORMING THE VISCOUNT

REQUEST YOUR FREE BOOKS!

HARLEQUIN®

HISTORICAL

Where love is timeless

2 FREE NOVELS PLUS 2 FREE GIFTS!

YES! Please send me 2 FREE Harlequin® Historical novels and my 2 FREE gifts (gifts are worth about $10). After receiving them, if I don't wish to receive any more books, I can return the shipping statement marked "cancel." If I don't cancel, I will receive 6 brand-new novels every month and be billed just $5.69 per book in the U.S. or $5.99 per book in Canada. That's a savings of at least 12% off the cover price! It's quite a bargain! Shipping and handling is just 50¢ per book in the U.S. and 75¢ per book in Canada.* I understand that accepting the 2 free books and gifts places me under no obligation to buy anything. I can always return a shipment and cancel at any time. Even if I never buy another book, the two free books and gifts are mine to keep forever.

246/349 HDN GH2Z

Name	(PLEASE PRINT)	
Address		Apt. #
City	State/Prov.	Zip/Postal Code

Signature (if under 18, a parent or guardian must sign)

Mail to the **Reader Service:**
IN U.S.A.: P.O. Box 1867, Buffalo, NY 14240-1867
IN CANADA: P.O. Box 609, Fort Erie, Ontario L2A 5X3

Want to try two free books from another line?
Call 1-800-873-8635 or visit www.ReaderService.com.

* Terms and prices subject to change without notice. Prices do not include applicable taxes. Sales tax applicable in N.Y. Canadian residents will be charged applicable taxes. Offer not valid in Quebec. This offer is limited to one order per household. Not valid for current subscribers to Harlequin Historical books. All orders subject to credit approval. Credit or debit balances in a customer's account(s) may be offset by any other outstanding balance owed by or to the customer. Please allow 4 to 6 weeks for delivery. Offer available while quantities last.

Your Privacy—The Reader Service is committed to protecting your privacy. Our Privacy Policy is available online at www.ReaderService.com or upon request from the Reader Service.

We make a portion of our mailing list available to reputable third parties that offer products we believe may interest you. If you prefer that we not exchange your name with third parties, or if you wish to clarify or modify your communication preferences, please visit us at www.ReaderService.com/consumerchoice or write to us at Reader Service Preference Service, P.O. Box 9062, Buffalo, NY 14240-9062. Include your complete name and address.

HH15

SPECIAL EXCERPT FROM

◆ **HARLEQUIN**®

HISTORICAL

*Runaway heiress Lorna Bradford must reach
California to claim her fortune, but when she's rescued
from robbers by fierce Cheyenne warrior Black Horse,
she's forced to remain under his protection!*

Read on for a sneak preview of
HER CHEYENNE WARRIOR, by
Lauri Robinson.

"Lie down, Poeso. Your day was long. You are tired."

Her glance was weary, and wary, and she shook her head.

"Black Horse protect you." Gesturing toward the doorway, he said, "No one will enter my lodge."

Still shaking her head, she whispered, "Who will protect me from you?"

Another whisper of understanding angered him, turned his insides dark. A man had hurt her. A bad man in a bad way.

"Black Horse protect you from all." He backed away and then moved across the lodge to repair his bed. Afterward he retrieved his pouch from where it hung on a lodge pole and pulled out the gun. Trust had to be mutual or it was nothing.

"Here is your gun, Poeso," he said, holding it out for her to take.

Her eyes were big and full of surprise, and her hand shook as she reached for the little pistol.

He laid it in her palm and wrapped both of his hands around hers. "I trust you, Poeso. You trust Black Horse."

She looked from him to their hands and back up at his face. "Are the bullets still in it?"

Her voice was soft, and the words cracked, but he understood she had to say them. "Yes." Letting go of her hands, he pointed to the buffalo hides. "Go to bed, Poeso, you are safe."

He waited, hoping his heart was right, that he could trust her, and then watched her scoot onto the furs. She kept the gun clutched near her chest, even after lying down on her side.

Black Horse moved to his bed. This might become a sleepless night. He had never slept next to a woman holding a gun. Once stretched out on his back, he listened for any movement she might make.

"What does *poeso* mean?" she asked quietly.

"Cat."

"Why do you call me that?"

"Because that is what you remind me of. The sleek mountain lions that roam the hills."

"Is that bad?"

"*Hova'ahane,*" he answered. "*Epeva'e.*"

"*Epeva'e,*" she repeated. "It is good?"

"*Heehe'e,*" he said. "It is good."

Don't miss
HER CHEYENNE WARRIOR by Lauri Robinson,
available June 2016 wherever
Harlequin® Historical books and ebooks are sold.

www.Harlequin.com

Reading Has Its Rewards

Earn **FREE BOOKS!**

Register at **Harlequin My Rewards** and submit your Harlequin purchases from wherever you shop to earn points for free books and other exclusive rewards.

Plus submit your purchases from now till May 30th for a chance to win a $500 Visa Card*.

Visit **HarlequinMyRewards.com** today

Earn **FREE** REWARDS
Join Today!
HarlequinMyRewards.com

MYR16R1